Praise for Frances McNamara's previous novels

"McNamara has a keen eye for zeroing in on how a metropolis can fuel and deplete the human spirit."
Chicago Sun-Times

"[*Death at Pullman*] convincingly recreates a pivotal moment in American labor history… Besides plausibly depicting such historical figures as Eugene Debs and Nellie Bly, McNamara throws in some surprising twists at the end. Laurie King and Rhys Bowen fans will be delighted."
Publishers Weekly

"McNamara…proves, if anyone was asking, that librarians make great historical mystery writers…[In *Death at Woods Hole*] so accurately portrayed is that small-town-in-summer feeling, when towns are overtaken by visitors, who coexist uneasily with locals… I'd follow Emily to any location."
Historical Novels Review

In [*Death at Pullman*] a "little romance [and] a lot of labor history are artfully combined… Creating a believable mix of historical and fictional characters…is another of the author's prime strengths as a writer…[she] clearly knows, and loves, her setting."
Julie Eakin, *Foreword Reviews*

"The combination of labor unrest, rivalries among loca and past romantic intrigues is a combustible mix, an edg that is laid out convincingly… A suspenseful recreation moment in American social history, as seen from the vie strong-willed, engaging fictional heroine."
Reading the Past

Also by Frances McNamara

The Emily Cabot Mysteries

Death at the Fair

Death at Hull House

Death at Pullman

Death at Woods Hole

Death at Chinatown

DEATH AT THE PARIS EXPOSITION

Frances McNamara

ALLIUM PRESS OF CHICAGO

Allium Press of Chicago
Forest Park, IL
www.alliumpress.com

Book and cover design by E. C. Victorson

Front cover images:
"Looking through Eiffel Tower to the Trocadero…
Exposition 1900, Paris, France" (Library of Congress)
Red velvet background by jsolie/iStockphoto
Vintage frame by Masamima/iStockphoto

Poem on pg. 10: "Upon Julia's Clothes" Robert Herrick (1591-1674)

ISBN: 978-0-9967558-3-2

Library of Congress Cataloguing-in-Publication Data is available.

To Colleen Farrell,
who traveled to Paris with me and who shares my love for that city

PROLOGUE

Paris. I haven't yet made peace with Paris. Say "Paris" and I still see the haughty wax figure in court dress. A fake tiara anchors a mass of perfectly waved hair above her smoothly vacant face. The choker of pearls surrounding the unnaturally long neck is anything but fake, though. And the court dress of heavy satin embroidered with pearls and trimmed with lace is the real thing. But it's the extravagant fall of the satin train, spilling down in a pool of fabric, trailing five feet behind, that catches the eye. That train and the kneeling wax figure of a seamstress who is carefully smoothing it out. The standing figure is regarding herself critically in a long mirror, so the eye almost misses the scuffed little black boots lying at an odd angle. At first you don't see it—a figure wearing a simple muslin dress printed with tiny flowers lying at the foot of that wax figure like a discarded handkerchief. No warm wax here, only cold, cold flesh with a face that is puckered in a grimace. A royal blue satin ribbon—that should have been tied around her waist—is knotted around that very young woman's throat.

And, once again, I desperately wish that I could somehow have prevented it. Like a sore tooth, it throbs and aches, that memory. If only I could have penetrated the layers of European artifice and misdirection sooner. So few Americans were capable of that. Certainly Bertha Palmer was not. She was too easily misled. Perhaps Miss Cassatt, with her artist's eye, saw through it. But not in time to save the girl.

We Americans were ruthless in our naïveté that long ago summer. Still, when someone says "Paris," I long to return to engage in that struggle once more, to see if I might not win and best them in this game of wits. But life with all its responsibilities prevents me. I have a family to look after. If the girl had lived, surely by now, she, too, would have been too busy with the cares of a family to remember it all. She would have moved on, like the rest of us, beyond the transitory excitements and seemingly critical discoveries of the Paris Exposition of 1900. For the rest of us, its wonders were gone in the blink of an eye, but she remains there forever, frozen on the floor of the exhibit, a sacrifice to the gods of modern Parisian fashion.

ONE

I was really in Paris. I sat in an open carriage with deep purple cushions on that fair spring day, being wafted through the town. The air was soft, the brightness of the sun broken by dappled shade from trees, as the horse clip-clopped down the broad avenue. From the Trocadéro to the Champs Elysees, we traveled in perfect comfort. I was a world away from the grimy streetcars of Chicago.

"I don't know how to repay you, I never can," I said. It wasn't the first time I had tried to thank the woman seated beside me for her generosity, nor was it the first time she had impatiently brushed away my thanks.

"My dear Emily, as I have tried to explain, providing you with an ensemble from the House of Worth is part of my plan."

Mrs. Bertha Palmer was regal but quite at ease in her corner of the carriage. She wore a high-collared jacket, stiff with embroidery in fashionable black and trimmed with narrow bands of red. A sweeping hat of black straw, decorated with satin bows and fluffy black feathers, framed her handsome, square face. Waves of silver hair were piled beneath the millinery confection and her eyes were a brown so dark they had been described as black. It was not strange that Mrs. Palmer had set out to visit the House of Worth on a fine spring morning in Paris. She had been dressed by the famous couturier for years. Even after the patriarch of that fashion house had passed away several years earlier, she continued to patronize his sons, who had, as long planned, stepped into the business. For an occasion as important as the Paris Exposition of 1900, Bertha Palmer would, of course, require an outstanding set of costumes. As the only woman commissioner in the American delegation to the fair, she was determined to excel in dress, as in all aspects of the job of representing her country. But no one could expect her to also purchase an outfit for a mere secretary. I knew she was doing so because I'd refused to accept a salary. How could I, when she had already been so generous to me and my little family? So, I was adamant in my refusal of any pay for my work. But she was just as adamant in her own right.

Back in Chicago, Mrs. Palmer had bemoaned the fact that she would face her duties at the Paris Exposition without the army of clerical staff she had employed during Chicago's Columbian Exposition in 1893. Miss Jane Addams had promptly recommended me for my organizational skills. I was flattered by her offer of a position, but I couldn't take it seriously. I had a husband, three young children, and a position lecturing at the University of Chicago. In different circumstances, I assured her, I would have loved to accompany her across the world to help organize activities for the United States Commission. But when I explained why it was impossible for me to travel to France, I had no idea what a strong will I was up against. Mrs. Palmer listened calmly to my objections and proceeded, just as calmly, to change all of the circumstances of my life. She had my husband, Stephen, invited to a congress of medical men and saw to it that funds were provided to support travel, not only for him but for his entire family. At the same time, she arranged for the university to grant me a sabbatical and even insisted that we bring our nursemaid, Delia, to care for the children. Finally, she arranged for our family to join the Palmers in the large house which they took for the duration on rue Brignole. It was a magnificent plan, and I soon found Mrs. Palmer was not to be denied. It was this lucky circumstance that had brought me and my family to the

City of Light on a trip that exceeded all of my dreams. And now she was taking me to the House of Worth for final fittings of her wardrobe, with every intention of improving mine as well.

We had already been busy with a whirl of letter writing, committee meetings, the planning of salons, and endless consultations. Today was a welcome respite from it all. The horse trotted along under dappled shade from trees in the Tuileries gardens. Mrs. Palmer's son Honoré, who sat opposite us, smiled at my protests. "You know Mother will not be thwarted. She truly means it when she says it's all part of her plan."

He was a solid young man only a few years younger than myself. He and his friend, Lord James Lawford, the younger son of an English earl, had decided to join us in our foray to the famous house of fashion. Their excuse was to carry the jewel case containing Bertha's fabulous pearl choker, one of many jewels her loving older husband had purchased for her. They assured me that men were welcome at the House of Worth and that the champagne and pastries offered to its customers were superb. The entertainment was enough to attract young men like themselves, even though it was really calculated to appease the older men likely to be responsible for payments. But the senior Mr. Palmer had scoffed at the idea of accompanying us ladies. Like my husband, he was content to remain at home with his papers.

"It's true," Lawford assured me. "Mrs. Palmer lays her battle plans like a general." He tapped my knee with the top of his ebony cane. He was a fair haired, tall, and stringy young man who had to fold up like a fan in order to fit into a conveyance such as the carriage. It was said that he went to great lengths to avoid socializing with other members of the English aristocracy, ever since he had escaped London for the French capital. He despised his fellow countrymen and loved nothing so much as the society of young Americans like Honoré. "The Queen of Chicago knows how to impress our Parisian hosts," he told me, capturing my attention by the steady gaze of his light blue eyes.

"The fact is, they have been nurtured on pictures of American Bloomerism, which terrifies them. They expect reedy spinsters in red shawls, who serve on committees and battle for women's rights." He feigned shock, while Honoré rolled his eyes and Mrs. Palmer gave her attention to the strolling Parisians beyond our carriage. "It's true! They are amazed by Mrs. Palmer. She is elegant, her French is impeccable, and her gowns are some of Worth's choicest productions. As such, she confounds them." The lady in question merely smiled at the hyperbole of the young man. "She has them eating out of her hand as a result," he concluded.

I saw what he meant. "Ah, and she cannot have someone at her side appear too much like the reedy spinsters, I suppose?"

"Now, now," Mrs. Palmer objected. "Lord James is correct in that I plan to impress our Parisian hosts with an adequate style. We do not wish to appear provincial in any way. But it is merely a requirement of the position, my dear. I am happy to provide you with an ensemble from the House of Worth since I require you to attend so many social gatherings during the duration of the Exposition."

I smiled. It was a good excuse. I couldn't dispute it, not that I would want to. We turned onto rue de la Paix where the great houses of fashion sat, waiting to fulfill the dreams of any woman who had the temerity and pocketbook to enter their doors. As we trotted up the broad avenue I watched the throngs of well-dressed people strolling along, looking into the glass windows. With florid names in gold paint above the glittering merchandise, the milliners, chocolatiers, and jewelers presented their wares on the street level. Halfway up the road, the House of Worth had an elegant stone façade with blue painted window and doorjambs. Directly opposite were the windows of Cartier. It was widely known that the two families would soon be joined, when the daughter of Jean-Philippe Worth became engaged to the jeweler's son. It would be a royal marriage of the two kingdoms of merchandise.

They made it so pleasant to arrive at the maison on rue de la Paix. When we halted, our coachman jumped down to place stairs for us to descend, and a doorman from the fashion house came over to assist. I took a last look at the broad street with all the strolling people. It was such an engaging scene on such a lovely day. I could hardly believe I was there.

Before I could gather my skirts and take the hand of one of the men to descend, a young woman rushed to the side of the carriage, grasping it and calling up to the young men in rapid French. I noticed that Mrs. Palmer pointedly ignored the girl, while Lord James's terribly pale complexion flushed and he responded in French. Honoré rolled his eyes and began to climb out over his friend, so as to be able to help me and his mother. The young woman, who was hatless, gestured to the shop she had come from and I saw it had a selection of hats in the window. I suspected this young woman was a milliner, a maker of hats, and that she wanted to catch the attention of our hostess, whose indulgence in millinery confections was as great as her acquisitions of other fashionable items, such as the gowns we were coming to view. I had heard that millinery was an occupation much favored by young women in Paris. It allowed a young girl some flexibility in her lifestyle, as she exercised her talents in decorating the massive hats that were such an important part of any lady's wardrobe at that time. But Mrs. Palmer managed to ignore her, even as the Englishman answered her in rapid-fire French. I had the impression he was embarrassed by the attention, and desirous of getting rid of the girl. I followed Mrs. Palmer, accepting Honoré's hand to help me descend.

"Jee – mee, Jee – mee" were the only words I could make out from the young woman's French. I knew Honoré's friend preferred to be called "Jimmy," disliking the more formal "Lord James," but I couldn't understand their conversation. Then she grabbed Honoré's arm in supplication. I took a look at her as I stepped to the pavement before following Mrs. Palmer through the door which was held open by the House of Worth man in his livery. She was a small girl, in a gown of figured muslin, a white background with pastel flowers. Around her neck a small locket hung from a black velvet ribbon. She appeared to be earnestly entreating the young men but they gently waved her off. As I turned away to enter the sanctum of the great house of fashion, I wondered about the lives these two young men led when they were out of our company. Of course, while they had many opportunities to go out and mingle with the everyday people of the city, Mrs. Palmer and I were restricted to more formal engagements with other ladies of our class. It made me just a little homesick for Chicago, where I traveled throughout the city to wherever my work took me. But I was aware, as I crossed the threshold into the luxury of the House of Worth, that in Chicago I was seldom called on to enter such lavish surroundings, and never with the object of being treated to the kind of attention I was about to receive. I sighed. If Mrs. Palmer commanded it, who was I to object? A certain excitement bubbled up in me, as I wondered what the famous designer would produce for me based on our visit and the instructions of my hostess. It hardly seemed possible, but I was about to be dressed by Worth.

TWO

As the large blue door swung open, Honoré stepped forward to offer his arm to his mother. Inside, a square foyer rose several floors to a skylight. The space was surrounded by open balconies. I took Lord James's arm and followed Mrs. Palmer and her son up a wide staircase. Along the edges, Chinese ceramic pots overflowed with peonies and greens.

At the top, we were met by a middle-aged woman in a dress of discreet black. It was made of a silk that was finer than anything in my wardrobe, and around her long neck there was a collar of finely spun lace. She and Mrs. Palmer greeted each other in French and then she led us through a series of rooms that provided my introduction to the ever-surprising delight to the senses that was the House of Worth.

The first room held yards of black and white silk, an austere display, as if to cleanse the sight for what was to follow. Overstuffed chairs and couches were scattered across the parquet floor. Glass cabinets trimmed in gilt stood in prominent places, and a large portrait of a man in a wide cloak and a soft velvet hat with a tassel hung on the opposite wall.

"The great man himself." Lord James ducked his head to whisper in my ear. "Father Worth. He passed away a few years ago but these were his collections." He gestured towards the cabinets. "Snuff boxes and antique fans, an amusement for lesser clients when they're kept waiting." My companion was amused.

It was obvious that we did not fall into the category of those who could be kept waiting.

We did not hurry but neither did we linger in that first room. I might have wanted to spend more time there, if I had not seen that the next room was such a vision that I gasped. Lit by large French windows, its cabinets held yards and yards of colored silks. A rainbow ranged along a palette from pale browns through yellows, greens, blues, and purples to pinks. It was not only the colors that invited. The textures made you want to reach out and caress the filmy fabrics. Liquid silks, gentle as breezes, lay beside figured satins and imported Italian brocades. While our guide stopped to point out one of the newest fashions, my companion whispered in my ear, "Needless to say, the silk makers of Lyon adore the House and will do anything to accommodate Jean-Philippe these days. His father brought back prosperity to that town singlehandedly." I barely heard him, I was so entranced by the display.

This was no accident. The way the bolts were placed, how much fabric was left pulled out, and whether it was flat or bunched to catch the light, it was all part of a masterful design. Beside me, Lord James softly recited,

> *Whenas in silks my Julia goes*
> *Then, then (methinks) how sweetly flows*
> *That liquefaction of her clothes.*
> *Next, when I cast mine eyes and see*
> *That brave vibration each way free;*
> *Oh how that glittering taketh me!*

I glanced up. He grinned. "I always think of that poem when I come through this room." He patted my hand. "But this is just the beginning."

We followed the others into the next room, as Mrs. Palmer and the saleswoman kept up a patter in French. This room was padded with plush and velvets. Here, bolts were pulled out to display wonderful designs of leaves or flowers, even butterflies figured on the velvet. There were panels of cloth draped across the top in deep royal colors and several velvet capes hung from a wooden frame. It was like the taste of a luscious cream cake, so thick and rich were those fabrics.

The next room was full of woolens, and Lord James proudly told me that many of them were of British manufacture. Tweeds and plaids were on the high shelves, with plain fine woolens in a range of shades below. It reminded me of crisp winter mornings in Chicago.

As we turned from the display to follow Honoré and his mother through the next doorway, I caught a glimpse of another open door. I was curious, and Lord James followed me as I stepped through an opening into yet another room. "Good lord," he commented, pulling back.

I smiled. Along one wall of the room a long table held a row of headless, legless mannequins wearing lovely bodices that were confections of lace, silk, and brocade. Each figure was unique, but they all had the hourglass shape of shoulders, bust, and waist that was the height of fashion. "I'm sure they keep the measurements of regular clients like Mrs. Palmer," I told him. "That way they can make up designs ahead of time when they know she's coming over from Chicago. I know she's been in correspondence with them about her wardrobe for the Exposition. It would take much too long to make up all of her order if they waited until she was here, you know."

The look of shock passed from his face and he stared down his long nose at me. "You women are such realists, it's alarming. Should we catch up with our party?" He gave a little shiver as he turned away and I laughed. It was true that the tour had led us through displays set up to engage the imagination. It was also true that any woman would be fully aware of the work it would take to transform the promise of the uncut bolt of cloth into a garment that could be worn without embarrassment. What young woman had not at some time cut into cloth and stitched it up according to a pattern, only to be deeply disappointed by the end result? I certainly had. It was why we could appreciate the art of an establishment like the House of Worth. I knew it was beyond male comprehension, however, so I gladly headed toward the final room, a high ceilinged, well-lit space of expansive proportions with clusters of comfortable looking tables and chairs ranged across the gleaming wooden floors.

But as soon as I crossed the threshold, I felt the tension. Mrs. Palmer and her son had stopped in front of a dapper man of medium height who sported a small goatee. Mrs. Palmer was, as always, unflappable, but the man seemed harassed. He had positioned himself to block the way to a central group of chairs, which was already occupied by a large party.

"Oh, dear," my companion whispered. "It's the Yanks."

THREE

I felt sorry for the couturier. It was M. Jean-Philippe Worth himself, the elder son of the founder, who stood before us uncharacteristically flustered and, soon, I understood why.

"I am *désolé*, madame," he told Bertha Palmer after I was introduced. "When we scheduled your fitting I was certain Mrs. Johnstone and her family would be gone before you arrived."

Mrs. Palmer raised an eyebrow. Squatting in the prime location was Amelia Johnstone, her daughter, and two other young women. Mrs. Johnstone was a social dictator in the tiny community of expatriate Americans in Paris. When her reign was rudely interrupted by the arrival of the Queen of Chicago society, Bertha Palmer, it was well known that Mrs. Johnstone was not content. In fact, it was said she was steaming when Bertha Palmer was appointed as the first and only woman commissioner in the American delegation. Earlier in the week she had left a party, angry that Mrs. Palmer had been given precedence in the parade into supper after the ball. It did not bode well for the rest of the summer that the ladies involved had already crossed swords. Bertha Palmer was not a woman to shrink from a fight. She had many advantages over Mrs. Johnstone, whose husband was nominal head of the delegation. But Amelia Johnstone had done little to aid her own position. Despite living in the City of Light for the past year, she had made no effort to learn to speak French. Bertha Palmer, on the other hand, was proud of the

French lineage of her family and had been fluent in French from a young age. But even beyond that, she had a cosmopolitan flair and a knack for politics. Amelia Johnstone just couldn't compete. Since our recent arrival, Bertha Palmer had already managed to convince the officials involved to increase the Exposition space allotted to the United States. And she had only begun her campaign.

Now, she smiled politely at M. Worth. She reminded me of a cougar I had seen when I visited the Lincoln Park Zoo with my children. The animal had bared its fangs in just that way. At the same time, I saw that the young men with us had retreated several steps, as if in expectation of some kind of outburst. Poor M. Worth looked harassed. "And Miss Cassatt as you can see… she, too, is kept waiting." He gestured helplessly towards a group of chairs close to the windows.

Before she could respond, I jumped into the breach. After all, what are social secretaries for if not an occasional rescue? "Miss Cassatt? Miss Mary Cassatt? Oh, Mrs. Palmer, do you think you could introduce me? As I mentioned to you, I've been so looking forward to meeting her. I admire her work so much!" At least that was no fiction. When Bertha told me she knew the American artist who lived in Paris, I had begged for an introduction. I still remembered her wonderful mural in the Woman's Building of the World's Columbian Exposition and, ever since seeing it, those images had haunted me.

M. Worth turned to me with a look of relief and over his shoulder I saw a glint of amusement in Bertha Palmer's eyes. While she was entirely capable of delivering a devastating remark within hearing distance of the obnoxious Mrs. Johnstone, she was under no absolute compulsion to do so. "Why, how lovely," she proclaimed. "Please, I have not seen Miss Cassatt since our arrival and there is so much to catch up on. Do you mind, M. Worth?"

I could see the man was overwhelmed with relief as he led us to the grouping of chairs in the light of the windows.

He snapped his fingers for additional chairs and refreshments to follow. Bertha introduced me to her friend after their very French exchange of cheek kisses.

Mary Cassatt was near Bertha Palmer in age, perhaps fifty, but she was taller and bonier than the Chicago matron. She wore a charming dress of muslin with fluffy lace under her chin. It was pleasantly light and airy for a warm spring day. She also wore a small hat with silk flowers pinned to the narrow brim perched on her head. The friend and companion with her was equally well dressed. It made me feel dowdy in my sturdy brown skirt.

They already had flutes of champagne on the low table before them, and M. Worth presented us with a choice of champagne or tea, both at hand on silver platters. I saw Bertha glance across to the party in the middle of the room, where a large pot of tea sat on their table. She rolled her eyes and waved over the champagne. The young men smiled as they reached for glasses and I saw Miss Cassatt suppress her own grin. Apparently, Mrs. Johnstone, like some other women in the American settlement, objected to French customs when it came to imbibing wine.

Content with her superiority, Bertha Palmer provided the poor couturier with even more relief. "M. Worth, I hope you will forgive us if we take a few minutes to catch up with our dear friend. We ladies must have our gossip, you know."

"Indeed, madame, please, take your time. Become comfortable. Let us know when you are ready to see what we have made for you." He rubbed his hands together. "It is magnificent. I know you will like it."

"Certainly. Honoré, give M. Worth the box." She gestured to her son and he stepped up and handed the box to Worth. "My pearls," Bertha told him. "We can see how they look with the evening gown." He accepted the box and beckoned to Mlle Arquette, the woman who had met us at the front door. Handing her the box of pearls, he whispered a few commands, then turned back to us.

"It will be marvelous, I promise you. You know, of course, my daughter, Andrée, is to be married? Yes, it is to the son of Cartier, the jeweler across the road. She has received the most beautiful gem, a sapphire, as an engagement gift. I must show you. I know how much you and Mr. Palmer appreciate fine jewels. I would be grateful for your opinion." He was fiercely proud, and Bertha smiled benevolently at him. "But not now, of course. I leave you to your gossip, and we will prepare the gowns. You will be amazed."

With that, he turned back to respond to the insistent waves of Mrs. Johnstone across the room. While Bertha and Miss Cassatt exchanged information about friends and travels, my attention drifted to the other group. I had placed myself where I could view them across the vast room that was very like a ballroom. The walls held multiple mirrors, so I had the uncanny experience of seeing my own figure beyond the group as I turned to watch. I had thought myself stylish enough when I dressed in the white shirtwaist, brown skirt, and straw hat that morning, but here in the House of Worth it was less than impressive. The sight of my plain figure and provincial air made me cringe, especially after viewing the magnificent raw materials in the rooms we had passed through. It was very clever, that. What woman wouldn't want to invest in a truly stylish garment worthy to be worn in the famous city after seeing her old clothes in such a reflection?

Across the room, Amelia Johnstone appeared to be arguing with M. Worth. The poor man looked distressed. A woman wearing a green velvet walking dress stood in front of them, turning this way and that on demand. I had seen Worth gowns on women in Chicago, wealthy women who took an interest in Hull House. The gown on display showed the unmistakable style of the dressmaker, but there seemed to be an excess of jet beading on the sleeves, hem, and even the back of the bodice. At least it seemed excessive to me, although, admittedly, I was no expert in the matter.

Bertha and Miss Cassatt could be considered experts and they were watching the demonstration as well. When M. Worth noticed their interest he turned back to the Johnstones, flapping his hands in exasperation.

"Poor Jean-Philippe," Miss Cassatt said. "They are the worst possible customers. For one thing they insist on green—which he hates. He told me no woman can support it but especially not an older woman."

"Oh, no," Bertha Palmer said, making a point not to look in that direction. "It's not for the mother, surely?" She coughed in a ladylike manner thereby disguising a burst of laughter. "And the jet. Did you see it?"

Miss Cassatt looked up. "M. Worth says it's the fault of the amateurs, as he calls them," she said. "A dress made for a discerning woman of fashion has just the right amount of trim, especially if that trim is of a certain type."

"Such as jet?" I asked.

"Correct. Such as jet. Anyway, the gown makes an impression at a ball or some such and immediately all the ladies come to him and demand this trim on any garment he is making for them. But, if Mrs. X has a certain amount of jet on her gown, then a woman such as Mrs. Johnstone wants twice as much and won't listen to M. Worth when he warns of excess. I dare say Mrs. Johnstone saw jet on one of your evening gowns, Bertha, and now she's insisting on it. M. Worth is devastated, but what can he do? The customer rules."

"Looks like a bloody lampshade," Lord James contributed and Honoré guffawed. The Englishman blushed. "Sorry, ladies, forgive my language."

Bertha shook her head. "Stop it, both of you." She glared at them and they buried their faces in their champagne flutes.

Meanwhile, the saleswoman who had led us through the maze of rooms stood awkwardly, as if she were reluctant to interrupt, although she obviously had a message. Bertha turned to her graciously. "Are the fitters ready for us, Mlle Arquette?"

"*Non*, madame. I am sorry. It is the Johnstone party. Mrs. Johnstone she asks me to invite the English gentleman to join them for a cup of tea."

I saw the satiric eyebrow raised on Bertha's face. It was an unfathomably rude request, inviting the young man but slighting the rest of us. Lord James was the only one of us they were interested in, it seemed. Even Honoré was amused.

"Oh, my," said the Englishman. "Oh, my, no, I don't think so. I mean, I have suddenly remembered a previous engagement." He put down his glass and gathered his top hat, gloves, and cane. "I do hope you ladies will forgive me, but I must away. I'm afraid I must leave immediately." The ladies smiled and nodded.

Mlle Arquette attempted to persuade him to greet the Johnstone party but he shied like a frightened horse and, before I knew it, he had disappeared out the door. Honoré gathered his own things to follow his friend, grinning all the while. "Excuse me, Mama, Miss Cassatt, Mrs. Chapman, ladies." He leaned in to me. "The only time you'll ever see Jimmy move that quickly is when he's afraid of being cornered. Mrs. Johnstone has been after him for her daughter all season. The one thing she would like, above all things, is to marry her daughter into the British aristocracy. The one thing he wants least in the world is to be dragged back into that same British aristocracy. Little does the lady know how much he will do to avoid the very society she seeks. The truth is, the joke's on her." He waved and hurried after his friend.

The Johnstone party watched with open-mouthed consternation as the young men disappeared out the doorway. But at least their departure accomplished what the House of Worth had been attempting since our arrival. Mrs. Johnstone began to collect her belongings in a move to finally abandon her roost. M. Worth looked relieved.

Suddenly, a flustered young woman hurried over to the couturier and pulled him into a corner. She gestured dramatically while she talked to him and pointed our way. Something was definitely wrong and it was difficult to disguise our curiosity. Then M. Worth returned to us, his hands clasped, his face red. He glanced at the Johnstone party and purposely turned his back to them. "Pardon, Mme Palmer, there has been some mistake. The box in which you brought your pearls...it is empty."

FOUR

Poor M. Worth. His anxiety was overwhelming. He turned and beckoned to Mlle Arquette who came over, bearing the red velvet case that had held the pearls. M. Worth took it and opened it. It was empty.

Meanwhile, Mrs. Johnstone was attempting to leave. As we were between her and the door, she veered towards us in a determined manner. Mrs. Palmer noticed and, frowning, she reached out and took the empty case from M. Worth. Closing it with a snap she handed it to me without looking in my direction. "We will deal with this later. We would like to see the gown regardless, please." Her command was obviously a relief to the couturier, who bowed and motioned to Mlle Arquette to go and do the customer's bidding.

Mrs. Johnstone stopped a few yards away. "Mrs. Palmer, how nice to see you again." Bertha Palmer turned a wide-eyed gaze on the woman and her contingent, quite as if she had been unaware of their presence. "You know my daughter, Lydia, of course, and these are her dear friends Miss Grace Greenway Brown of Baltimore and Miss Edith Stuart of Philadelphia." Mrs. Johnstone was short and plump. Her daughter, in contrast, was tall with an oval face and a long thin nose. The hat that she wore sported a spiky feather that only emphasized her height. The other two women were smaller and dressed in lighter colors. Miss Brown, in particular, was a pretty young woman with hazel eyes and a warm smile. Miss Stuart was small and pert looking with blonde curls framing her face.

Mrs. Palmer gave them a cool nod. Mrs. Johnstone seemed to think it a slight. Her eyes narrowed. "I must say, in the future, it would be kind of you not to keep all the young men to yourself. I've seen Lord James here before and I was sorry to see you send him away. We mature women must let the young ones have a chance, you know, and not begrudge them the company of the young men."

I nearly choked on my champagne at this attempt to chide Bertha Palmer, but she ignored the slight altogether and turned away to introduce the rest of us. At that point, the young women in the Johnstone group gaped and exchanged glances. Lydia Johnstone spoke up. "Miss Cassatt? Miss Mary Cassatt? Is it really Miss Mary Cassatt?" It seemed they were all taking art classes during their stay in Paris and they were very excited to meet the famous artist. They were so effusive in their praise of her paintings that I could see Mrs. Johnstone cringe. Their enthusiasm took her completely by surprise.

M. Worth rejoined us then and, beyond him, I saw another figure come through the door. She was easily the most beautiful woman in the room. Slight and thin, with porcelain skin, she wore a suit in a gray shimmery fabric with a long coat over a flat skirt and a creamy silk blouse with a bow under the neck. Her face was partially obscured by a large hat with a filmy veil. She walked carefully, leaning on a silver-headed cane. Behind her came a young woman in a white lawn dress with flounces at the hem, a tight blue jacket, and a blue satin sash. Her auburn hair fell down to her shoulders from beneath a perky little plate of a hat. Bertha Palmer also noticed the quiet entrance of the two women, which caused Mrs. Johnstone to turn to see what had caught her attention. When she saw the woman in gray, her eyes opened wide and she glanced at M. Worth. He, too, turned towards the door.

"That woman! Well, if that isn't the limit," Mrs. Johnstone huffed. "I'll not have my daughter and the others exposed to people like that. I never. Lydia, come. We're leaving. *Now*." She looked at Mrs. Palmer, as if expecting her to join in the protest. Meeting only a stony glance, she herded her group towards a door, away from where the newcomers were headed.

The speedy exit of the Americans was only too obviously rude. Bertha Palmer clucked and shook her head, while M. Worth watched with horror. The group rushed out with only a few backward glances by the young people.

Bertha shook her head again. Reaching out to pat the couturier's arm she said, "M. Worth, I see the countess and her daughter have arrived. Won't you ask them to join us?" I saw she was going to some lengths to repair the damage Amelia Johnstone had done. M. Worth hurried to the side of the woman with the cane and ushered her and her sylphlike daughter over to our group. She was introduced as the Countess Olga Zugenev and her daughter's name was Sonya. I sensed there was some story about the beautiful woman and I wondered exactly what had caused the Johnstones to hurry away.

The countess and Bertha exchanged greetings in French and Mary Cassatt joined the conversation. In deference to me, they changed to English, which the countess spoke with an accent I assumed was Russian.

"It is the first time you have come to Paris?" she asked me. "And how do you find it?" She had a soft breathy voice and large dark eyes with long lashes. She was so petite she looked like a girl herself, but there were fine lines at the corners of her eyes and lips that showed her age. I couldn't guess exactly how old she was, though. She was small enough to seem almost swamped in the glittery gray of her long boxy jacket.

"It is wonderful. We are so thrilled to be here and it's all due to the generosity of Mrs. Palmer and her husband."

"Nonsense, Emily. Mrs. Chapman here is my social secretary and I'm working her hard," Bertha told them. "Oh, my, look at that."

We all looked up to see a woman walk through the room in a magnificent evening gown of figured velvet and satin in shades of gold. The skirt fell to the ground in a simple A shape, with a train spilling off the back. On the front the fabric was patterned with stalks of corn, which appeared to grow from the ground, with long gracefully crinkled leaves falling away, like stalks swaying in a gentle breeze in a golden sunset. The bodice had a square neckline, gently puffed sleeves, and a black velvet sash around the trim princess waist. It was a tour de force, perfect for Bertha as the representative of the great plains of the American Midwest. It had been designed specifically for her to wear at official receptions during the Exposition.

There followed a lengthy technical discussion of the dress, the shoes, and the accessories that would accompany the ensemble. The pearls were mentioned again, and M. Worth looked distressed, but Bertha brushed aside any questions and promised to bring them to the final fitting. She had brought some handmade lace they decided to add to the neckline of the bodice and there was talk of some additional flourishes down the front. When they finished the model left the room, then returned a few minutes later, wearing a different gown. I realized that her physique resembled Mrs. Palmer's. The second gown was an afternoon dress with delicate stripes of ribbon woven through a gauzy fabric. It was judged complete and ordered sent on to the Trocadéro house.

A walking suit for Miss Cassatt was shown next. It was worn by a different woman, who was shaped more like the artist, being taller and lankier. It was of a dusty blue silk, with the smooth seams of a princess line running from the neckline down to the hem. The flared skirt looked short enough for walking, although it was fuller in the back. Pale white lace trimmed the high neck and fell down the front of the bodice. The suit was completed by an unusual metallic lace bolero with tapered sleeves, which ended in a strip of tiny buttons to the wrist. The ensemble evoked a style of the past, perhaps from a Renaissance painting, which made it rather grand. It would be perfect for the artist. While we were watching, Bertha was trying to recruit Mary to be a judge for the artwork at the Exposition. But Miss Cassatt was adamantly opposed, and impervious to all the coaxing turned on her by her very persuasive friend.

"But, Mary, you must do it. Do you know how few women there are on the award panels? We must have more women. Come, you must do your part." I noticed that Countess Olga quietly sipped her champagne without joining this debate.

"M. Worth, the suit is splendid. You can pack it up." Miss Cassatt turned to Bertha. "No, my friend. I have told you already. I don't believe in these competitions. They are insidious. They do nothing but harm. I saw it when I was young. All anyone ever wanted was to be shown and to win. It was corrupting. You have no idea. Young artists are forced to bend their styles to please the judges. It's all wrong."

Bertha Palmer frowned, but then she turned her attention back to the blue walking suit, as the woman modeling it walked away. "That suit is very fine, M. Worth. Do you know, that is just the sort of thing I had in mind for Mrs. Chapman."

Despite my protests, I was made to stand, walk, and turn, while Bertha Palmer and the couturier consulted. "Yes, I see it," he said. "Just the colors of autumn, as you say, for the academic lady. And perhaps a little watch chain, a chapeau for the head with a little feather, yes?"

I was sent to the fitting room, where the capable Mlle Arquette and her minions swarmed over me with measuring tapes after removing my outer garments. It was all done so quickly and efficiently I was back with the group before I knew it. It left me with the uneasy feeling that I had left behind more intimate knowledge of my physical faults and failings than anyone else in the world had ever been privy to…even my husband. But it was done so swiftly and comfortably I could hardly complain. Would I, too, be represented by one of those headless, legless, stuffed bodices?

When I returned, the women were viewing a ball gown in champagne-colored satin damask worn by Countess Olga's daughter Sonya herself, rather than by a mannequin. The bodice had a chiffon overlay that repeated the floral pattern in the satin. There was lace trim on the round neckline and an irregular fall of lace from the shoulders for the short sleeves. A tuck at the back provided for a small train. It was embellished with pink ribbons and fabric roses at the shoulders, halfway along the neckline, and at the waist. It made the slender young woman look like a fairy or one of the Three Graces in spring.

"How charming," Bertha commented. "I am so sorry Honoré and his friend left before you arrived. I was hoping he would meet you, my dear." She turned towards the countess, who held her champagne flute in a hand with a wrist so small and white it looked quite delicate. "You will come to the opening of the House of Worth exhibit, won't you? I'll send an invitation. I've been helping them plan it. It will provide the perfect opportunity for Sonya to show off her new gown."

"Ah, but even before that, we will see all of you in my gowns, I hope." M. Worth stood over our group. "I have invited all of you to the party for my daughter's engagement. You will come, will you not?"

FIVE

When we arrived at the large stone house that the Palmers were renting on rue Brignole in the Trocadéro, I hurried to the first floor suite set aside for myself and my family. I still found it amazing that these rooms, with their very tall French windows opening into a walled garden, were all for our use. When I was growing up, it was common for my wealthier relatives to make annual trips to Europe. But this was the first time my husband and I had done so, and we had never expected to be so well situated. The suite of rooms was all for us, our three small children, and Delia, who had come as their nursemaid. It was a fantastic gift that made the whole trip a fairy tale for us. I reveled in the glory of it, as five-year-old Jack and four-year-old Lizzie clattered across the shining wood floor to greet me. Delia stood smiling behind them holding three-year-old Tommy in her arms.

Seeing my little family, away from the surroundings that we were so used to back in Chicago, took my breath away when I realized what we had become. Gone were the days when my only preoccupation was the next assignment for a class. There was a time when I'd felt overwhelmed by the responsibilities I'd taken on as a wife and mother. The birth of my third child, Tommy, had come in the midst of a year when I not only taught at the university but also managed several of the ongoing campaigns for better government at Hull House. Much to my surprise, I realized that the more I did, the more I could do. When I thought of the past few years, I realized how busy we always were. Stephen had continued his research, running experiments and publishing results. He had stopped work on the dangerous X-rays, although he kept in touch with Emil Grubbé. Somehow, we had managed to return to Woods Hole each summer, which provided a sun-filled break for me and the children. I loved that very much, as it reminded me of my own summers on the Cape with my mother's father, digging in the sand to find clams and rushing at the waves. While Stephen labored over test tubes and tanks of squid, the children, Delia, and I played on the beach or waded around with buckets for specimens we brought to the Marine Biological Laboratory. They were always willing to accept our offerings and to show the children other special prizes in the tanks. We would all miss that trip this year, but the opportunity to travel to Paris was not one we could pass up.

In Chicago, I helped Jane Addams fight against Alderman Johnny Powers, who had tried to drive the Hull House women out of the West Side. But I also brought Jack and Lizzie to the kindergarten there, where they tumbled around and listened to stories alongside the children of immigrants. They enjoyed it and Stephen felt it was a better education for them than being kept apart in some kind of sterile isolation. I had worried about that but, in the whirlwind of activity that was our lives, we all seemed to be bumbling along free from any lasting harm.

Stephen set aside time to spend with the children on the days I lectured. Jack was getting rambunctious, but Stephen seemed to love that challenge. Lizzie, meanwhile, had quite a temper and could easily bring down the house with a tantrum. But she would listen, if I promised to take her with me the next time I left the house. Even at such a young age, she had a way of approaching the world as if she were a warrior happily on attack.

And Tommy was a cuddly little bear who loved to eat. Where Jack was bright and inquisitive, and Lizzie was adventurous, little Tommy was content as long as he had something in his mouth. He spoke later and less often than the first two, but we thought he was probably overwhelmed by the loquaciousness of his siblings. He couldn't get a word in, between Jack's statements and Lizzie's questions. I worried about him sometimes, but Stephen laughed at my concern and Delia liked the way he clung to her during the day.

In short, our world had become hectic, sometimes filled with frustrations, and always demanding a huge amount of energy. But, when we were suddenly set down in Paris and I could look across the sea to our life as it was back in Chicago, I had to admit it was very satisfying. I couldn't tell exactly where we were heading, or what the children would become as they grew, but we were underway and on a course, rough though it might sometimes be.

Looking at them now, in the green warmth of the little garden flooded with afternoon sunshine, I felt a thrill once again. I never would have imagined that we would be in Paris…all together.

I removed my hat and jacket, then changed my boots for slippers before I joined the children in the garden. It was only after I'd visited with them for a while and heard about how they'd been chasing a white cat all around the garden, that I remembered the empty velvet box I'd carried back from the House of Worth. I would have to return it to Mrs. Palmer, and I was uneasy about what would happen when she told her husband the pearls were missing. With a sigh, I stood and straightened my skirt, then I left to find my way to Mrs. Palmer's rooms on the second floor. I needn't have worried. But I didn't know that, as I carried the box up the stairs. Just as I reached the corridor I almost bumped into Honoré.

"Oh, excuse me, Mrs. Chapman. I'm sorry. I'm just going to join my father for an outing to the races." His glance fell to the box in my arms and I saw his face slowly turn red. It was especially noticeable with his pale skin, open face, and thin mustache. His eyes opened wide and I saw him swallow, but he made no comment on the box. "Excuse me, I mustn't keep Father waiting." He hurried away, as if I was contagious.

Hugging the red velvet box to my chest, I knocked and the maid admitted me to Mrs. Palmer's rooms. Bertha had changed into a flowing tea gown, which was designed to allow a woman to discard her confining corset while at home. It was pink silk chiffon, in a faint floral print, with a froth of transparent chiffon and delicate lace at the round neck. A dainty lace bolero had sleeves to the elbow, where several layers of lace spilled down to her wrists.

She was working again, seated in a gilt chair at a large, ornately painted desk that might have been from the seventeenth century. The rooms in this part of the house were even taller than those on the first floor. Their ceilings featured carved moldings and painted ovals of cherubs floating in blue skies. Back in Chicago, such tall rooms with colorful decorations existed in institutional buildings, such as banks and offices, where they were calculated to impress. But, in Paris, a private home seemed to be a place built for giants of another time. I had come to the conclusion that they were designed to emphasize the vast difference between the aristocrats and the lower orders of an earlier era. Perhaps it had been such disparities that had incited the French Revolution.

Bertha used the sitting room adjoining her bedroom and dressing room as an office. The tables were spread with private and official communications. On a side wall hung the Renoir painting she took with her wherever she went. It had been in the sitting room of her mansion on Lake Shore Drive in Chicago. Then it had hung on the wall of her stateroom on the transatlantic trip and now it held the place of honor in her Paris rooms. In it, two young girls who were circus performers stood, accepting applause in the middle of a sawdust ring. One was turned so she could gesture to the crowd. The other hugged a half dozen oranges in her arms. I wondered if they had been juggling them, or if they were tributes thrown by the crowds. In the upper corner you could barely make out the figures of several well-dressed men sitting and watching. I couldn't help thinking there should have been children applauding, rather than those businessmen. I had come to think that Bertha Palmer must have identified with the girls. She and her sister, Ida, had been quite young when they first appeared on the social scene in Chicago. Had it seemed like a stage, perhaps, where they were called upon to perform? Like the girls in the picture?

I had heard how Potter Palmer, who was more than twenty years older than Bertha, had met her when she was still a schoolgirl. He'd been patient for a long time and, despite the other suitors who'd appeared by the time she was of age, she chose him in the end. From a really young age she must have known her own mind. I imagined that something in her girlhood must have made her feel a special sympathy for the two young girls in the painting.

"Emily, our visit to the House of Worth was very satisfactory, don't you think?" Bertha's dark eyes gleamed and she smiled with mischief, so I knew she was thinking of Mrs. Johnstone's retreat. I was sorry to poke a hole in her bubble of satisfaction but I held out the empty velvet box without comment.

She reached for it. "Yes. I know. I've just questioned Honoré about it, and he insists it never left his hands. I will have to make inquiries." She opened and shut the box, frowning. "It's a delicate matter, Emily. One cannot raise a hue and cry without having suspicion fall on some poor servant or saleswoman. Even the breath of such a scandal could absolutely ruin them, you know. No, this will take some quiet investigation, so as not to stir things up."

I collapsed onto the gilt chair opposite her. "It was a very valuable piece of jewelry, though, wasn't it?" I was no expert on jewels, but her choker with seven strands of pearls was quite famous in Chicago.

"Hmm. Yes." She lifted an eyebrow. "Over two thousand pearls and seven diamonds, actually." She sighed and folded her hands in front of her on the desk. Looking directly into my eyes, she said, "We must *not* mention this to Mr. Palmer."

"But perhaps you'll need to speak to the police. Wouldn't you want Mr. Palmer to know about that?"

Bertha grimaced. "The police…no, I don't think we want that. You see, Emily, sometimes Mr. Palmer believes I'm careless with my jewels. He's been known to sleep with them under his pillow when we travel." She shook her head in disapproval of this habit, but I had heard tales of how she'd dropped a diamond bracelet in a box at the symphony in Chicago, never noticing it was gone until it was returned by a conscientious usher. Mr. Palmer had reason to be concerned.

"You may not know that Mr. Palmer was quite ill in Rome last year. I really do *not* want him worried." I could see she was sincerely concerned about her aging husband. Despite the difference in their ages, and sometimes their interests, I had rarely met such a devoted couple. "You need to promise me, Emily, not to mention this to Mr. Palmer."

"Certainly."

"We'll find the pearls before he ever knows they were missing."

It seemed to me to be more than a mix-up, but I had to defer to her wishes.

"It may be that Honoré has done something foolish," she admitted. "And that would be even more upsetting to Mr. Palmer than my misplacing the pearls, you see. Meanwhile, what did you think of the Countess Olga and her lovely daughter, Sonya?"

"The countess is quite beautiful."

"And no doubt her daughter will be just as much a beauty. But I must warn you about something. You saw the way Mrs. Johnstone snubbed her? Of course you did. She's a terribly small-minded woman. The Countess Olga is married to a Russian count. He's distantly related to the tsar. Of course, it was an arranged marriage.

He's rather a brute, apparently. You saw the cane. She's never explained her injury. There are things that are not mentioned. But they live separately now, by arrangement of the family."

I realized she meant that the countess's injury must have been caused by her husband. It was a terrible story. I had met women in the tenements around Hull House who had been mistreated by their husbands. But I had foolishly assumed such behavior was caused by poverty. I had not thought to hear of it in the upper reaches of society in Europe. It seemed very sad to me.

"It's a shocking story. But the Europeans, the other aristocrats, they understand that sometimes it's necessary to make such arrangements. It's our own Mrs. Johnstone who makes a fuss, as if the countess were the baker's wife in her hometown and had chosen to leave her husband."

"Can't they divorce?" I asked. It was an extreme measure but I knew that Florence Kelley—a social activist I had worked with at Hull House—had survived a divorce. She had moved to Illinois with her children to finally become legally free of a husband who'd deserted her.

"In England or America, it might be possible, but they are Catholics of some sort and it's not permitted. Really, is it too much to ask to grant the woman a little leeway? Can't she just live in Paris in peace? I find Mrs. Johnstone's attitude very embarrassing. And the French think she's quite mad. But she tries to get the other Americans to follow her lead in this. It's just disgraceful."

"I can see it's not something you would do."

"On the contrary, I find the countess charming and I believe that Sonya would be a wonderful match for a nice young American." Her eyes glowed with the excitement of it. "Especially, a nice young American with political ambitions. My niece Julia married into the Romanian aristocracy, you know. I think it only fair that we should bring home a Russian bride!"

Julia was the daughter of Bertha's sister, Ida, and the granddaughter of President Grant, as Ida had married the former president's son Fred. Lacking any daughter of her own, Bertha was extremely fond of her niece. She'd told me that, since the young woman's marriage, she sorely missed her company. And I even suspected that I myself benefited from that absence. Bertha yearned for a young girl to mother. It made me glad I had a daughter of my own, as well as two sons.

"That's why you were disappointed Honoré left before they came?"

"Don't you think it would be a wonderful match? Of course, I would never try to force the issue, but she's a charming and beautiful young woman and he's a carefree young man."

"So nature might just take its course?"

"You never know." She tapped her fingers on the desk. "And a young man needs a wife, if he's going to start a political career."

"A political career?"

"Alderman. He'll be standing next year. Plans are underway."

"Well, in that case, I'm sure he'll win."

"I certainly hope so. But can you imagine the impression he would make in Chicago with the daughter of a Russian count on his arm? The campaign will still take a lot of work, but I have the assurance of support. I was very disappointed with President McKinley. He promised Mr. Palmer an ambassadorship but never fulfilled that promise. I let him know exactly how disappointed Mr. Palmer was, so I expect a good deal of party support for Honoré."

I suspected that Mr. Potter Palmer might not have been as disappointed as his wife when he was not named ambassador. But I certainly believed Honoré would have a great deal of support for his election. And he would have a hard time resisting the beautiful daughter of a Russian count, if his mother turned her attention to making their meeting inevitable. Few men could resist Bertha Palmer when she set her mind to something.

We spent the rest of the afternoon planning attacks in her other current battles. She was on the offensive to get more women appointed to the awards committees for the Exposition.

In addition, she had succeeded in expanding the space for the United States exhibit and would meet with a committee to decide where the additional paintings by American artists would hang. Winslow Homer and Whistler would be prominently displayed in the fine arts exhibition in the Grand Palais. The United States was already well represented with paintings by those artists and others, such as Eakins and Sargent, but some lesser painters, whose work had not been accepted for the Grand Palais, still needed to be hung elsewhere. So Bertha had identified space in another pavilion. Negotiations were more often concluded in salons than committee meetings for this type of issue and, by nature of her connections and fluent French, Bertha had wangled invitations to the most useful of them. The French were charmed by the "Queen of Chicago," despite the fact that they were originally dismayed by the appointment of a woman to the post of commissioner to the Exposition.

"Mary Cassatt will not be persuaded to act as a judge. And she refuses to submit her own work anymore. However, she may be persuaded to attend our little tête-à-tête with the young American artists." It was one of the social engagements she had delegated to me to arrange. "But you must convince her to get M. Degas to come as well. She was his protégé for a long time, you know. They do have their little tiffs, these artists, and they are on the outs again. But I'm sure you can convince her to invite him, and they are such old comrades, I'm sure he's just waiting for her to ask. She'll be at the engagement party for M. Worth's daughter. She has a swarm of relatives visiting from Philadelphia, but she wouldn't miss it. Oh, and we all need to wear Worth. The man would be completely insulted if we appeared in anyone else's designs."

I looked at her with alarm. I certainly had nothing suitable among the dresses I'd brought to Paris, let alone a gown by Worth. I was looking forward to the day ensemble Mrs. Palmer had promised me, but a ball gown was a different matter altogether.

SIX

The next day, Bertha Palmer arranged a special treat. She rented a boat, so we could cruise the Seine between the banks where the Exposition buildings had been erected. She announced her plan at the breakfast table and described it as a family outing, inviting me to bring Stephen, the children, and even Delia. Mr. Palmer was allowed to decline this particular invitation, but Honoré's attendance was demanded and he had been told to encourage Lord James to join us. I was charged with delivering an invitation to Countess Olga and Sonya.

At Bertha's suggestion, Stephen and I left early to take the children to a matinee performance at the Théâtre des Bonshommes Guillaume. We took a taxi to the Place de la Concorde and herded the children and Delia down an incline, along a walk shaded by tall trees, to the little theater building. Delia carried Tommy, who sucked his thumb contentedly, while Jack and Lizzie ran ahead. They came to stop in front of the fantastical little building and looked up at the frieze above the door, where some figures were dancing along.

Lizzie pointed. "Puppets, puppets, puppets!"

I took her hand. "That's right. We're going to see marionettes. They're a kind of puppet that has strings. You'll see."

"More of the new art," Stephen commented. He grabbed Jack's hand to prevent him from running further on. "This way, my boy."

As we waited in a short line to purchase tickets Stephen and I took in the building. It had the wavy, swirling lines of what was now being called "Art Nouveau." Slim columns, like vines, twisted up and turned down to form arches. It looked magical, like it might move at any moment. This was also the style of the entrances to the new Metropolitan, the underground trains that had been built in time for the Exposition, and for many other new buildings. It was a style for the new century.

Inside there were only about a hundred plush seats and the children bounced up and down in excitement and joy as they saw the marionettes marching and jumping around. The story was in French but it was easy enough to follow from the actions of the puppets. The visit was a great success.

When we emerged into the sunlight again we took the children down to the river, where a flat boat with a green- and white-striped awning was pulled up to the dock. Mrs. Palmer waved from a seat at a table laid out in the stern and we were helped aboard. The children ran to the railings to look at the water, and Stephen and Delia kept a hand on each of them to be sure they wouldn't jump in. But I knew they were used to boats from summers at Woods Hole and I was sure they would behave themselves.

"This is wonderful," I told Bertha.

"Yes, it is nice, isn't it? There are more tables and chairs, and even a small set for the children. Seward has seen to it all. Do sit down. We're just waiting for the others." Seward was Bertha's butler and his presence meant all would run as smoothly as butter. The goodies for the tea would no doubt have been prepared by Bertha's wonderful cook.

As I sat down, Honoré and Lord James came back from the bow of the boat just in time to help Countess Olga and her daughter Sonya step down into the stern. They exclaimed over the surroundings. When everyone was settled the boat began to shake a little and then, very gently, it moved away from the dock. Seward had two maids pour the tea and set out plates of petit fours and little sandwiches. I helped get the children something to eat and that captured their attention, for the time being.

Sonya came to meet the children and she talked to them for a while. I could see Bertha Palmer wore a satisfied little smile and it made me wonder if she really had plans for her son and the young woman. A rehearsal for a future daughter-in-law? It seemed that Countess Olga also took notice.

"This is quite splendid, Mrs. Palmer. You have outdone yourself," Lord James said. The countess agreed.

"A little excursion before the real work of the Exposition begins," Bertha said. "I thought we would all benefit from it."

"I haven't had time to visit the exhibits yet," Stephen said, addressing the two young men. "I know you two have been out there. What do you find most interesting?"

"The Palace of Optics," Honoré said. "They have the largest telescope in the world. You've got to see it."

"You should see the Palace of Electricity. There's a waterfall in front of it and it's all lit up at night," Lord James said. "But what's really amazing are the huge dynamos behind the building. They power everything in the whole exposition."

Stephen pulled out a map and laid it out on a padded seat that ran along the stern of the boat. He was too excited to eat but I sipped tea at the table with Bertha and the others. Soon the two young men were standing again to look at the passing sights.

"So, the main gate is back there," Stephen said, as he pointed up the river, "at Place de la Concorde, and we are sailing down the middle of the whole thing. This is like the grand canal at the Columbian Exposition."

"Similar," Bertha said. "But that was an artificial body of water. Here in Paris, it is the Seine itself. They insisted the Exposition be right in the center of the city. In Chicago that would have been too disruptive, it never would have worked with all the thousands of visitors. But in Paris, they make it work."

"Well, most of it's temporary," Lord James said. "And,

of course, they had a previous exposition in 1889. Put the whole thing up then tore it down, all except the Eiffel Tower. That remains, they even repainted it." He pointed and we all looked to the left, where we could see the metal webbing of the tower standing, as if striding at the top of the Champ de Mars.

"The Grand Palais and Petit Palais are not temporary," Countess Olga said. "And the new Pont Alexandre III, those were all built to be permanent."

Bertha sat back, enjoying her tea from a fine porcelain cup with a pattern of tiny violets. Today she wore a walking suit of pink velvet with lace at the neck and elbows. A straw hat with a wide band of ribbon and an arrangement of black fabric flowers and feathers on one side was perched on her head. The countess wore a white lace jacket over a gray dress with a wide-brimmed hat, while her daughter wore a sailor-style navy blue dress with a wide white collar and a white straw hat. I had dressed the children in little sailor outfits as well and I could see Lizzie eyeing Sonya's outfit and comparing it to her own. She seemed to like the young woman.

"Here are the Grand and Petit palaces, and the new bridge," Lord James told us. He was standing, with his hands in his pockets and he bent at the waist to look over the right side of the boat. Honoré stood behind him, eating a sandwich as he surveyed the right bank. The new buildings were heavy with stone but topped with glass, like a conservatory.

"That bridge is quite a construction," Stephen said. "It was dedicated by the Russian tsar, wasn't it?" I craned to look towards the front of the boat to see the bridge we were fast approaching.

"That is so," the countess said. "It is named for Tsar Alexander III and the first stone was laid by Tsar Nicholas." I remembered that her husband was supposed to be somehow related to the tsar and glanced at her. She hid in the shadows of her broad-brimmed hat as we slid under the bridge. When we came out the other side we could look back at the ornamentation. There were candelabras perched on pylons along the length of the bridge and the arches below were strung with garlands, accented with gold. At each end there were even taller pillars holding statues of winged horses in gilt bronze. The countess pointed to the right. "Originally the statues were to be of both French and Russian figures, but in the end they are all French. The alliances, they are a bit unsteady I think."

In the New World, the Columbian Exposition had been built on empty land south of the city, and everything was freshly made, from scratch. Here in Paris there was so much history, so many tangled alliances, that nothing was simple and they were always building on the bones of what had come before. This exposition, like the one in Chicago, was meant to show the progress that would take the whole world into the future. But in Paris, the past hung much more heavily over all that was new.

While the rest of us were looking behind, Lord James was watching ahead and he pointed to the right bank. "There's the Horticultural Building."

"It is so beautiful…you must go inside…the flowers are amazing," the countess told us.

"Ah, that's Old Paris." Honoré had moved behind Lord James and he pointed to the next set of buildings on the right bank as we slid slowly down the river.

The children came out from under the awning to see what was happening. I took Tommy from Delia and held him on my lap, while Stephen moved so that he could keep a hand on Jack's shoulder. Delia followed Lizzie, who had to run back and forth a few times before joining the group at the railing. The young men made room for the children and pointed out some of the buildings of Old Paris. It was a reproduction of the city through time, with parts representing different eras—Medieval, Renaissance, and seventeenth century. Stephen was even more interested than the children, so the young men, who had already visited the attraction, told him about it. I sat back contentedly, after feeding Tommy another petit four. I ruffled his hair and he snuggled against me good-naturedly. He liked a lot of attention, my little Tommy.

We were coming to the Trocadéro, on the right bank, and the Eiffel Tower, on the left. The Champ de Mars, which housed the greatest number of exposition buildings, extended beyond it. On the Trocadéro side, there were pavilions for all of the colonies of the various European powers. The most curious looking structures were located there, as they represented exotic cultures. It made me think of the Eskimos and the Africans who had been exhibited on the Midway in Chicago. The number of peoples represented here was much higher and the very fact of it made me a bit uncomfortable. The European nations had spread out to conquer these many places and peoples around the world and had now brought them all here to be put on display. This led to a discussion between my husband and the young men about the rights and wrongs of having colonies.

"Well, we in the United States were colonies once…but that didn't turn out too well," Honoré said. "'No taxation without representation,' that's what we said."

As we passed by slowly I could see, behind Lord James, buildings of various shapes on the land between the river and the Trocadéro Palace. He looked down from his height with a supercilious expression. "That may be in the past, but I see your country is about to change its line, what with the conflicts in the Caribbean and the Philippines. What are the Philippines if not a colony for America?"

"We're just helping them to get an independent government set up," Honoré protested.

"Yes, you see, and that's what Britain is doing in Africa and India. We're helping the natives."

Stephen had picked up Lizzie to let her lean out to see what was coming ahead. He held her with his good arm and said, "Some Americans don't think we should have suppressed the locals in the Philippines. In Chicago, Jane Addams is helping to start a group that opposes getting involved in colonialism. What's it called, Emily?"

"The Anti-Imperialist League," I said. "They opposed the war against Spain that led to the acquisition of the Philippines." There had been some tense moments when Miss Addams had opposed the popular war. I could remember it only too vividly, which made me glad to be floating on the Seine drinking tea. "Not everyone agreed, but some prominent Americans, including Andrew Carnegie, think it's completely against our principles." I took a sip of my cooling tea. With milk and sugar, it tasted of home, where I would have a cup while playing with the children. I surprised myself by almost feeling homesick for our little apartment in Hyde Park.

"Look at that," Lord James said. "Now isn't that something?"

"It is the Pagoda of Vishnu," the countess said. "And that is a Chinese exhibit beside it. They do regular Brahmin religious ceremonies there every day."

It was a white, crenelated stone structure with many balconies carved with spiky decorations. There were several odd-shaped domes that looked somewhat like corncobs sticking up. We could hear some faint chanting. Beside it, there was a brightly colored red and green pagoda, which housed the Japanese exhibit.

While the men discussed imperialism, Bertha, the countess, and I sat looking out the back of the boat as we passed under the bridge. Behind us we saw the Eiffel Tower on the left bank and, in front of it, a huge sphere set into the top of a colonnaded stone building.

"That is the Celestial Globe," Bertha said. "It marks the extreme west end of the fairgrounds. There are two inner spheres and if you look up there, you can see a terrace with a wonderful view of the whole Exposition." The globe was covered with astrological signs and the terrace hung out near the top, where it was tilted towards the Eiffel Tower. The tower was by the river and the Champ de Mars was off to the right, leading down an avenue of large buildings to the Palace of Electricity at the end.

The boat pivoted and we headed back down the river, under the bridge again. Sonya pointed out the nearby Palais Lumineux, the "Luminous Palace," a small building all of glass, complete with a staircase of crystal. Jack was slumped on Stephen's lap in the stern of the boat and even Lizzie was getting tired, although she was still standing, clutching Delia's skirt and lifting one leg and then the other, as she continued to look around like a little bird perched and ready for flight. Tommy slept peacefully with his head resting on my shoulder.

The others discussed the pavilions of the various countries, as they slid past on our right along the Quai d'Orsay, where the rue des Nations, or Street of Nations, was located. We could see the United States pavilion squeezed between two others. Bertha had an office there, so I was already familiar with that building.

The young people moved to tables behind us to eat the last of the petit fours and drink the last of the tea before we docked. The countess thanked Mrs. Palmer for a marvelous afternoon and I echoed her. It was Bertha's nature to truly enjoy arranging things so that other people could easily and efficiently enjoy themselves. I could tell that she was satisfied with the results on this day.

"And we will see you all again tomorrow night at M. Worth's party for his daughter, will we not?" the countess said. "Sonya's gown will be finished. They deliver it tomorrow. We must all display the gowns of M. Worth for him to admire his work, is it not so?"

Bertha Palmer agreed, but I felt the panic I had experienced before. "But I'm afraid I really cannot do that." I said. "I don't have a gown from M. Worth. I'm sorry, perhaps we shouldn't attend." I looked at Stephen, knowing he would not care if we missed that particular engagement.

"Nonsense," said Bertha.

SEVEN

D on't be silly, of course you should wear it. What's all the fuss about?"

My husband looked quite fine in the formal evening wear that is so uniform for men. Only his studs were not fully attached, so I was fixing them for him. Then he held out his arms so I could fix the cuff links as well. The Palmers had offered servants to help us dress, as they couldn't imagine doing it without help. But I had protested, finally accepting only the assistance of Bertha's French maid with my hair. She had created an elaborate arrangement of curls for me and then left us to complete our toilettes together.

"It's too much. Really it is." I finished helping Stephen and stood, hands on my hips, looking at the two gowns spread out on our bed. It was true, my pink satin did look a little out of style compared to the one that Bertha had sent over, with the message that it was an older gown she had decided not to wear during her stay in Paris. It was a silk taffeta with a shiny light tan background on which clusters of cherries were painted. The bodice had a square neck trimmed with a band of lace and feathery capped sleeves. Affixed to the wide silk ribbon around the waist was a little bunch of artificial cherries. The ribbon tied in a large bow in the back. It was quite simple but marvelous all the same.

"She wouldn't offer it if she didn't want you to wear it. Besides, Mrs. Palmer did say Worth would be insulted if women arrived in gowns he didn't design. How can you refuse?" Stephen was forty-two now and, while his face seemed a little gaunter, and there were some small gray hairs beginning to show at his temples, I thought I had never seen him look happier. He adored our children and this trip meant so much to him because he could finally visit the institute founded by the famous Dr. Pasteur, who was his idol. His only regret was that the great man had died in 1895, before he could meet him. Nonetheless, he spent most of his time with the scientists he'd met at the Institut Pasteur and had even learned some French from them. Now he stepped to the bed, gathered the beautiful dress, and held it over my head.

Defeated, I let him pull it down and I shrugged into the fabric. Using his good arm, he helped me fasten the eyelets and tie the bow, then put his hand on my shoulder and marched me over to the mirror. "You see. Mrs. Palmer knows you only too well. It's a perfect fit." I couldn't disagree. "Besides, if you want to repay her, perhaps you can help her find her pearls."

I turned to him. "You haven't told Mr. Palmer, have you? I promised to keep her secret." The one thing that could draw my husband from the clutches of the French scientists was the opportunity to accompany our host on his occasional excursions to the racetrack and other mostly male entertainments in the city. Stephen was always available to join him. The older man's health was still delicate, although he pooh-poohed any attempts by his wife and son to take special care of him. Nonetheless, I thought he appreciated having my doctor husband by his side and Stephen, for his part, had quickly formed a friendship with the older man, different though their backgrounds must have been. You never knew with men.

"No, no, I wouldn't mention it," Stephen reassured me. "Although I do believe there's nothing Mrs. Palmer could do that would provoke even a mild scolding from him. He's completely enthralled by her, even after all their years of marriage."

"I know. She won't say it, but I think she's afraid Honoré might have something to do with the disappearance of the pearls, and she's worried that would upset his father. You don't think that's possible, do you?"

Stephen considered this, as he watched me in the mirror. "Honoré is a pleasant enough young man. He does share his father's love of fast horses, though. Both to ride and to bet on."

"But he wouldn't take his mother's pearls for a debt, or something like that. I'm sure he wouldn't. Is that what you're suggesting?"

"Not at all. But what I do think is that you would be doing our hosts a great favor if you could find the pearls without anyone being the wiser."

"I don't know how you think I could do that. It's not like it is in Chicago where I can call on Detective Whitbread for help." I thought that should be the end of it, but he just took my arm with a suspicious smile on his face as he gathered up my cape and led me downstairs. I had the feeling he was not going to let the matter go.

M. Worth had borrowed the chateau of one of his clients to stage the ball in honor of his daughter Andrée's engagement to Louis Cartier, the son of the jeweler. We descended a marble staircase into the gilded ballroom, where the gowns and jewels provided a stunning display of the work of the House of Worth. When we reached the floor, Bertha immediately drifted away on a quest to secure for M. Worth a more favorable location for his exhibit in the Palais des Fils, Tissus et Vêtements at the Exposition. The couturier had complained to her that the House of Worth was relegated to a dark corner and she had resolved to try to right that wrong.

Stephen and I remained with Potter Palmer, sipping champagne. The older man's eyes followed his wife as she circulated, primed to pounce on her prey when she spotted the requisite official.

"Cissie is looking especially grand tonight, don't you think?" he asked me. "Cissie" was a nickname used only by Bertha Palmer's family. I would never presume to use it myself, but Mr. Palmer called her that whenever he was regarding her with proud affection, as he was that night.

"She looks magnificent," I agreed. At the age of fifty her hair had turned a beautiful silver but that only served to complement the red velvet gown she was wearing. Another Worth masterpiece, it flowed smooth and soft from bodice to floor, with transparent silk chiffon draped from the shoulders to half-length sleeves that were embellished with silver sequins. Pinned to the left side of the bodice were two rich velvet roses, complete with green silk stems and leaves. As further ornamentation, she wore a magnificent set of ruby earrings and necklace, and another red velvet rose in her hair.

"Those rubies are marvelous," Lord James said as he joined us, followed by Honoré, who also looked at his mother with pride. "They must have cost a fortune."

"And worth every penny," Potter Palmer told him. "A woman like Cissie is not to be kept cheaply. I've always said, when I die I'll need to leave a tidy million to the man who marries her next. He'll need it to keep her."

By Honoré's grin I realized this was a well-known joke in the Palmer household. Lord James kept his peace by swallowing another mouthful of champagne, but his eyes were wide with amazement. Stephen suggested to the senior Palmer that they retreat to a smoking room where they could sit in peace and perhaps find a game of cards. I knew Stephen would be sure he was entertained without unduly tiring him. At seventy-two years of age he was, after all, older than most of the men present, even if he had no intention of admitting it.

A few minutes later I saw Bertha Palmer bearing down on us with the Countess Olga and her daughter in tow. At just that moment, the noise stopped and all eyes were drawn to the top of the staircase where a handsome young couple stood. M. Worth was on their left, and an older couple, who must have been M. Cartier and his wife, stood to the right. Both young people had glossy black hair—his in curls, hers like silk and arranged in an elaborate pile with a spray of jewels above one ear. She wore a deep blue satin ball gown embellished with a black velvet pattern of leaves and geometric designs. The scooped neck was hung with white lace and at the shoulders were little lace cap sleeves. Around her neck was a fantastic filigree of tiny diamonds that held a very large blue stone.

"Good lord, it's a star sapphire," Lord James whispered. "I'd heard Cartier provided a jewel for the engagement, but I had no idea. Magnificent taste, really, to settle for one large perfect jewel rather than a string of second-rate ones. They are very good, those two." He nodded towards the fathers as we all raised our glasses in a toast.

The formal announcement was followed by music, and the young couple took to the dance floor.

"M. Worth must be very happy with all of this," Bertha commented. Then she looked significantly at Honoré. "You young people really should join in."

Her son snapped to attention and offered his arm to Sonya. Lord James insisted on leading out Mrs. Palmer. Left standing with the countess, I saw she was smiling at the sight of her daughter, leaning on her cane as she watched.

"Mme Palmer is very considerate. I am so grateful to her for her kindness to us," she said.

"I also benefit from the kindness of the Palmers," I told her. I found a chair against the wall for her to sit on while I continued to stand, watching the whirling figures. When the waltz ended, our party flocked back to us. Then M. Worth approached, bringing his daughter. He presented the flushed young woman to Mrs. Palmer and myself then sent her to a side room to have a minor repair done on her beautiful deep blue gown.

"Mlle Arquette is available with several of the sewing women," he explained. I thought he gave a slight nod of approval to me. He must have recognized the gown I wore.

The countess stood up, balancing against her cane. "If you will permit, I will take Sonya to your vendeuse as well. The sash needs some attention." Sonya was wearing the gown she had shown us at the House of Worth, the champagne-colored damask with the garlands of pink fabric roses that looked so spring like.

"But, of course, allow me to take you." He led them away. I sensed that Bertha Palmer was disappointed to see Sonya parted from her son so soon.

Lord James had his own plans. He clapped Honoré on the shoulder. "Well, what do you say? Shall we do our duty and beard the lioness in her den?" He nodded across the room to where Mrs. Johnstone and her daughter stood. "I'll need some support." He grabbed Honoré's arm and started dragging him away. "There's a dearth of males over there and I can't take them all on, you know."

We watched, as the American matron was stunned to silence by the unexpected onslaught of the young men. Lord James led her daughter, Lydia, to the dance floor while Honoré politely invited one of her friends. Bertha sniffed, but she soon lost interest, looking beyond them at the crowd. I knew she was still searching for the official who was her prey in her plans to help M. Worth get a better space at the Exposition. When the couturier returned he brought along two other men. He introduced the older as his brother, Gaston, and the younger as M. Paul Poiret. Then Bertha quickly led him away as she had spotted the man she planned to corner. She was always at work at these social events.

It turned out that M. Gaston Worth, an older and plumper version of his brother, spoke no English. It was left for M. Poiret to translate and amuse me. He was quite capable and, I thought, probably accustomed to charming American women with his accented English. Of medium height, he wore his hair slicked down and parted in the middle, sported a neatly trimmed beard and mustache, and was attired in an elegantly tailored evening suit. He told me he had been hired by M. Gaston for a very particular purpose. "He said to me that the House of Worth was like a great restaurant which would refuse to serve anything but truffles. It was necessary to create a department for fried potatoes. M. Jean, he does not care for the fried potatoes. And, of course, his designs are superb, elegant, like the gown you wear so well tonight, madame." I felt an unaccustomed pang of pride at his assessment. No wonder women longed for a Worth gown, if it inspired such admiration. The gown did suit me. "He had always refused to make the simple and practical garments, you see. But M. Gaston knows the clients are not always at the ball. They must go out in the carriage to the visits or the shopping. For this, something more plain is needed."

"Fried potatoes."

"Indeed. They are very popular, the fried potatoes, the walking suits and simple gowns."

"I'm sure they would be more useful for someone like me." I explained my work and how my husband and children had come to be in Paris. I also confessed the Worth gown I wore was loaned to me.

"Of necessity. M. Jean would have been wounded if you had not worn something from the House!"

"Especially to a celebration for his daughter, I know. It's too bad her mother could not see her looking so beautiful and so happy." I assumed M. Worth was a widower.

M. Poiret raised an eyebrow, then took a couple of flutes of champagne from the tray of a passing waiter. Handing one to me, he raised his own in a toast. "To the lovely Mlle Andrée." After sipping he went on confidentially, "M. Jean was never married. Mlle Andrée is the result of a liaison. The mother has never been acknowledged."

"Oh." I wasn't sure how else to respond.

"But she has had all the advantages of a legitimate child. She was a favorite of her grandfather and the connection to the Cartier family is a great boon. In France, you understand, this is not so uncommon."

"I see. Well, her father certainly seems to dote on her." At that moment I saw Lord James glide by with the tall Miss Lydia in his arms. He winked at me, like a conspirator. Honoré passed by right afterwards but he was too concentrated on his dance steps and his partner to acknowledge me.

"But, madame, you must dance also. Is your husband not present to oblige?" When I explained that my husband was keeping Mr. Potter Palmer company in the smoking room, M. Poiret insisted we join the next dance, another waltz. So I found myself swirling around the room in his arms and, after that, in the arms of Lord James.

It was only when we stopped and stepped to the side again that I noticed a tall, magnificently gowned woman wearing a brilliant diamond tiara making her way through the crowd towards us. She had almost reached us when I finally recognized her. "Consuelo Vanderbilt."

Lord James jumped and appeared startled. "The Duchess of Marlborough?" With a quick look over his shoulder he immediately started to move away. "Excuse me, Mrs. Chapman, I'll just go look for Honoré. I can't imagine where he's gotten to." And he was gone by the time the regal looking young woman reached me.

"Miss Cabot? It *is* you, isn't it?"

I'd met Connie the year of my own marriage when she was a seventeen-year-old debutante in Newport. At the time, she was being groomed by her mother to be married into the European aristocracy, a plan that had since come to fruition. She was wearing a gown of white satin with a pattern of curlicues embossed in black velvet. It was a striking design, with cap sleeves and a long train. It reminded me of some of the swirling wrought iron Art Nouveau designs we'd seen on our boat excursion. There was a fluffy white feather in the dark mass of curls on her head, and she wore a choker of pearls and diamonds. I particularly noticed her long, graceful neck as it reminded me of the iron brace I'd seen in her room in Newport. Her mother had insisted she use it to train her to keep her head up. Presumably, she no longer suffered such indignities but she still appeared like a slender birch tree that would bend to any strong wind. I remembered how she had envied the comparative freedom of my friend Clara and myself, as university students. From her happiness at seeing me, and her questions about Clara and myself, I sensed that she still felt some yearning for a simpler life. Entrenched as she now was in British society, I assumed she must have recognized Lord James.

"Oh, of the Lawfords? No, I didn't see him. I do hear that he despises living in England. He came over here some years ago and the family finally gave up trying to force him back when his older brother succeeded to the title and provided an heir. I think they leave him alone now."

I saw her being beckoned from across the room by a bejeweled older woman and I thought she might have also envied Lord James his freedom. With a sigh and an apology, she drifted away, and soon I saw her led to the dance floor by an aging man in formal military attire and a chest full of medals. I was looking around for other members of my own party when I felt a change in the room. The orchestra was still playing but there was a sudden tension. It moved through the room like a stiff breeze suddenly rushing through a stand of trees, or rippling across a body of water.

Bertha Palmer appeared at my elbow. "Have you seen Honoré? I cannot find him."

"Not since he was on the dance floor." I didn't see him among the couples still twirling by. I noticed the crowd was thinning. "I believe Lord James was scared away by a duchess. Perhaps he took Honoré with him when he escaped."

"Of course, I'm sure that's it. Come, we must find Potter and Dr. Chapman. I don't want Mr. Palmer to tire himself." I was surprised that she wanted to leave already but she leaned in and whispered in my ear. "There's been an incident. Mlle Andrée's star sapphire has disappeared."

EIGHT

The next morning, while I sat relishing my café au lait and croissant, I was summoned to Mrs. Palmer's boudoir. With a sigh, I left the sight of my children rolling on the grass. The maid was alarmed. She told me that a policeman had arrived.

I found Bertha where I found her every morning, ensconced behind her desk, wearing one of her elegant morning gowns. It was a lilac silk taffeta wrapper with a print of blue hydrangeas, voluminous sleeves and skirt, and flounces at the wrist and hem. It was a subtle message to the policeman that she had not arranged to receive him in one of the more formal parlors downstairs. She retained her air of command even in such an informal setting. At my arrival, the man opposite her rose from the delicately gilded chair where she had placed him—to his disadvantage, I thought. He was a tall man, with broad shoulders, a square face, and a substantial mustache, wearing a well-tailored coat with velvet lapels. Introduced as Inspector Marcel Guillaume, I learned much later that he was young for his rank, only in his early thirties. He had recently married the daughter of the Commissaire of Police. Perhaps envy of his sudden rise had led to this assignment. It must have been uncomfortable to be sent to interrogate important foreign visitors about the theft of valuable jewels. He gave me a formal bow, then we both sat down opposite Bertha.

"Inspector Guillaume has come about the theft at the reception last night," she told me. "I've been telling him that we didn't see anything helpful." At her nod, I described the evening in my own words, while he sat listening attentively with his hands folded in his lap.

"That is very helpful, madame." He turned back to my employer. "It would also be helpful to speak to M. Palmer and the young M. Palmer. Are they at home?"

It soon became apparent that Bertha was not going to be obliging on this point. "I'm afraid that won't be possible, Inspector. My son has gone out with his English friend, Lord James Lawford, and my husband's health is rather delicate. I really would prefer that you not bother him with this matter. He doesn't like to admit it, but he really is not very well and I cannot allow anything to happen that might cause a relapse. We nearly lost him last year in Rome, and I must insist that he not be imposed upon."

"My husband was with Mr. Palmer the entire time last night, I believe. He has gone to the Institut Pasteur this morning but I can ask him to come to you at your office," I offered. "He didn't mention seeing anything unusual but I'm sure he would be more than happy to tell you that himself."

Inspector Guillaume blinked several times then turned back to Bertha. "Your son, madame, perhaps you could arrange for an interview later in the day?"

"Well, I think he and Lord James had already left the ball before the theft last night, but I'm sure he could arrange to speak with you. You may leave your information with our butler and he will give the message to Honoré. If that is all..."

"Not quite, madame. There is the matter of your own pearls. I understand they also disappeared last week?" His broad face was very placid as he brought up a topic for which we were both unprepared. How did he know about the missing pearls?

Bertha was nonplussed. "I...no...well, yes. That was a mistake. We thought we had brought them to a fitting at the House of Worth but we were mistaken."

"I see, and they were found when you returned here, then?"

Bertha pursed her lips. I was certain she would have told me if she'd found the pearls, and I was also sure she would not have told her husband they were missing. Certainly she would not have told the police. "M. Worth told you about that, I suppose?"

"And other members of his staff. Of course, when the sapphire also disappeared they remembered this incident. Did you find them?"

"No, but we are still investigating. I didn't want to have suspicion fall on an innocent person, you see. It needs to be handled discreetly. It's certainly possible that they've just been misplaced temporarily."

"But they are very valuable, is it not true, madame?"

"Yes, yes. But, you see, I didn't want my husband worried by that either. I really am very concerned about his health. I don't care how valuable the pearls are, they are nothing compared to my husband's well-being and peace of mind." I thought that what she really wanted to spare her husband was not so much the loss of the pearls, as the faint suggestion that their son might be involved.

"But what if the pearls were stolen? What if the same thief stole the sapphire last night, don't you want him found and the jewels returned?"

"Yes, of course I do...of course."

I wanted to help Bertha, to distract the inspector from her dreaded suspicion, so I asked about the investigation. "Do you believe one of the guests stole the sapphire?"

He turned his dark brown eyes on me. Bertha suddenly spoke up. "Inspector, you should know that Mrs. Chapman has experience working with the police back in Chicago. She has done a lot of work with them. Perhaps she could be of assistance."

I was appalled. "Oh, no. Certainly not. I'm a university lecturer, Inspector. It's true that I work with a detective of the Chicago police, but it is mainly for the research we're doing. A study in sociology. That detective has an interest in scientific investigation." I tried to think of how to convey the true nature of my involvement with the Chicago police. "We have studied Lambroso and collected identity information on the lines of your own Bertillon."

"I see. Yes, M. Bertillon is an important consultant for the Sûreté."

Bertha was about to press her point, but I interrupted her. "That is the sort of involvement I have with the police. I'm certainly no investigator, myself. Of course, we want to help you as much as possible. It is in the interest of all of us to recover the jewel for Mlle Worth. And if Mrs. Palmer's pearls have also been stolen, we would be grateful for your help in recovering them, as well. I think Mrs. Palmer just wanted to ensure that the pearls were indeed stolen and not just misplaced. It's difficult to know how they might have been taken by someone outside the household. That's all."

"Yes, madame. Your establishment here, and the premises of the House of Worth, not to mention the chateau where the reception was held, none of these are open to the public. You are protected behind your walls. Only the known members of your society, and the trusted and watched staff, are allowed in. For this reason, it is most difficult to identify the thief. It would seem that everyone saw the famous star sapphire on the neck of Mlle Worth last night…as she was presented, as she danced. It was all very exciting for the young lady. It was only when her father found her later in the evening that they saw it was gone. Tell me, do you remember seeing the jewel?"

As I thought about the question, Bertha Palmer spoke up. "I noticed it when they had the toast to the young couple but, I confess, I had my own affairs to attend to last night. I only became aware of the loss when Mlle Arquette mentioned it to me just before we left."

I remembered something. "The last time I noticed the necklace was when I saw M. Worth take his daughter to have her dress repaired. It was the first I'd heard that Mlle Arquette and some of the staff of the House of Worth were in a side room… to help the ladies with any minor repairs, I guess."

"Oh, yes. It's commonly done," Bertha Palmer explained. "Of course, you don't usually have help as skilled as the seamstresses, hair dressers, and milliners from the House of Worth. I took advantage of that myself, when I noticed a thread pulled on my bodice. It was when I went to her for assistance that Mlle Arquette told me the sapphire was missing. Naturally, I clutched the ruby necklace I was wearing and decided we should leave. How very embarrassing for poor M. Worth."

It had to have been not only embarrassing but also very alarming for poor M. Worth. The place was full of his wealthiest clients. How could he accuse any of them of the theft? "Surely the people attending were all too wealthy themselves to be thieves," I suggested. But I hastened to amend that. I didn't want to suggest that the poor staff of the House of Worth were the logical suspects. "And the House of Worth staff like Mlle Arquette must always be dealing with the jewels of those people. Why would they suddenly turn to theft?" I thought of the red velvet case for the pearls that had been handed to M. Worth and returned empty.

Inspector Guillaume raised his bushy eyebrows. "Indeed, it is a puzzle. But a puzzle not without…how do you say it?…a precedent."

"You mean this has happened before?"

"During the last exposition, in 1889, there was a similar outbreak of thefts. Several very famous jewels were stolen. It was believed to be a gang."

"A street gang?"

"*Non*, nothing so crude. It was a group of young women and men, some of them imposters."

"You arrested them?"

"The young ones, yes. But we believe there was a ringleader.

He was not found and none of them would admit to who he was. They were young people, some of them from good families but with money problems. They were seduced by someone, a kind of Pied Piper. They came from other countries—Germany, Denmark, Italy. For the most part, they came from families who paid back for some of the stolen jewelry."

"You never found the Pied Piper? But you know it was a man?" I asked.

"As I said, no one would identify him. But it was thought it must be a man."

I wondered about that. Why not a woman? Bertha had been listening attentively. I knew her major concern was that her son Honoré should not be implicated. The inspector's story seemed to relieve her. No one could accuse her son of being an imposter. But perhaps the Parisian police didn't know that. "The Palmers are very well-known members of society back in Chicago," I told him. "And Mrs. Palmer is a commissioner to the Exposition for the United States."

He raised his hands in protest. "But of course, of course, no one would suggest Mme Palmer or her family are anything but genuine. Only it is possible that others might have taken advantage of them. So I would very much like to speak to M. Palmer, father *and* son."

"My husband has done very little socializing here," Bertha told him. "He is not involved in the Exposition. He's gone out only with Honoré and Dr. Chapman. It's true that Honoré has gone out among others much more." She looked at me. "Honoré is very young. It's possible he could be fooled."

"Inspector, last night I arranged with Honoré and Lord James to meet them at Notre Dame this morning. Perhaps you would want to come with me?" I offered.

Bertha protested. "But Honoré is no imposter, you've already admitted that. Surely you can't think Lord James is one?"

"No, no, madame. The aristocracy do tend to all know each

other. It is not the known families from which such an imposter would come. It is unlikely an imposter could exist for long in such circles. No, we look for someone who envies the wealthy and titled. But someone who can befriend them, or who can influence, perhaps, some of the young people who have enough entrée or connections to do the thefts. It is not your son and the English lord we would suspect...they are the big fish, if you will. It is the little fish who swim around them, that is who we wish to ask them about. Mme Chapman, I would be most grateful for your company. We will find the young men and question them gently. We do not wish to alarm the smaller fish. We will simply spread our net to catch them."

NINE

Inspector Guillaume had a motorcar, complete with a driver. We climbed into the back, which was enclosed, and I clutched a handle on the side as we jolted a bit across the pavement of the broad boulevards. By the time we reached Notre Dame we'd crossed a bridge, and the streets had become narrow and more uneven, so the motorcar rocked every few feet. I was glad when we stopped and I could climb out.

I had no idea exactly where to meet the young men, but Inspector Guillaume took my elbow and led me through a large wooden door. I had never been to the famous cathedral before. It was when I had confessed as much the night before that Honoré and Lord James insisted I join them. Apparently they were planning to propose such an excursion to others— young ladies, I suspected. I could tell they wanted me to act as a chaperone. It was soon after my agreement to this plan that the young men had disappeared from M. Worth's ball.

I had been amused, wondering exactly which young women would appear, but that was before we'd heard of the theft of Mlle Worth's sapphire, and before Inspector Guillaume had called on Bertha that morning. I was no longer amused.

But I was impressed by the cathedral. We stepped from the bright spring sunshine into its cool stone shadows and I realized how very alien a place it was. A vast expanse of stone pillars rose to high stories where strips of multicolored stained glass, like bright ribbons, were set into the walls. It was all vertical, rising high above us and then leading down to the altar. Wooden pews filled the floor, leading up to a set of carved choral screens around an elaborate altar, which was set far back from our view. Of course, I knew that the gray stone buildings of the University of Chicago, where I'd spent so many of my days, were designed in imitation of medieval churches such as this. But they were mere pencil sketches, faded watercolors, perhaps muffled echoes of what I was seeing here. This was something unique. Whoever had built this, they were people very different from the modern workmen who had built the broad boulevards and clean, elegant buildings where we had been spending our time. This was a remnant of the medieval Paris that Baron Haussmann had ruthlessly struck down in order to fashion the modern city.

But the work of the medieval master craftsmen who had built this towering monument to the god they believed in, could not be destroyed so easily. The huge slabs of stone fashioned into the floors and pillars were darkened with the dirt and blood of many ages. Looking down that magnificent nave was like listening to a hymn in a language I could not understand, while enjoying the music of it, nonetheless. What had the artists been thinking when they embroidered story after story in the carved figures or the painted stained glass? How had they managed to stitch it all together with such harmony?

The building seemed heavier and more grounded than anything I had ever seen before, in Paris or anywhere else. It was so much itself. It imposed its image on me so strongly that I forgot every other thing for a few minutes after I entered the door. Finally, I got my bearings and turned to Inspector Guillaume.

"This is your first visit, madame?" he asked me.

"Yes. It is very beautiful."

"But, yes." He smiled as he gazed down the long aisle. "Even we Parisians, born here, are impressed. It is always there, like a gray stone heart of the city." He nodded behind us. "Perhaps Mme la Comtesse can help us to locate M. Palmer and his friend."

I pulled my gaze away from the vast interior and looked back. Between the doors were a few hard benches. On one of them Countess Olga sat, talking to a young woman. I thought I recognized the white muslin dress printed with small flowers. It was the young woman who had spoken to us outside the House of Worth. She wore a squared-off straw hat with a dark blue ribbon and a blue shawl was wrapped around her shoulders. The countess wore the same shimmering gray suit and matching veiled hat that she had worn at the couturier's salon. She introduced the younger woman as Denise Laporte. The girl seemed embarrassed, and quickly slipped away.

"She does not speak English," the countess explained. "She is a milliner. She often works for M. Worth."

Inspector Guillaume had produced a formal bow for the aristocratic lady, and now he spoke. "Mlle Laporte attended the reception last night as well. She was assisting the staff of the House of Worth in the cloakroom. We have already spoken to her, as we did to you, Mme la Comtesse."

"She helped the other staff in the room with Mlle Arquette, of course. Have you found the thief yet, Inspector?"

"Unfortunately not yet. We must continue our interviews." He explained that we had come in search of Honoré and Lord James.

"Ah, yes, the young men left before all the excitement last night. They are here." She gestured towards the colonnade. "They tour. My daughter is with them. Last evening at the reception the young people arranged to meet here. Sonya acts as the guide. She has been here many times, of course. Ah, you see, here they come." She pointed her silver cane towards the left side where a chattering group of young people erupted from the far aisle.

Lord James had Lydia Johnstone on one arm and her friend, Edith Stuart, on the other. They made an unbalanced grouping. Lydia was nearly as tall as the English lord. She wore a tailored walking suit in yellow watered silk with jet trim that trembled with every step. On her head was one of the largest platter-like hats that I had ever seen. It was made of black straw adorned with gauzy trim and several yellow satin roses. It added to her already substantial height so much that it rose higher than Lord James's top hat. On his other arm, Edith Stuart wore a stylish walking gown with white flounces punctuated by lace trimming and large yellow bows, topped by a small black bolero. She wore a trim little felt hat with a yellow and black feather, and yellow leather gloves. But she was barely as tall as Lord James's shoulder, so she had to trot along, trying to keep up with the taller pair.

The gentleman appeared to be in his element, talking and gesturing. The young women were animated as well. I wondered at his courting of the young lady he had appeared to be avoiding during our visit to the House of Worth. I'd heard him complain humorously of the title hungry American heiresses and he'd claimed to be besieged by them. But, at the moment, he seemed happy enough in the company of two of the breed.

He recognized us. "Mrs. Chapman, how lovely that you could join in. We'll have to apologize for starting without you. It's the young ladies. They were impatient." He detached himself from the young women and bowed.

Meanwhile, Honoré followed more quietly, escorting the countess's daughter, Sonya, and Lydia's other friend, Miss Brown. Those three were better matched in height and quieter in demeanor. Sonya wore white muslin with ruffles and lace, a blue sash, and a short jacket with a little plate-like hat on the side of her head. Miss Brown wore a lilac silk suit with a cream blouse, which had delicate pleats tucked into a trim waistline and tiny embroidered violets at the neck and wrist. I thought Bertha would be pleased to see her son with Sonya. But the young man seemed embarrassed and he, too, greeted me formally.

"This is Inspector Guillaume of the Sûreté," Countess Olga told them. "He wishes to speak with you, as he spoke to the rest of us last night. About the theft of Mlle Worth's sapphire."

"Was it really a theft, then?" Honoré asked. "We left before it went missing."

"We heard about it this morning from the young ladies," Lord James added. "But we thought perhaps it might be found. After a thorough search, you know."

"Alas, monsieur, the jewel has not been found," Inspector Guillaume told him.

"Well, I don't think we can help you," Lord James said. "We left before it happened."

The police inspector regarded the young men for a few seconds. It had become a slightly uncomfortable silence when he finally spoke. "We are not sure yet exactly when the stone was taken," he told them. "But it seems unlikely that it was misplaced. There is another matter in which I hope M. Palmer may be able to assist us."

"Me?" said Honoré.

"Yes. We have heard that the pearls of your mother have also been lost. We would like to talk to you about that."

"Oh, but that was just a mistake," Lord James told him. "They were just left behind. Someone didn't put them in the box, don't you know. They weren't stolen."

The inspector turned his eyes on the tall Englishman. "Unfortunately, we learned from Mme Palmer that the pearls are still missing and have not yet been found."

Honoré's face turned red. Lord James stammered, "Oh, but really...I don't think Mrs. Palmer had decided to call the p-p-police, now had she?"

"Yet, it would seem the sapphire of Mlle Worth *was* stolen, and so soon after the disappearance of the pearls. You can see that it would be most helpful for us to interview the young M. Palmer. It might help us to find the thief." This was met with an uneasy silence. The young people were dumbfounded.

Finally, Honoré swallowed and spoke. "Certainly, Inspector, anything I can do to help."

"Very good. If you would be so kind. You may not be aware, but the prefecture is only a few blocks away and my motorcar is waiting. If you would come with me. Ladies, please excuse us." He extended an arm to shepherd Honoré out the door.

"Oh, dear," Lord James murmured. He looked at me. "I can't let them just take him away. I'll go with them. Tell Mrs. Palmer she's not to worry. I'll be there." He tipped his hat goodbye and hurried after them.

What would Bertha think? I saw no way that I could accompany them. It would be best to let Lord James use his influence to find out as much as he could. I turned back to the young women who looked alarmed. My head was full of imaginings about imposters. Perhaps the young women could help to clear Honoré's name.

TEN

The young ladies were stunned to be so suddenly deprived of their male companions. Countess Olga noticed and she attempted to rally them. "Mrs. Chapman has not been able to see the cathedral yet. Sonya, you must act as guide."

They seemed to shake themselves, reminding me of little puppies shaking off rainwater, and we sorted ourselves out. Edith Stuart decided she was tired and she slipped onto the bench beside the countess. When she sat back with a sigh, I realized the soft yellow leather boots that matched her outfit so well must be pinching her feet.

Sonya and Miss Johnstone were still full of energy. It seemed they had formed an unlikely friendship and they strode down the center aisle arm in arm, chattering away. That left Grace Greenway Brown and myself to follow.

"Is this your first trip to Paris, Miss Brown?" I asked.

"Yes. Miss Johnstone, Miss Stuart, and I are all students at the Pennsylvania Academy of Fine Arts. I am very lucky to be able to travel with Lydia and her family. It is the greatest desire of all the students at the academy to come to Paris to study art. Miss Cassatt studied there, you know. A long time ago, before she came to Paris. And Miss Cecilia Beaux is a more recent student. Did you know that one of her paintings was accepted in the main exhibition? It's a great honor. Something we all dream about."

"And has Paris been living up to your expectations?"

She was walking slowly, her eyes raised to look at the stained glass windows in the upper story. She held a Baedeker's guide in her hands. Reluctantly, she pulled herself back from her contemplation to answer. "Oh, yes. The museums and churches, the sculptures and paintings, they are really magnificent. Of course, we've been studying copies in Philadelphia—plaster casts and copies of paintings. But it's so very different to see the real pieces of art and in the places where they belong. It's quite amazing, actually."

I wondered if she felt the church to be as alien as I had. "Different from the copies?"

"Why, yes, of course. Not quite so pristine. You'll think that odd, but when they make copies they smooth out the borders. They make them so serene. When you see the real works, so often they're much more vibrant, perhaps more violent, even. And much less perfect. There are chips and rough edges. It makes them so much more real."

I glanced at her. She had quite a serious expression on her face. "I'm no student of art, so I think I must trust you on that. Certainly I've never been in a place quite like this before." I gestured to our surroundings. "For me, it makes me curious about the people who built it. A lot of people must have been occupied for a long time to get this built. Were they all artists?"

"All craftsmen, I think. All working towards the same goal, wanting to glorify the Blessed Virgin." She laughed. "It's certainly very different from the First Methodist Church of Baltimore where I attended church every week back home."

"I know what you mean. I've had the same thought. It's so huge and ornate compared to the Unitarian churches I attended back in Boston."

She stopped then, and read aloud a paragraph from her guidebook. It said that it had taken two hundred years to complete the building of the cathedral. By then we had caught up with Lydia and Sonya who had turned into a side aisle halfway down.

They were putting francs into a little tin cup and lighting candles that were mounted on a black iron stand with several dozen rows of candles, some lit and some not.

"I light a candle in memory of my grandmère," Sonya explained. She touched a thin stick into a lit candle and carried the flame to an unlit one. The others copied her actions.

Somewhat reluctantly, I lit a candle for my mother, although I wondered what she would think of such a ritual. Compared to the plain decorations and prayers of the Unitarian churches we had attended, the rituals of the Roman Catholic Church had always seemed comparatively alien and superstitious, hardly Christian, as we thought of it, at all. And, yet, she was always patient with the unusual customs of others, so I assumed she wouldn't object.

Grace noticed my little grimace, and she commented, "I know. It seems strange, doesn't it? Yet, when you think of it, people have been lighting candles here for hundreds of years."

Lydia and Sonya turned away to continue down towards the main altar. I noticed Grace watching them. "And how are your companions on your trip? Are you enjoying their company?"

"Oh, certainly. Sometimes I think I'm too interested in the study of art and not enough in the practice of society for them, though." She glanced at me to see if I disapproved. "I'm not accustomed to socializing with European aristocracy. I find Mrs. Johnstone and Lydia are forever having to correct my ignorance about people's titles and things like that. I'm afraid I didn't grow up having to address dukes and countesses," she said drily.

I laughed. "I can sympathize. I'm acting as Mrs. Palmer's social secretary, so I've had to attend to these matters closely. On the boat over I was given several thick volumes to study and we rehearsed how to address dignitaries. It took quite a bit of practice."

We reached the altar railing. Looking back to where we had started, down the long nave, we could see the great rose window above the doors. The glass was primarily of royal blue and vivid red, all pieced together in stories and outlined in black lead. When

I looked back at the delicate wisps of material that made up the gowns of the young ladies, it seemed a pale and fleeting attempt at decoration compared to the majesty of the stone and glass in the cathedral. It made me realize that when we were all long gone, "Our Lady of Paris," which was dedicated to the Virgin Mary, would still endure.

"It seems that Mrs. Palmer, like Mrs. Johnstone, is most anxious to befriend the aristocracy over here," Grace said. I was sure she was thinking of Lydia and her mother's pursuit of the English lord and Bertha Palmer's patronage of the countess and her daughter.

"Yes, I've heard that a good many young Americans come looking for a noble husband. But is that true of you, Miss Brown? Do you long to be a duchess or a countess, yourself?"

She raised an eyebrow, watching Lydia and Sonya who were whispering together. "It's my understanding there is a trade involved in such engagements. The American brings money and the European brings a title. My parents have a comfortable living but they aren't wealthy enough to buy a title. So, no. I come in pursuit of art, not a titled husband." She was staring down the aisle towards the door now. "I believe I see Mrs. Johnstone has arrived to collect us. She'll be disappointed that Lord James had to leave. I'll tell the others she's looking for us."

While she went to convince Lydia and Sonya to return to the back of the church, I headed down the aisle to where Mrs. Johnstone lingered in the doorway. She was keeping one of the large wooden doors partially open, yet she seemed hesitant to come in. I greeted her and followed her back out into the sunshine, assuring her Grace had gone to summon the others.

"Lydia and her friends wanted to see it...this church. For the art, don't you know. I'm not at all fond of the Gothic style, myself," she confided. "It all seems rather dark and spooky. We have an American church in our quarter where we attend services. It's very new and clean and the pastor is from Connecticut, a very educated man. I know some people are very fond of this church and the other old ones. The girls even wanted to come to a mass here, one of the services, don't you know. But I put my foot down at that. Art is one thing, but religion is quite another." She was dressed in a stylish pink walking suit with black jet trim. A frilly black parasol hung from one wrist. Her big plate-like hat was similar to her daughter's but not as large. It was just as well. She had a much shorter figure and could not have carried it off. I had the impression that she was superstitiously afraid to enter the cathedral. It also occurred to me that she might have seen Countess Olga inside the church and wanted to avoid having to acknowledge her.

"I saw Miss Stuart with the countess in there," she said, as if she read my mind. "Of course, I knew the girls had also arranged to meet young Sonya when they arranged to meet Lord James and Mr. Palmer. I suppose the mother had to bring her." She looked around impatiently, then turned back to me when no one else came out the door. "I know Mrs. Palmer believes it's necessary to be civil to all these European counts and countesses and dukes and princes, or what have you. But I must caution you, Mrs. Chapman. Not all of them are worthy of your respect. I know Mrs. Palmer's niece is married to one of those Russians but they are not all of good repute, you know." She shook her head. "She thinks I'm being provincial, and what might be scandalous back in Omaha is accepted here, but I'm not so sure."

It occurred to me that Mrs. Johnstone had no problem with the English aristocracy in the person of Lord James Lawford. It was only some of the others who appeared to be unsavory to her. I wondered if it might really be a religious objection. No doubt the Englishman was a good Protestant. A change of subject was called for. "How long have you been in Paris, Mrs. Johnstone?"

"Oh, most of the year this time. We took an apartment on avenue Matignon. It's not as grand as what the Palmers have, but it's quite acceptable and fine for hosting soirees. We're able to hold larger receptions at the embassy or the exhibition pavilion."

"Have you visited Paris in the past?"

"Oh, certainly. We were first here in '89. Mr. Johnstone is in business with his brothers, you see, in Omaha. He's the one who travels. He came in '89 to set up the exhibit. It was quite a success. I had my two boys over with me that time, but they're both married and settled now. It's only Lydia, this visit. She's our youngest. She's very headstrong, but she's the apple of Mr. Johnstone's eye. She insisted on going to the academy in Philadelphia and when Mr. Johnstone was appointed to the American commission we said she could come. Then she begged to bring some of her friends from school so, of course, we agreed. But I've made it clear to her that I expect her to return to Omaha with us and to settle down herself...if she doesn't make a match over here, of course."

At that moment the young ladies came out into the sunshine. "But where are Lord James and Mr. Palmer?" Mrs. Johnstone asked, somewhat indignantly, I thought.

Lydia was not at all surprised by the question. "Didn't Mrs. Chapman tell you? She came with a policeman and he took them away."

ELEVEN

Mrs. Johnstone had hired a spacious Victoria to take herself, the three young ladies, and the two young men to rue de Rivoli for lunch. Annoyed by the defection of the young men, she hurried the young women into the carriage. It was no disappointment to me that she stopped her daughter from extending an invitation to me, and perhaps Sonya, to join them. I had no desire to appear to support the rival of my patroness, Mrs. Palmer, so I ignored Lydia Johnstone when she attempted to get my attention. I noticed that Miss Brown had the good sense to also ignore this and Miss Edith Stuart was too concerned with her own feet to pay any attention. It wasn't a particularly congenial group in any case. I watched from the steps of Notre Dame as they drove off.

"Are you engaged to go somewhere, yourself?" I heard Countess Olga ask at my elbow.

I thought about that. Mrs. Palmer would be busy at a luncheon. When I did see her, she would expect me to inform her about the progress of the police investigation, but I would have nothing to report. I sighed. "No, in fact I'm completely free."

She seemed to sense my frustration. "Then perhaps you would like to explore the Latin Quarter? Sonya and I are going there."

I was tempted. I had been so occupied with Mrs. Palmer's concerns that I had not had time to explore the oldest part of the city—where the Sorbonne, the university of Paris, had been located for hundreds of years. If I were honest, I would admit I was somewhat homesick for the academic community where I spent so much of my time in Chicago. And I was curious about how it would compare to such an ancient European university. "I'd like that."

"Hmm. Sonya, *allons-y*." The countess regarded me with some calculation as her daughter sighed with disappointment at not being included in the party with the young ladies. "I think, first, we must visit the *bouquinistes*."

Sonya brightened. "*Les bouquinistes! Allons-y!*" She raced ahead of us towards the bridge to the Left Bank.

"*Les bouquinistes?* What is that?"

"You will see. Come!" Countess Olga took me by the elbow and directed me across the river where she ignored the busy streets of the Left Bank, to turn me down the walk along the Seine. It was shaded by trees and ran above the quays. You could look over a low stone wall and down at the water as it flowed along. The riverboats passed below us and, every now and then, there were stone steps down, but we stayed up at the street level. There were plenty of people strolling in the sun and shade and soon we were at the start of a line of stalls along the wall.

"Books!" I exclaimed. Green wooden boxes rested against the wall in long rows and they were full of books with their spines displayed temptingly. Wooden slats stood up from the boxes to display layers of engraved prints of various types.

"Yes, books. You are interested?"

"Of course. Oh, how wonderful." I had been to several English language booksellers in rue de Rivoli but always with a particular title in mind for myself or Mrs. Palmer, a guidebook or a novel. But here I found a plethora of all kinds of books, most of them old, laid out like a tasty buffet just waiting for some hungry reader to pluck them out and riffle through the pages to taste the goods. Of course, most of them were in French, although with the help of Sonya, I quickly found some English translations of Voltaire and Zola and an illustrated edition of Dickens. There was a wonderful large French translation of Shakespeare's *Midsummer Night's Dream* with fantastic prints and one stall specialized in gorgeously illustrated medical tomes that I knew would fascinate Stephen. I couldn't stop myself from purchasing a small illustrated volume of fairy tales even though it was in French. I was sure, between us, Stephen and I could make up the stories to go along with the pictures.

We must have spent an hour perusing these treasures, with Sonya every bit as excited as I was, before I realized poor Countess Olga must be tired of being on her feet, leaning on her cane. She smiled and assured me it was a favorite activity for her and her daughter. But, as we all realized, we had amassed a surfeit of books and were hungry for actual food, so she suggested we make our way to a café she knew well. One of the many policemen we had seen helped us to cross the street. At the café, the countess was recognized as a frequent customer and we were soon tucked into a little table in a prime location under the red canvas awning and against the glass windows. We had a wonderful view of the other customers and passersby, many of whom looked familiarly academic.

I had visited some of the splendid sidewalk cafés near the fashionable rue Royale, where plenty of Americans and other foreign visitors sipped coffee and nibbled pastries. But this was a much humbler establishment and homier in a way, relaxed and comfortable. The countess ordered simple omelets for us, which were served hot with bread and wine. The space was even more cramped than at the cafés on the grand boulevards but it was obvious that concern for food and drink was only a secondary object of the customers. The primary goal was watching. Watching passersby who hurried or strolled. Watching the bouquinistes and their patrons along the river. Watching carriages and motorcars duel for space on the street, and listening to the whistles of the policemen and the cries of the drivers. Watching fellow customers at the café was also expected. None of them were in a hurry to leave. Some read newspapers, a few wrote letters, others had muted discussions with companions, but most sipped their wine or coffee and regarded the world as it went past. Our table was a tiny green iron one with a white linen cloth, and the unexpectedly comfortable chairs were of cane. I discovered that it was easy to sit back, as if you were in the most comfortable armchair of your own sitting room, and watch the ebb and flow of the people passing by. I suppose the glasses of wine I had imbibed may have intensified the experience, but suddenly I realized why there were so many cafés all over Paris.

"Do you know why it is called the Latin Quarter?" Countess Olga asked.

"Because that was the common language of the scholars who came to the university."

She smiled. "That is correct. Over there is boulevard Saint-Michel, which leads to the Sorbonne. The streets are still narrow and old. Baron Haussmann has not had his way here." She turned to her left. "And over here is Faubourg Saint-Germain, where many of the old families still have residences. That is where Sonya and I live." She looked down at her coffee cup. "My husband's family has always had a house there, you see." Looking up, she exchanged a few words with her daughter who rose and hurried off after saying goodbye with a little curtsy. "Sonya studies with a tutor. She must leave now to be on time."

I found this most interesting. I was sure my mentor, Marion Talbot, back at the University of Chicago, would approve of this young woman pursuing her studies. "That is very good. Does she attend the Sorbonne? What is she studying? I lecture at the university in Chicago, you know."

Countess Olga appeared a bit distressed. "It is not a course of study at the university. That is not what I meant to say. Sonya studies Russian history and literature. You see, she has been brought up mostly here in Paris, not in our native Saint Petersburg, so she must be tutored to know about her own country's history and customs."

"I see. Yes, well that must be good for her." The circumstances that had caused the countess and her daughter to live in Paris, separated from her husband and his family, seemed a topic to be avoided. But there was something else I wanted to ask her. "It sounds as if you've lived in Paris for some time. Tell me, were you here for the big exposition in 1889...when they built the Eiffel Tower?"

"Yes. I was here."

"I ask because the policeman, Inspector Guillaume, said that at that time there were a number of jewel thefts that might be similar to the theft of Mlle Worth's sapphire. Do you remember anything like that?" I imagined that she must have moved in the circles of society where the thefts would have occurred.

She frowned. "It was a difficult time for me. Sonya and I had moved to Paris permanently. I did not see as many people as I do now, you see. I do remember hearing of some jewels disappearing. It seems to me people were trying to be discreet. I think it was much later that I actually heard something about it, from someone who had lost a jewel, but later she received recompense, I think."

"Yes. He mentioned something like that. He said there was a gang of young people from good families who were involved. Some of them were caught eventually and their families paid back some of the value, but they never caught the ringleader. The inspector referred to him as the Pied Piper."

"The Pied Piper? Oh, yes, the fairy tale. I see. No, I'm afraid I do not know anything about that."

At that moment, the countess was greeted by a gray-haired man in a top hat who was passing by. They exchanged some words and he gave me a brief bow, then turned back to the young woman at his side and took her arm, which he had dropped while speaking to us. She was a young blonde woman in a stylish suit of white satin with red stripes and streams of red ribbons from a side bow at her waist. Her hat was as broad as Lydia Johnstone's, with two long white plumes held by a broach with a ruby at the center. Countess Olga saw me watching her as they walked away. "His *maîtresse*—his mistress, as you would say." She must have noticed my raised eyebrows. "It is not uncommon to be seen so. Of course, he would never invite her to salons or to the homes of his friends, but to be seen on the street may be overlooked, you see."

"Oh, dear. But isn't he worried his wife would hear of it?" Certainly back in Chicago such indiscretions were closely guarded secrets. You would hardly expect to meet one of the Prairie Avenue magnates in the street with a woman who was not his wife. "It's not a scandal?"

"Ah, I have learned that what you Americans consider a scandal is not quite what Parisians would blink at. To marry below your rank would be scandalous here, to take a mistress is considered normal."

I thought of Stephen and Potter Palmer. I couldn't imagine either one of them indulging in such a thing. But this was a foreign country and it hardly seemed right to expect the French to have the same customs as us. Yet, it seemed wrong. Perhaps it was that so many of these visiting Americans were anxious to copy the fashions and manners of the French, especially of the nobility they met here. I thought of Bertha Palmer and Mrs. Johnstone, so anxious to marry their children into this society, and wondered if I would share their aspirations when my own children were old enough to marry. I thought not. And then I pictured Stephen's face and I was sure that would never happen.

The countess gestured for the bill. "No, no, Mrs. Chapman, I am here all the time. It is my pleasure to invite you. But, now, I must return home. Can I help you to find a cab to return you to the Trocadéro? One of the waiters will be glad to find one for you."

"No, thank you. I'll walk a bit. There's something I need to do."

TWELVE

I left the countess and walked back to the pont Saint-Michel. Across the river I could see the gray stone of the Prefecture of Police. That was where Inspector Guillaume had taken Honoré Palmer and I knew I could not return to the Palmers' house without finding out what had become of their son. I sighed. The pleasant part of the day, when I could act as a tourist, was over.

I owed it to the family who had been so good to my own, to find out what I could. It just seemed that Bertha Palmer had impossibly high expectations that I would be able to gain the confidence of the Parisian policeman. I doubted that very much. To him, I must appear to be a mere secretary to a wealthy American woman. I had no history with him, as I did with Inspector Whitbread back in Chicago. That was an entirely different situation. Whitbread knew me. We had shared experiences that had challenged us and we knew each other's strengths and weaknesses. It was true that, if we were in Chicago, I could have gone to Whitbread, and he would have found a way to include me in the investigation. He was, in many ways, my mentor. And I had always felt, with him, that the fact that I was a woman was a good thing. Theoretically, he saw no reason for that to be an obstacle to my understanding of the techniques of investigation and, practically, he considered the thought that women were not expected to understand such things a challenge he was sure he could overcome. It was an attitude unique to my old friend and not one I could expect to be shared by a different policeman in a foreign country. Yet, both Bertha and my husband thought I could somehow solve the mystery of the jewel thefts.

I forged ahead, overcoming a natural trepidation. After all, since when had I ever let that stop me? Surely my husband and my mentor would both be disappointed if I failed to at least try. I trudged across the bridge to the large gloomy building that was the Prefecture of Police, determined to find Inspector Guillaume. Before I entered, I looked down the cobblestones of the old boulevard. Across the way was the Conciergerie, where Marie Antoinette had been kept before being led out to the guillotine. What a contrast that was to the Paris I was experiencing. Paris was about strolling by booksellers and sipping coffee in cafés, while the world passed in front of you, yet it was also the city where the mob had set up the guillotine and publically executed hundreds of the aristocrats of the time. I shook my head and walked firmly through the doorway.

With my lack of French and my unorthodox request, it took more than an hour to reach my goal. I was shuffled around to various waiting rooms, including one with hard benches where several bareheaded young women gave me angry stares, and another filled with ordinary people with worried looks on their faces. At last I followed a uniformed young policeman up some stairs to a small corner office where I found Inspector Guillaume.

He looked bemused as he sat me down in a chair opposite him, across a desk of scattered papers. There were framed charts of various criminal statistics on the walls, above bookcases filled with volumes similar to those in Whitbread's office but, of course, these were in French. On the corner of the broad wooden desk, which filled up most of the room, was a small red guillotine. I learned later that it was really used to cut the ends off cigars, but it seemed a most ominous sign at the time. It was meant to be. Apparently the inspector would handle it during an interrogation to delicately remind suspects of the consequences that were in the balance. I suppressed a shiver.

But he was calm and pleasant with me, as he had been before. His deep brown eyes considered me thoughtfully. He was such a large man that he was by no means overwhelmed by the proportions of his desk. But it all felt very foreign. Of course, it *was* foreign. I was in the Prefecture of Police in Paris, France. Somehow the realization of that made me homesick for Detective Whitbread's office, with its window opening onto a brick wall and his poster listing maxims for life, such as "Don't wait to do tomorrow what you can accomplish today." I bit my lip to remind myself of where I was.

"And what can I do for you, Mme Chapman?" This reminded me of the poem I'd heard about the spider and the fly, although Guillaume was much too substantial to in any way resemble a spider.

"I wanted to find out how your interview with Mr. Honoré Palmer was concluded. He did not return to us at Notre Dame."

"And you must go back to the very impressive Mrs. Palmer and let her know what happened to her son?" Before I could respond he raised a hand. "Do not bother yourself, madame. The young man answered my questions and then he was rescued from my clutches by the amiable English lord."

"Lord James?" I was relieved to hear this. I had some idea that the French justice system would allow them to hold a man without actually charging him.

"Yes, the Lord James. He began by demanding to see me but he became quite friendly when he was allowed to join us. He agreed with M. Palmer that they saw nothing of use and that they left the ball before the theft was discovered. The English lord attempted to suggest that the sapphire might have been misplaced, as the pearls of Mme Palmer were supposed to have been misplaced, but, alas, that is not the case. The star sapphire was most definitely stolen."

"You are sure?"

"Very sure. A most thorough search was made of the house,

and all of the guests and staff who remained were searched. Most discreetly, you understand. Every person who was present has been interviewed and the premises were searched multiple times. It is unclear who is the thief and how they got the stone out, but it was most certainly stolen."

Guillaume and his men must have been up all night to accomplish such a conclusive search. But my main concern was Honoré. "So, Mr. Palmer was allowed to return home?"

"But of course." He leaned towards me. "Surely you did not think that we would detain the young man? That is perhaps what your police in Chicago would do?"

"No, no, of course not." But that was the concern that had compelled me to find out what happened to Honoré before returning to his parents.

"You must report back to your employer, no? She was very worried about her son this morning. Is it because, with a mother's feeling, she senses something is wrong with her son? Has he gotten drawn in by bad companions? A bad crowd, perhaps?"

"I don't believe so." He was right, however. Bertha *had* been overly concerned about her son.

"He is a young man in Paris. Perhaps he stays out too late at night? He goes to the races? He gambles?"

"Well, of course, he does those things. But, so does his father. Mr. Potter Palmer is quite fond of the races. My husband goes with him. He is rather frail, as Mrs. Palmer said, and my husband is a medical doctor. But I suspect he wagers a lot more money than his son does."

"Hmm. But perhaps he also has a lot more money at his disposal?"

"He's a very wealthy man, yes."

"You think it unlikely that the young Mr. Palmer might have taken his mother's pearls, or Mlle Worth's sapphire?"

I was surprised he seemed so interested in my opinion. It was flattering, but I was wary. This policeman was very different from any other I had met. He was nothing like Detective Whitbread, who was one of the most forthright people I have ever known. Guillaume looked large, but not threatening, as he sat across from me, considering me with a quizzical smile. "No, I don't believe Honoré would steal," I told him.

"I see. And what about the young ladies who were at Notre Dame today? They were also at the reception, were they not? The young M. Palmer is gallant. Perhaps he would help the young ladies, if they were in difficulties."

"What do you mean? Are you suggesting that he would steal jewels for them if they needed money? Is that what you think? But these young women have no 'difficulties' as you say. Miss Lydia Johnstone has enough money that her mother wants to marry her off to an aristocrat. And, besides, Honoré is not interested in the young Americans. If anything, he'd be interested in Miss Sonya Zugenev, the daughter of Countess Olga, and she has no need of jewels."

"Ah, yes, the American comes over with the intention to buy a title. You believe this is true for M. Palmer?"

"Well, I don't know. His mother thought it would be nice if the young people met and liked each other." I waved my hand a little helplessly. This sort of matchmaking was not something I wanted to be involved with. And, yet, I was also a mother. How could I know how I would feel about it when my children were Honoré's age? I couldn't even imagine it. I pulled myself back from such speculation as from the edge of a cliff. I needed to make the inspector turn his suspicions away from Bertha and her family. They could have no reason to steal. The idea was absurd.

"Really, Inspector, isn't it more likely that someone on the staff at the House of Worth is the thief? All these young people... they don't need jewels."

"And yet, the young people who followed the Pied Piper before, they also seemed to have no need."

I stared at him as he let that hang in the air. Finally, he looked away. "You must not think that we ignore the staff of the House of Worth. I can assure you that we are keeping a close watch on them. It is something you can convey to Mme Palmer." He folded his hands on the desk. "M. Worth prepares for the opening of his exhibit tomorrow night. You and the Palmers will attend?"

"Of course." Bertha had succeeded at the last minute and the long awaited exhibit of the House of Worth would have a more prominent place in the Palais des Fils, Tissus et Vêtements. A reception to unveil the exhibit was planned for the next evening.

THIRTEEN

Y ou will accompany us to the opening tomorrow night. And you will escort the Countess Olga and her daughter for the entire evening." Bertha Palmer had summoned Honoré to a family dinner in the formal dining room of the rue de Brignole house. I had noted her great relief, despite her attempts at a stoic demeanor, when I reported on my conversation with Inspector Guillaume. "You will remain in our party for the whole evening, as well." Her gaze was stony as she pronounced this sentence on her son.

"Another occasion for the ladies to wear their jewels," her husband pointed out blandly as he was served the fish by a white-gloved footman. "It would be awfully bold for this thief to attack again at another party of Worth's, but I suppose he must be bold to carry out the thefts he already has." Potter Palmer had yet to mention the missing pearls, at least in my presence. But there was a wicked gleam in his eyes. "A sapphire was stolen the last time, from what I've heard. You must wear yours, perhaps, my dear. Surely having stolen a star sapphire the thief would not stoop to notice the rather plebeian stone in your filigree set, don't you think?"

"Dear Potter, of course, if you wish it. But I'm not convinced the pearls were stolen, really I'm not," Bertha said.

"I hope your optimism is rewarded," he said. "But even if by some miracle your choker should appear before the reception, it would be wise to leave it here in the safe. No sense tempting fate." As his father spoke, Honoré shook his head, whether in disbelief or frustration I couldn't say. Bertha resolutely attacked her plate of fish, determined not to respond to her husband. Unsuccessful in his attempt to needle her, he turned to his son. "I trust the outing will not result in another visit to the prefecture for you, Honoré. It won't do for that to become a habit. Being seen in the company of the police too often might lead you to be taken for a police spy and get you barred from the track. We couldn't have that now, could we?"

Bertha was unhappy with this suggestion, although I saw my husband smirk into his dish. "There's been quite enough frequenting of the horse track," Bertha told them. "We came to Paris to enjoy society, not horses."

Potter raised a wiry eyebrow. "Unfortunately, over here, the equine stock seems better behaved than the humans," he told her. "You don't see the ponies banding together to pick the pockets of the spectators, whereas these drawing rooms and palaces seem to have a band of well-disguised confederates just waiting to prey on the necks of the ladies." He seemed quite satisfied by his comparison.

The following day, I found Bertha at her desk fretting because Honoré had left the house early. However, he was back in plenty of time, and he took a rented carriage out to escort the Countess Olga and her daughter to the evening reception. Stephen and I were both impressed by his gallant behavior towards the Russian women as he made sure their carriage was at rue Brignole by the time the large Victoria was brought for the rest of us. Just at dusk we formed a procession and started towards the fairgrounds.

One of the most popular features of the Exposition was the moving sidewalk, "le trottoir roulant" as the French called it, which circled most of the grounds and was a must for any visitor to experience. We had already taken several turns on the moving platforms—which had a lower, slower level you could hop onto, and then a higher, faster moving level to step up to—on previous visits. On that night we had passes that allowed us to take the carriages into the grounds and right up to the Palais des Fils, Tissus et Vêtements—the Textiles Building. The event called for evening clothes so, once again, I wore the lovely gown with the cherries at my waist and, this time, Bertha had insisted on lending me an evening coat as well. The "sortie-de-bal" as it was called, was a lovely white satin, embroidered with stars and clouds. The sleeves and hem were finished with pleated chiffon and satin ribbons gathering the feathery fabric at my wrists. Bertha was wearing her official gown with the stalks of corn figured in the velvet. The antique lace had been added to the squared-off neckline of the bodice and a thick, black velvet ribbon surrounded her waist. Her evening coat was also of black velvet, figured with flower stems in white and trimmed with white ruched chiffon. We both wore evening slippers that never would have allowed us to traipse through the fairgrounds or ride the moving sidewalk.

Instead, we sat in the spacious carriage, Stephen and I facing the Palmers. We rode through the main entrance on the Place de la Concorde. This was a large arch tiled in white, green, and blue terracotta. At the top was a female figure whose attire had been designed by the couturier Jeanne Paquin. It was very characteristic of the City of Light that the main symbol for the huge exposition would be a Parisienne, a woman of fashion. I had a great admiration for Mme Paquin herself. Mrs. Palmer had pointed her out to me at the opera, where she was surrounded by her models, who wore ensembles she'd designed. I was most impressed by the filmy pastel pink gown that she wore, herself. Another one in pastel blue had shimmering vines embroidered along the hem and, on a third, fur trimmed the sheer black silk. It was a surprise to find that she was a young woman of about my own age. I learned that she and her businessman husband had opened a house of couture next door to the House of Worth, then expanded to London. They were so successful that Mme Paquin was chosen by her fellow couturiers to be the president of the fashion section of the Exposition. It was thrilling to think that a young couple could put their stamp on the world of fashion as they had done. It seemed to me the mark of a wonderful new century that a woman could be so successful.

As we passed under the arch, we were flanked by two giant turbaned male figures who looked like genies. Inside the grounds to our right were the Grand Palais and the Petit Palais, where the all-important fine arts exhibits were displayed. To our left was the Pont Alexander III, which crossed the Seine to the Hôtel des Invalides. But we continued along the banks of the river to the next bridge, opposite the Trocadéro. That led to the prize from the last exposition in 1889, the Tour Eiffel. And, like Chicago's Columbian Exposition, this exposition had taken electricity as one of its most dramatic exhibits. So, already the Eiffel Tower was outlined in electric lights, and as we passed under it and down the Champ de Mars, we could see, at the other end, the fountains lit up in front of the Palace of Electricity.

But we stopped halfway down on the left, at the Textiles Building. It was one of a series of white fronted, colonnaded buildings constructed for the Exposition. They all led down the Champ de Mars to the fountains backed by the Palace of Electricity. There was a line of carriages waiting to disembark their passengers and, as we waited our turn, I looked up at my husband. Stephen smiled at me. He, too, remembered the night we had walked beside the water of the grand Basin at the Columbian Exposition in Chicago. It was before we were married. It, too, had been illuminated by electric lights in an amazing display and we had been on our way to a concert in the Music Hall, an event that led to an adventure that had brought us together. I couldn't help but be reminded of that night. How far away it seemed now.

We descended from the carriage and waited for Honoré, the countess, and Sonya to join us before we entered the building. Inside, the high ceilings were formed by the tracery of iron supports. There was an immense space broken up by glassed-in exhibits of weaving and silk making and other fabric related demonstrations. But we were herded past all of these to a wing that was dedicated to modern fashion. I saw the designer Jacques Doucet's exhibit with headless mannequins in evening gowns. Passing another for Paquin that was similar, we plunged on further into the bowels of the building. Soon, we were relieved of our evening coats at a table in the corridor. Mlle Arquette greeted us and took the lovely coats, patting them with affection and appreciation, like a mother patting her child's head. She seemed excited. The House of Worth's staff must have been working all day to get the exhibit finished. There had been a delay, thus its opening was the occasion for this special celebration.

We entered the large room via a reception line where we had a chance to greet M. Jean-Philippe Worth, his brother Gaston, his daughter Andrée, and her fiancé, Louis Cartier. It was a way for poor M. Worth to recover from the debacle at Andrée's engagement party. When we reached the end of the line, I saw that they were taking no chances. Inspector Guillaume stood by in evening dress, and there were many uniformed policemen stationed around the edges of the room. Surely no thief would be bold enough to try to steal jewels from the guests with all of these policemen watching. The inspector greeted us quietly but I saw Bertha bristle. Her eyes scanned the room until she found a distraction.

"Come," she said, taking my elbow. "There's Mary Cassatt. She's here with her brother and his wife. He's one of the most powerful men in America these days. He took over the Pennsylvania Railroad, you know." Mary had spotted us and waved. Bertha whispered in my ear as we traveled across the shiny wood floor to get to the group. "One of the few things that can make Mary really angry is when people assume she's supported by her wealthy relatives. She's made her own way by selling her paintings for years and she's fiercely independent."

We reached the painter, who was dressed in an elegant Worth gown of pale blue satin with delicate pink butterflies embroidered along the hem and flying up the front of the skirt. A swath of pink tulle lay across her neckline, from one shoulder to the other. Little puff sleeves of transparent tulle capped each arm and a simple string of milk-white pearls hugged her neck. She wore elbow-length kid gloves, with a thin bracelet of tiny sapphires on one wrist. Her ensemble reminded me of an early morning sky at the beach, when the light was still soft. We were introduced to Mr. and Mrs. Alexander Cassatt, her tall brother and his rather short wife, who wore a heavy white damask gown that was loaded down with appliques and pearl trim. I recognized the gleam in Bertha's eye, as she zeroed in on the powerful man. Her husband also recognized a kindred spirit in the railroad magnate.

While they talked, I looked across to Honoré, who had Sonya and her mother on either side of him, clutching his elbows with gloved hands. He was looking in the direction of the Americans. The countess wore a gown that flowed in a gently flowered set of silk panels, open in the middle to a waterfall of pastel chiffon. A swath of chiffon swept across the bodice, emphasizing her collarbones, between which a small sapphire pendant hung. Silk flowers were pinned in her hair. She still leaned on her silver-headed cane. Her daughter wore a bright pink gown with a chrysanthemum pattern in a lighter shade. The voluminous gathered skirt was pulled into her small waist with a band of ribbon, and the large puffy sleeves were topped by layers of lace. They made a lovely pair hanging off Honoré's arms.

I stepped back and took a look around the large room, quickly spying Lord James. His tall figure stood out from the group of Americans, and I was surprised to see that he was escorting Lydia Johnstone and her mother. Mrs. Johnstone wore a gown of pale satin that was heavily loaded down with fantastical gold-toned circles embroidered all along the hem and covering the bodice.

Lydia's gown was of cream silk with a jade velvet pattern of ribbons and garlands. She stood tall, with her blonde hair piled high and her shoulders bare and thrown back. She was proud to cling to the Englishman. I raised an eyebrow at that but, when the crowd parted and I could see the exhibit of Worth gowns finally revealed, it distracted and amazed me.

FOURTEEN

J ean-Philippe Worth had not been content to display his
gowns on headless mannequins, as Doucet and Paquin had
done. Instead, he had dramatized a whole story, laid out in
a long corridor, and peopled entirely by wax figures of women.
The plaque on the flowered black ironwork at the bottom of the
long glassed-in case was labeled, "Going to the Drawing Room."
The figures each had individual features and were placed in
various poses that were quite lifelike. The background was of
cream-colored walls with moldings of garlands. Panels of pale,
striped fabrics were inset on the walls, and a large French door
with mirrored panels stood, closed, in the middle of the corridor.
Perhaps that led to the drawing room they were preparing to
enter. Several other mirrors set throughout helped to make the
area seem even larger than it was.

Entranced, I moved through the crowd of talking and
drinking live people to get to the beginning of the scene at the
far left. It started with two women who looked as if they had
just come in from the outdoors. One was lounging on a plush
sofa with her arms spread out along the mahogany back. She
wore a gauzy evening gown, the train of which was draped on
the seat beside her. There were flowers pinned to her chignon.
At her side stood a woman wearing an elaborate hat tilted over
one eye and a short jacket. Just beyond these two figures, a maid
was arranging a samovar and small teacups on a table. One of

the things that made the tableau so lifelike was the inclusion of some figures in less formal dress. A tall woman wore a hat with a fur fringe and a magnificently embroidered walking suit made up of a long coat over a full skirt in vibrant colors. She appeared to be talking to a woman in a silk evening gown of gorgeous panels printed with a flower motif.

Two more women in high-necked, elegant day dresses, and large hats with veils, were to the right of the center mirrored door. The second wore an outfit of black chiffon and taffeta that was extremely sleek and modern. The transparent chiffon stretched across the arms and shoulders alluringly, fell in generous folds around the arms, and then was gathered at the neck and wrists. The mist of black chiffon and the sheen of the taffeta clinging to the figure made it seem a perfect fit for the woman. It was a style I had seen few in the salons of Paris carry off successfully.

These women appeared to be watching another wearing full court dress who was being helped by two servants, one of whom wore street clothes and might have been a seamstress come to help with final adjustments. She knelt and seemed to be straightening the yards of material that made up the immense train of the satin and lace gown. The other servant wore a maid's apron and stood beside the court figure with her arms extended to hold a fantastically embroidered evening cloak, as if it had just been handed to her. The main figure had her back to the viewers as she put the final touches on her bodice, viewing herself in a gilt-framed mirror. The placement allowed you to appreciate the magnificent needlework that went into the production of her dress, which was encrusted with pearls and sequins.

I was about to step closer, to try to get a better view of the figure's front in the mirror, when I noticed M. Paul Poiret talking to a short man with a waxed mustache, who wore stylish evening dress. The young couturier's eyes rose from the man's face and he recognized me. He started, as if alarmed. Turning so that his back was to my approach, he spoke to his companion, who then quickly slipped away. Poiret turned back to me, composed this time. "Mme Chapman, we meet again at a celebration. I sincerely hope this one will come to a much better conclusion than the last excursion at which I had the pleasure of meeting you."

I put my hand to my neck where I wore the small string of pearls I'd gotten from my mother. They were not worth much compared to the jewels owned by the other women in this room but they were important to me. Poiret noticed and raised an eyebrow, which caused me to blush. "Tut, tut," he said. "I see we are all being quite modest in our display of the bijoux tonight. Don't be alarmed. It is only to be expected. The last thing M. Worth would want is another incident such as at the engagement fête." He shook his head.

"Surely no such thing will happen with all the policemen present," I protested.

"We hope not. But come, how do you like our exhibit? It is good, no? I can tell you that there were endless discussions about it, and disputes about what each madame must be doing."

"I think it's marvelous." I moved up to the railing, which stopped a viewer about a foot from the glass wall of the exhibit. "They're so lifelike, one could almost think they're actually talking to each other in there."

"Yes, yes. That is it. These two down here are telling the lady in the court dress how she is to behave and what she should change in her appearance before she enters."

"And the woman who is straightening her train, even her dress is quite lovely, and I like that hat." The figure kneeling was more like a member of the staff of the House of Worth come to assist, than an ordinary maid of the house. She quite realistically wore a simple dress of black with white dots and a band of white lace on the arms. A black silk rose was at the high neck of the dress and the hat was a modest one with a brim over the eyes and a soft plush crown. "Is that one of your fried potatoes?"

"Indeed, you have guessed it! I am delighted that you appreciate it. Yes, to make it more real the servants, as well as the mesdames, are present."

"I was just trying to see the front of the figure looking in the mirror," I told him, standing on tiptoe and straining my neck. "There seems to be something familiar about her."

"Ah, but she is not real, madame. Real as she may appear, she is wax, like the others. I don't know who Worth used as models for the wax figures, but she is not real, I assure you. Even we would not make the mannequins to stand for such a long period of time. It would be cruel!"

"No, it isn't that. It's something else." I strained to see. There was something bothering me about the figure and, at first, I couldn't think what it could be. But then I noticed the choker of pearls around the neck of the mannequin. *Surely, it couldn't be?* If only I could see the front I might rid myself of the suspicion forming in my mind. "M. Poiret, is there any way I could get a closer look at that figure? It's the pearls, I just want to see them." Poiret looked at me as if I was a little mad. "I know it sounds odd, but I really think you should look at those jewels."

"Well," he said, taking a look around, "it's really not permitted. But, of course, there is a door in the glass that we used to go in and dress the figures and to stage them. I don't believe anyone is paying attention. They have started to serve the champagne, and everyone speaks." It was true, the buzz of conversation had become a roar as people filled the room, and no one was actually paying attention to the exhibit. They were all catching up and exchanging gossip before the speeches started, I presumed. Poiret's eyes sparkled. "*Allons-y.* Come. *Vite.* Quickly, and no one will see."

He grabbed my hand and pulled me down to the far right end of the exhibit then, bending down, he released a catch so that the piece of glass swung out towards us. He helped me step up into the scene before he stiffened, as someone spoke his name.

I glanced back and saw M. Worth, with an angry look on his face, making his way through the crowd. That made my mission even more urgent. I turned back and moved deliberately into the tableau until I could see the front of the figure in court dress. She looked down at me coldly but suddenly I realized I was right. Around her neck were seven horizontal rows of pearls, divided by vertical strings of tiny diamonds, with a large pearl hanging on a pendant in the front. It was Bertha Palmer's pearl choker!

Before I could say that out loud, my eyes were pulled down the front of the heavy satin dress, where more pearls had been sewn on in curling designs, to the floor at the wax figure's feet. Lying at an angle were a pair of plebian, scuffed little black boots of worn leather. Just as I began to wonder who had left them so incongruously, I realized they were on feet, and peeking out from the magnificent evening cloak, which hung from the hands of the wax servant girl, was a pile of white muslin with little red and blue flowers printed on it. Perhaps I should have screamed or fainted, but I never do that sort of thing. Instead, I strode forward and roughly pushed aside the heavy cloak to see the rest of the figure. The young milliner I had first seen outside the House of Worth lay on the floor in her flowered dress, with the royal blue satin ribbon that should have been around her waist garroting her throat. Her eyes stared unseeing, and her mouth grimaced in a ruined face that had a bluish tinge to it. The girl was most definitely dead.

FIFTEEN

Poor M. Worth must have believed he was cursed. First theft, and now murder. This was not the kind of notoriety he sought for the House of Worth. It seemed there was nothing he could do to stop the disasters that kept happening, going from bad to worse to catastrophic.

With Inspector Guillaume and his men already present, it was all quickly under control. The broad-shouldered policeman climbed into the case with me and viewed the prone figure. He spoke quietly to the assistant who had followed him, and then asked me a few brief questions before he shooed me out.

Soon, all of the guests had been herded out to the porches, where tables had been arranged in the soft summer air. It was a lovely arrangement. The tables were set with linen and crystal, and candles in protective glass jars. Gentle gaslight shone from fixtures on the walls. From this side of the building we could see the illuminated fountain in front of the Palace of Electricity. I found myself seated at a table with the Palmers and Countess Olga. My husband listened to my whispered explanation, then put his arm around me protectively. I was relieved to sink into his shoulder.

"It is quite unbelievable," Bertha said, hardly moving her lips as she looked around. Her husband shrugged. Waiters moved through, pouring champagne, and the guests murmured quietly as they gulped the sparkling wine. Few knew about the gruesome discovery, but everyone suspected something had gone terribly wrong.

I sipped the cool, fizzy liquid, suppressing a shiver as I remembered the figure of the little milliner. Over the rim of my glass, I saw Inspector Guillaume heading towards us. Unable to speak, I nodded, and Bertha Palmer twisted around to see what had caught my attention.

"At last," she said. "We should get some information from him."

Her husband raised an eyebrow skeptically as he twirled the glass from which he had just taken a sip.

But the policeman was ambushed before he could reach us. Several tables down from us, I saw Mrs. Johnstone rise from her seat to step in front of Guillaume. "What has happened?" she demanded. "Why can't we leave? We asked them to call for our carriage but they refused. I want to know what is going on."

The men at her table, including the tall and gangling Lord James, rose awkwardly. The woman's husband rolled his eyes and took another gulp from his glass. They had to remain on their feet as long as she did.

"Pardon, madame. There has been a tragedy. We must ask for your patience."

"Nonsense. I demand to leave now. I assume this is another case of jewel theft. We have lost nothing. But I won't have my daughter and her friends exposed to such things."

The tall detective stopped and regarded the short woman. "Alas, madame, it is no longer theft but murder with which we are concerned."

This caused a stir as the news was whispered to the other tables.

"Murder! What do you mean? Who was murdered? You can't keep us here. We could be in danger!"

"I assure you, madame, we are doing our best to protect you. The unfortunate victim was a young milliner named Denise Laporte. Were you acquainted with her?" Guillaume ostentatiously took out his notebook. If Mrs. Johnstone wanted to be the first to be interviewed, he appeared ready to accommodate her. She took two steps back.

"I have no idea…no idea at all, but we saw nothing. Our party arrived together, and we stayed together the entire time. We saw nothing. We could not have done anything. None of us."

"Ah, yes, madame. But it seems the young woman who was strangled did not die tonight. It seems it was this afternoon that it happened."

I remembered touching the body of that poor girl. She was cold, but she was also stiff. In fact, she had felt as hard as stone, especially her face, which was rigid in that terrible grimace and her hands set as hard as lobster claws. I knew from other deaths I had seen, and from Stephen's explanations, that it was some hours after death that this kind of stiffness took hold. "Rigor mortis," he whispered in my ear and he smoothed my hands, for I had clutched them in my lap as I listened.

Inspector Guillaume paused, with his pencil over a page of his notebook. "You would like, perhaps, to account for your whereabouts this afternoon, madame?" he asked Mrs. Johnstone. "After which, my associate will take your information and you will be able to return to your house. This is your wish?"

The woman appeared to be dumbfounded. But her daughter was not. Lydia bounced up and pushed past Lord James to face the policeman. "Well, that's all right then," she told him. "We were all together. We were here, at the Exposition. We were riding the wheel." She gestured into the night towards the lights of the great Ferris wheel, which could be seen slowly turning off in the distance. It, too, was lit up festively with electric lights. "We had to wait in line for the most awfully long time, didn't we?" She turned to Lord James for confirmation. Looking surprised, he nodded. "Of course, my parents were home," she continued, "but you couldn't seriously suspect them, could you? In any case, I'm sure the servants can vouch for them. And we were all together for dinner and then we came to the reception. There, that should suffice for you."

"And Denise Laporte. Were you acquainted with the young woman?"

Lydia looked at him blankly, then she looked at Lord James and her friends Miss Brown and Miss Stuart. "Well, of course, it's possible she may have *served* us. But we wouldn't have *known* her."

Inspector Guillaume stared at them just long enough to make them uncomfortable, before introducing his associate who would take their particulars. Then he resumed his considered pace towards us.

I was aware that Bertha Palmer was glaring at her son, although she was holding her tongue with some effort. By the time the policeman arrived, she had retrieved her sangfroid and she turned to him politely. Inspector Guillaume apologized for keeping us, and was particularly polite to me, saying he hoped I was not overcome by the experience of finding the body. Finally, he pulled up an iron chair and got down to business. "As you may have heard, the young woman was killed in the afternoon. This was made clear to us by the medical staff that we summoned. I myself was present from before the guests arrived, but it seems the death of this poor young woman had already occurred." He seemed just slightly exasperated. There must have been much planning that had gone into protecting the reception from another incident, yet the worst had come to pass anyway. "You understand, we must ask all of the guests whether they knew her and where they were in the afternoon."

Bertha and I had seen the girl but knew nothing about her. My employer and I had also been together for the whole afternoon, working on her correspondence. Stephen had been at the Institut Pasteur. Countess Olga and her daughter were at their home with Sonya's tutor. Guillaume turned politely to the Palmer men. Honoré was slightly flushed. "I'm afraid I was out walking. I don't think anyone saw me."

The inspector raised an eyebrow and looked back at the Johnstone party, who were gathering their things to leave. "You were not with the other young people, perhaps? At the wheel?"

Honoré flushed even more red. "I'm afraid not."

"And I was home taking a nap," Potter Palmer announced. "I doubt anyone looked in on me." He stared brightly at his wife. "My son and I might have attended the races, where we could have been seen by any number of people, but we were told in no uncertain terms that we did not come to Paris to go to the races! So neither one of us can vouch for the other, I'm afraid."

Inspector Guillaume had to be aware of the tension around the table, but he quickly wrote in his notebook. When he finally looked up, I let my breath out. I was not even aware I had been holding it.

"Well, thank you. You will all be remaining in Paris for the Exposition, I know. If for any reason you feel you must leave the city, you will be so good as to come to us for permission." Nodding to a uniformed police officer, who was standing by, the big inspector rose heavily and wished us a good night.

The officer, we soon realized, was assigned to keep us always in his sight. Not all of us, perhaps. Honoré Palmer was his main concern and, when Bertha Palmer realized this in the following days, she was furious.

SIXTEEN

Bertha Palmer was beside herself by the end of the week. She couldn't believe the police were serious about her son as a suspect, and she was furious with young Honoré for having been on an unexplained outing the afternoon of the murder. It was all the more frustrating since it was her own decree that had kept him from going to the horse races with his father. Had they done so, he would be as beyond suspicion as the others.

"The inspector is wasting his time having a man follow Honoré like this. It's ridiculous. Surely his time would be better spent looking for someone who actually had a motive to kill her. Why would Honoré want to harm a young woman like that? It's absurd."

I bent my head over the correspondence we'd been working on. I didn't want to be the one to suggest the obvious. Guillaume must believe there was a relationship, perhaps a romantic entanglement, at the center of the case. Or, perhaps he suspected she was an accomplice in the jewel thefts. Neither were theories that Bertha Palmer would consider, and I had no intention of bringing them up, but I couldn't help thinking they would have been obvious to the police who didn't know the Palmers.

"A young woman like that…she had access to all the wealthy clients of M. Worth. Surely they must suspect that she was in league with the Pied Piper and that she'd threatened him with exposure or something. What do you think, Emily? What would your detective friend in Chicago think?"

Knowing Detective Whitbread, I was quite sure he would have thought the same thing the French police were thinking. But, unlike Inspector Guillaume, it wouldn't occur to him to try to spare the feelings of a Bertha Palmer. He would have been even more blatant about his suspicions and, by now, he would have dragged Honoré into the police station for a searing interrogation, rather than having him discreetly shadowed. How was I to explain this to Bertha? "The police have a duty to find the murderer," I told her. "If the dead girl were your daughter or niece, you would want them to do everything they could to find the culprit, wouldn't you?"

"But I cannot understand why they're concentrating on Honoré. He wasn't even acquainted with the woman."

I wondered if that were true. Bertha's endless speculation was not helpful. She was driving herself to distraction, pacing back and forth before the painting of the two young circus performers. I feared she would make herself ill.

"Can't you go to see Inspector Guillaume and find out what he's doing?" she asked.

Even with all that the Palmers had done for me and my family, I couldn't see how I could help with this problem. I was useless to her. "I really don't think Inspector Guillaume will share information about his plans with me." Bertha turned on her heel and headed across the rug again. How could I approach the policeman? It was impossible, impractical, unthinkable. But perhaps there was another avenue I could explore. "Surely the staff at the House of Worth must know more about the young woman's background."

She stopped pacing. "Yes, yes, Emily, you could go and find out from them."

"Well, I'm not sure I could just ask..."

"Yes." She came and took my hand. Presented with an idea, she immediately had a plan. It was so like her. "The walking suit they're making for you. I'll tell them it's required for an outing next week. They'll need to have you in for a fitting at once." She hurried back to her desk. "I'll write them right now."

So it was that I found myself once again at the House of Worth, three days after the body of Denise Laporte was found in the Worth exhibit.

This time I was led to the sacred precincts on the upper floors. I followed Mlle Arquette up two flights to the ateliers where the real work was done. Here the ceilings were low. There were rooms with wide tables for cutting lengths of fabric, there were rooms fitted with sewing machines being worked with foot pedals, and there were rooms where women hunched over vast swaths of satin, doing hand embroidery or adding pearls in swirling patterns.

We passed on to a room with a skylight and a raised platform. Mlle Arquette translated as two buxom women in shirtsleeves and aprons helped me to remove my outer garments and step into the skirt and jacket of the new ensemble. It was a marvelous plush fabric in golds and browns, but I hardly had time to look at it. They pushed and prodded, then gestured to me to step up onto the platform where they adjusted various seams and made marks with chalk. I raised and lowered my arms as commanded, and moved in imitation of them as they considered the fit. Finally, they required me to stand still as one of them moved around the bottom of the skirt, pinning up the hem.

I took the opportunity to ask Mlle Arquette about Denise Laporte.

"Tragic, so tragic. She was so young," she grimaced. "It has greatly alarmed all of us to have so terrible a thing happen." The other women responded to the mention of the dead girl with shaking heads and a couple of sharp comments. I looked at Mlle Arquette for a translation. Reluctantly she told me. "They say the young Denise was a coquette. She was only young, though. Her parents were dead. She worked for her uncle's wife in the milliner's shop next door." Mlle Arquette tut-tutted at more remarks in a quick exchange between the other two women. She sighed. "They say she bragged about a wealthy lover who was going to take her away." She exchanged a few words with them, and they motioned for me to turn a few steps to my right. "But I don't believe it."

"What are they saying about her?" I really wanted to know. Not being able to understand was frustrating to say the least.

"The girl was a model, for painters sometimes. These young women who have no family, sometimes they do things they shouldn't. Working in the shop they see the nice things the wealthy ladies have and all they think about is the latest finery, how to get ribbons and feathers for their caps. With no one to stop them, they can make money posing for the painters. And then they are in the studios and the galleries, they go to the dance halls with the men and women they meet there. I can understand how a young girl, like Denise, would be attracted to the little flashes of light and music and happiness." Perhaps she was remembering a time when she had been like the little milliner. I couldn't picture her posing in an artist's studio, or dancing under the stars at one of the outdoor cafés we'd seen. Mlle Arquette was the one who kept the women workers in order, but she must have had a different life when she was younger.

I needed to find out more about the dead girl. "Did they believe her about the wealthy lover?" Mlle Arquette looked at me curiously but she translated. They said the girl had seemed to disappear and live away from her uncle's house for a while and had only recently returned. There was a lot of discord with her aunt about that, but she'd been taken back, albeit grudgingly. They assumed she'd taken a lover but been discarded by him when he tired of her. It was not an uncommon story. A girl like that was a leaf blowing in the wind and could so easily be detached from the tree and buffeted to the ground. She was lucky to be able to return to her uncle's house, although it must have been unpleasant for her.

I asked if they thought she could have been involved in the jewel thefts. That made them look very uncomfortable, even resentful. Mlle Arquette reluctantly translated their remarks. "They say they would never let her near the jewels of the ladies. But she had insisted she would be getting money and would not have to live with her uncle any longer. They didn't believe it. Girls like that are always dreaming. Certainly she was jealous of the sapphire of Mlle Andrée. They all were, madame. You know, don't you, that Andrée's mother started as a seamstress, here in the atelier? M. Jean fell in love with her and he took her as his mistress, set her up in a home. Later, he raised the girl as his legitimate daughter, so they all think it could have been them. But it is not so common, that. Like all of them, Denise would have thought that if things were only a little different, it might have been her with the handsome, wealthy young husband and the star sapphire jewel. That could have been *her* engagement present." She shook her head. "Dreams, all fantasy."

"But you don't think it's possible Denise was involved in the robberies?"

"She was helping in the room with the dresses and hair, but no one would allow her near jewels." There was more back and forth between the women but she spoke sharply to them.

"What did they say?"

"They are gossips. They say M. Poiret stole the sapphire because M. Jean does not appreciate him. It is not true. M. Paul and M. Jean do not always agree, but it is just the disagreement of artists. M. Paul will be a good designer in his own right eventually, but he needs to obey M. Jean who has so much more experience. M. Gaston hired M. Paul, and M. Gaston is a good businessman."

She listened to them again. "No. They say M. Paul is angry because, with Mlle Andrée marrying now, her husband Louis will come into the business, and M. Paul will not rise. I don't believe it. M. Cartier has plans for his son in his own business. It is Mlle Andrée who will do what her grandmother did, wearing the new styles and socializing with the aristocracy to lure the new clients," she told me. When she translated her comments back to the women there was a burst of argument. "Oh, oh," she turned back to me. "What they say is true. They are not so interested in the aristocrats. You would be surprised, madame, how many of them order the finest dresses and then don't pay their bills. Oh, yes, we are very interested in the nice Americans like Mme Palmer who order the best but always pay for it. Unfortunately, it is not always the same with the aristocracy. So the designs of M. Poiret for the more ordinary, they are still very important. The fried potatoes, as M. Gaston says. At least the customers of the fried potatoes pay the bill right away."

"M. Poiret designs the more ordinary garments, isn't that so?" I asked. "Did he design my suit?"

They laughed. "No, no, for the secretary of Mme Palmer, M. Jean himself, of course, does the design. Come." She held out a hand to help me down two steps and over to a full-length mirror so that I could see the walking suit.

It was wonderfully stylish suit but understated. There was a high-necked, cream silk blouse with a lacy bow at the neck and a ruffle of lace down the front. The skirt and jacket were of a tawny brown with gold highlights. It was made of light velvet that had a quilted texture, soft and plush. The trim down the edge of the front skirt panel, and at the shoulder and elbow, was a dark chocolate brown. There was a wide belt in a matching dark brown, from which hung some copper chains with a small metal change purse and a tiny little metal book. The skirt was a smooth bell shape, while the jacket was long, with a pinched in waist, a flare below that, and modestly gathered sleeves, with long cuffs to the elbow. The amazing thing to me was how very well suited it was for me. I could see myself wearing it on the grounds of the university. I had not expected M. Worth and Mrs. Palmer to be so very correct in their assessment of what would be suitable for me. I felt a little thrill of excitement, thinking of how I would look to my colleagues back in Chicago. I was hugely grateful to Bertha and determined to do anything I could to repay such generosity.

I was reluctant to step out of the new garments but, with the help of the seamstresses, I did. They told me there was a hat that I must see at the milliner's next door that was required for the suit to be complete, so I was to stop there before returning home. This fit well with my own plans, as it would allow me to try to find out more about the dead girl. As I descended the stairs, I heard a commotion on the second floor where there were offices. I saw a short man with a waxed mustache shoot out one of the doors and hurry down the stairs to the large blue door out to the street. He was followed by M. Jean-Philippe Worth, who was growling at him and waving his arms. Down below, I saw a startled looking M. Poiret, who quickly took a step back into the shadows. As the short man turned and yelled something up the stairs just before he exited, I realized I had seen him before. It was the man M. Poiret had been talking to when I met him at the exhibition.

SEVENTEEN

Stepping through the blue door into the sunshine, I nodded to the doorman and walked the few steps to the milliner's shop next door. It was a small storefront with a multi-paned window displaying hats at different levels, all decorated with gauze and flowers. One of them sported what looked like a dead bird, whose beak would rest on a woman's forehead. I had seen women wear such things but couldn't imagine actually buying something like that.

I pushed the door open and a bell jangled to announce my arrival. There were tables and shelves lining the walls, all holding a mixture of hats and trimmings. In between were a variety of standing mirrors. But my attention was immediately drawn to the counter at the back where a tall, red-faced woman in a high-necked dress of black bombazine was arguing with a short young woman in broken English.

"The money. It is owed. You must pay." She had a piece of paper in her hand that she was waving in front of the other woman's face.

"No. No money. Just look at this hat, look at this lining, it's ripped. That's the way it was delivered. I'm bringing it back. I won't pay for this. No one would pay for this. Just *look* at this." She waved the hat back at the saleswoman's face.

It was Lydia Johnstone's friend Edith and the hat with the ripped lining was the one she had worn at Notre Dame, on the day I had met her there with the others. It was of creamy white satin on a straw crown, decorated with sharp yellow ribbons and silk roses. The yellow silk lining had a vicious rip from which threads hung. She turned the hat to expose them and thrust it into the face of the angry woman before her. "I won't pay for such shoddy work. And I'll tell everyone I know about how awful you were to me, Mme Laporte," she announced with a sneer. Then, tossing the damaged hat on the counter, she turned on her heel and flounced out of the shop. I think she recognized me as she passed, but she made no acknowledgement, continuing on to slam the door shut behind her. The bell jangled.

The woman at the counter, who I now realized must be Denise Laporte's aunt, was in a rage, picking up the hat and muttering what I'm sure must have been curses. For a moment I was carried back to fairy tales of my childhood, she was so much like a witch in one of the stories. Of course, the poor woman had just lost her niece and, besides, I thought Miss Stuart might have tricked her about that hat. I was certain she'd been wearing it in the church, so her claim that it was delivered with the damage seemed unlikely. It was not my place to tell Mme Laporte that, though.

When she recovered herself she turned to greet me. Her English was good enough to serve her British and American clients, especially those from the House of Worth, which obviously had an arrangement with her to cater to their customers. When she heard my name she was happy to seat me and go to find the hat that had been designed to go with the walking suit. It was perfect, a plush little felt toque in chocolate brown with a fluffy brown feather on the side. She placed it on my head, at a slant and showed me how it looked in the mirror.

It was better than any hat I had ever owned, and I said as much. She was pleased with my response. "I am so sorry about your niece," I told her.

She frowned, but her shoulders also fell from the stiff stance that must have been her normal posture. "Denise, she was niece of my husband. Not a good girl. We raised her, we gave her position, but always she is wanting more. It was bad, bad for her to go and help at Worth." She nodded in the direction of the blue door of the House of Worth. "We thought it would be good. She could learn something, meet more clients. But all she does is to want more. I told her it is not for you to want, it is for you to find out what the rich lady wants and make it for her. But she wouldn't listen. Always, I am like the wicked stepmother. We only wanted to help her, but she wouldn't be helped. The young ones, you cannot tell them anything."

I was surprised that she would say so much to me, a stranger, but it seemed she must have had all of this buttoned up inside her since her niece's death. And I suspected she probably knew that the women who worked with Denise—like the seamstresses I had talked to—thought she had driven her niece away. I was a convenient listening post to get her side of the story expressed, I suppose.

She walked over to the window and, reaching down, she gathered up a broad-brimmed hat with a wave of gauze and several floppy silk flowers. She turned to show it to me. "You see, she was very good. She made the very fancy designs. But for something like this," she pointed to the hat for me, "that was not good enough for her to work on. And the painters." She shook her head and placed the large hat carefully on the table in front of me. "When she went to the painters we almost threw her out. She should know no good girl is a model for the painters. But she said she needed the money. What good is money if you ruin yourself? I asked her. She said it wasn't only the money. It was the dancing and the cafés. That is what she liked."

"Young girls are attracted to the lights and music, I'm sure," I said. "Did she actually move away from you at that time?"

She looked at me. What I'd just said confirmed for her that others were talking about the dead girl. "I know what they are saying." She nodded in the direction of the House of Worth. "So foolish, so very foolish. She moved away for a man. She didn't tell us so. She just disappeared. But my cousin saw her in the Montmartre district, in a café, with the artists. But it wasn't an artist, she insisted. It was a gentleman, an aristocrat, a man with much money she said. I didn't believe her. She came back to us with nothing a month ago. He died, she said. I didn't believe that, either. He just got tired of her. She said he couldn't tell his family, they wouldn't approve. I tried to make her tell me who it was. I know he wasn't dead. She was still secretive. She was still sneaking out to see someone. I told her she must tell me. He must help her. But she refused. So foolish the little petite, the foolish, foolish girl. My husband, he would kill the man if he knew him. That's why she wouldn't tell me. But I told her he had to know about it." She looked up at me, her eyes red and blurry. "She was *enceinte*. She couldn't hide that from me, I know. I had no babies myself, I couldn't carry them to the end, you see. But I knew the signs, and she couldn't hide it. She had to admit it. She was afraid of what my Henri would do, but I could tell." There were tears in her eyes. "*Ma pauvre petite fille*. To the end she thought the man would take care of her. They are so foolish the young girls."

"Oh, my. *Enceinte*. She was with child when she died?"

"*Oui.*"

EIGHTEEN

Bertha was unusually quiet when I told her. She was quicker than me to jump to conclusions. "Is this why the police are following Honoré? Do they think that, because she was with child, my son must be the father? He would never do such a thing. It makes no sense."

"She was telling people the man was an 'aristocrat,'" I said. "Surely they would see that she couldn't have meant Honoré. Wouldn't Lord James be more likely?"

"I'm afraid Lord James is much more sophisticated than my son. I cannot believe he would be so foolish as to have had an affair with a milliner. Inspector Guillaume should be able to see that. But Honoré…" She shook her head. "He is the naïve young American. The police must think he could be foolish enough to have an affair with a young girl like that. But they are wrong. He would never do that, but they don't know him. But I do know that he's keeping *something* from me. I asked him point blank if he knew the girl and he denied it, but he couldn't tell me where he was at the time the police are asking about. There *is* something wrong. I never should have made him come to Paris. It was all my idea and I forced him to come join us here after his grand tour. Oh, how I regret that now." She dropped down to the seat in front of her elegant desk and put her head in her hands. The lacy sleeves of her white tea gown fell in delicate folds, but her face looked gray and drawn, much older than I had ever seen her.

"Even if she was with child by Lord James, or someone else, surely that would not be a reason to strangle her." The thought of that ugly, distorted face with the bulging eyes, lying below the beautifully dressed mannequins, was disturbing to me. I shook myself slightly. "Isn't it much more likely that she knew something, or saw something having to do with the jewel thefts? They said she was in the changing room at the reception for Mlle Andrée. But she could not have been near the jewels of the ladies, they all said that. Perhaps the man she was involved with was the jewel thief, the Pied Piper. She was telling people she would soon be taken care of." It must have been galling for the young woman to have to return to her uncle and aunt after they'd warned her against her lover.

"We know they suspect Honoré of being the thief, though what reason they think he would have for that, I cannot imagine. He is so stubborn. He must have gone somewhere that afternoon but he refuses to explain."

"Whatever he's hiding from you, it's not that he strangled that girl. Knowing him, I'm certain of that."

"But Inspector Guillaume might not consider it as we do."

"By now the police must have discovered the girl was with child. If I could find that out, surely they could. Inspector Guillaume does appear to be a conscientious investigator. Eventually he'll see that your son was not involved."

"But why do you believe that? They *are* following my son. In him they have a likely scapegoat. Wouldn't it be easier for them if they could blame an American? It's a great embarrassment for the French to have this jewel thief operating during their exposition. They're in competition with us to prove their fair is better than the one we had in Chicago, you know. I have it on the authority of some of the officials who are friendly to me. They believe it will save face if the thief is caught and he is a foreigner, and you can be sure Inspector Guillaume has been told as much. And now, with that poor girl strangled, it's more than an embarrassment, it's an outrage." She stared up at the ceiling. "I am at a loss as to what we should do. The plain fact is that Honoré is living under a cloud of suspicion, and there are those—even in our own commission—who would gloat if he was charged with these crimes. I don't know what to do to stop this madness. I've ordered him to act as an escort for Countess Olga and her daughter and to refrain from any activities that might in any way be misinterpreted. I think…at least when I told him he was being followed…he finally paid attention. But he's so stubborn. He insists on his innocence, as if that matters, if there is the appearance of indiscretion. I very much fear that he will have to learn the hard way that appearances are critical. I'm so worried about Potter, Emily. He presents a good front, but if anything were to happen to our son he'd be devastated. You know he's not nearly as robust as he would have people believe."

I did know that from Stephen, who was keeping a careful eye on the older man. Bertha shook her head in frustration. "He's as stubborn as Honoré. Neither one of them will believe there is a real danger here. But I can sense it in the way people act towards us, and the satisfaction in the faces of those who are jealous of me and my position. What they don't realize is that the very public nature of my work here puts my son in a perilous situation. They refuse to recognize it!"

I could tell that she was deeply disturbed. She sat for a while, just shuffling through the invitations and papers that she usually attacked with such gusto. She was truly afraid of what could happen. I dearly wanted to be able to reassure her, but her mind would not be at rest until the real culprit was found, or her son was proven innocent in some definitive manner. But what could be done? To withdraw completely from the activities of the Exposition would give the appearance of guilt, yet to continue risked another occasion when Honoré Palmer could be present if there was a jewel theft.

"I assume you have asked the countess to keep an eye on Honoré, when he is with them, so that there can be no question of his being implicated, should this jewel thief strike again?"

"I did beg her to be vigilant and I'm confident she'll do everything in her power to protect his reputation. She's quite grateful to us for our support of her in a few awkward social situations of her own." I knew she was thinking of Mrs. Johnstone and her campaign to try to expel the countess from any events sponsored by the Americans. Bertha had quashed that movement and the countess might well be grateful for her support. "But Olga can do nothing about the vicious rumors and gossip that some people are spreading. How anyone could think that Honoré would actually strangle a young woman like that is impossible to contemplate but there are those who would have it that he did." She was bitter.

I couldn't stand it anymore. "All right. I'm quite certain the inspector will not give me any information about their investigation, but it must be possible, at the very least, to track down who the man was who fathered Denise Laporte's child. They lived together for some time, so someone must be able to tell us who he was. If we could find that out, the police would have to treat the man as a suspect and, in any case, we could counter gossip with facts." She looked up, a glimmer of hope apparent in her eyes. I only hoped I wouldn't disappoint her. "I've been thinking. If Mlle Laporte was an artist's model, and if that was how she met this man, perhaps Miss Cassatt could help us find out who he is by finding out what artists she sat for. Surely they would have some inkling as to who the man was."

She sat up straight. I had provided her with a course of action. The thing that frustrated Bertha Palmer most was the lack of a plan of action. Once she had something she could do, she brightened considerably. "That's an excellent idea. I'm sure Mary could help, or she can find someone who can. Yes, I'll write to her immediately and beg her to use her contacts to find out who painted the girl."

I was relieved to see how much writing the note and dispatching it by hand improved her mood. Once she had done that, she was able to turn back to the tasks at hand and begin to deal with them. She was still laboring under a great deal of worry, but she seemed less strained.

Miss Cassatt was prompt in responding. The following afternoon Mrs. Palmer received a note announcing that M. Edgar Degas had been one of the girl's employers, along with an invitation to attend a gallery reception where he would be present. Mrs. Palmer asked me to go, and I readily agreed.

NINETEEN

The Palmers' carriage took me to the gallery of Paul Durand-Ruel on rue Laffitte. If rue de la Paix was where women went to pay top price to decorate themselves from head to toe, rue Laffitte was where connoisseurs could go to view and purchase, even invest in, art with a capital "A." It was a street of galleries and Durand-Ruel's was a premier example.

The small, rotund man greeted me at the door. His fluffy white hair and beard made him seem to be a miniature Saint Nick. "*Alors*, we are invaded by the mesdames today," he told me. "Mlle Cassatt, she has brought the Americans who are always welcome." There was a shine of joy in his eyes.

I had heard that wealthy Americans, like the Palmers, were directed to M. Durand-Ruel by Miss Cassatt and others. I only hoped he didn't expect me to be able to actually purchase something. If so, he would be disappointed.

He called out and gestured to a young man who led me to an inner room, where Mary Cassatt was holding court surrounded by other women and the four large walls were hung with more than a dozen of her pictures. They portrayed women and children in oils and pastels, and a few sets of prints. The walls vibrated with the flowing strokes of her brushes and bold lines of ink. It was like stepping into a place I knew, although I wasn't familiar with any of the women in the paintings. Some were portraits of wealthy women wearing Worth dresses, accompanied by a daughter just as well dressed. Others were more ordinary women, drying infants just plucked from a bath or doing other everyday things. They were unsentimental but filled with the sense of encompassing connection that I felt, as a mother, in the company of my own children. She had captured something of that, in a way I had never seen before in a painting. It was intrinsically feminine, and as strong as it was soft.

I had to pull my eyes away from the framed pictures in order to meet the other women in the room. Louisine Havemeyer and her daughter were old friends of Mary Cassatt. They could have been lifted from one of Bertha Palmer's receptions. Sarah Choate Sears was just as fashionable in a gray walking suit with a wide band of black velvet at the hem and cuffs. She was a wealthy heiress but also an artist whose watercolors had been accepted for the main salon exhibit at the Exposition. She told us that she had a show of her photographs coming up in Paris, along with a group of new artists. Cecilia Beaux, who Grace Greenway Brown had mentioned to me earlier, was also there, along with another woman, who they told me was a student of Camille Pissarro.

Mary also introduced me to Miss Theodate Pope, a woman of about my own age who had designed her parents' home in Connecticut. "Mary's show here is quite successful," she told me. "No matter that she doesn't submit to the judgment of the Exposition judges. No need for her to do that anymore, when she can sell pictures here and in New York, as well."

"So she told us. My employer, Mrs. Palmer, says they need more women on the prize committees but Miss Cassatt refused. I can see, with such a wonderful display of so much of her work here, having one or two pictures in the Grand Palais would not be that important to her."

"That's not the only consideration," Miss Pope told me. "It's a matter of principle for her. Isn't it, Mary?"

"Yes. I was lucky enough to be one of the founders of the Independent Exhibition and our principles were: no jury, no medals, no awards. Our first exhibition was in 1879 and it was a protest against official exhibitions, not really a grouping of artists with the same style, you know. We've been dubbed 'Impressionists.' That might apply to M. Monet but not necessarily to M. Degas or myself. We exhibited cooperatively in order to free ourselves from the tyranny of a jury. Surely no profession is as enslaved as ours. I don't want to serve on *any* jury. I could never reconcile my conscience if my decision served to effectively shut the door in the face of a fellow painter."

She had caught the attention of the other women painters in the room. "It must have been quite an honor to be invited to join the independents," Cecilia Beaux said.

"It was." Mary spread her large hands. "At last I could work with complete autonomy without concerning myself with the eventual judgment of a jury. I admired Manet, Courbet, and Degas. I hate conventional art. At last I began to live." She looked around at them. "I am independent! I can live alone and I love to work."

I could see that she was encouraging the young American artists to dare to live the kind of life she had. As they turned away to look at her show in more detail, she put out one hand to touch my arm. "Mrs. Chapman, I have something to show you."

Nodding to some newcomers, she led me up a winding staircase to another room and stopped in front of the picture of a young girl in a blue dress. I thought it might be Denise Laporte. The title of the work was 'The Milliner' and the subject sat beside a hat stand with a box of trimmings on her lap and a bunch of red silk roses in her left hand. She wore a light blue dress that was decorated with lace and satin ribbons at the neck and wrists. Her dark hair was pulled back from a face still rounded with the plumpness of childhood. She must have been very young, perhaps only about fifteen. I asked Miss Cassatt who the painter was.

"Eva Gonzalès," she told me. "She was a student of Manet. She died in childbirth in the early eighties, the same year as Manet. She was only thirty-four."

"Denise modeled for her?"

"No, that is her mother. She was also a milliner. She also had a child with no father who would recognize her." It seemed that Mary already knew that the girl had been with child when she died. Mrs. Palmer must have told her in the note she sent asking for help. "She worked in the brother's shop, too. It's not known if Denise's father was one of the painters, or some man her mother met while she was creating hats for wealthy women. Milliners and other shop girls only earn a little money and are exposed to the life led by the wealthy. Who can blame them if they want something more from life than the drudgery of work? The mother died when Denise was born. The uncle and his wife took her in. You can imagine how angry they were when they learned that she, too, was modeling for painters. For one particular painter, in fact. Come, I hear the master." She said that somewhat ironically and I followed her out to the landing where we could look down on the gallery entrance.

Standing beside M. Durand-Ruel was a man in a top hat and cape carrying a cane. He was of a similar age as the gallery owner and their discussion was heated.

"It's Degas," Mary told me. "Seeing his work was the most important thing for me. I used to go and flatten my nose against the window of an art dealer to absorb all I could of his art. It changed my life." I'd heard that he was the one who'd invited her to be part of the independent Impressionists exhibition.

"We've been friends for a long time, but we go through periods of disagreement. We had a huge argument the last time we met. It made him furious that he couldn't find a chink in my armor. There have been some months when we just could not see each other. But, as always, I painted something new for this show, and that has brought us back together." She led the way down the stairs.

After a profuse greeting and pecking of cheeks, all carried on in French, Miss Cassatt introduced me, and told the older painter that I wanted to see his painting of a milliner. M. Durand-Ruel gestured to a room that was off to the side and down a few steps, so we moved there. On the walls were numerous paintings of the theater, of dancers rehearsing, and one of a horse race where a man had fallen to the ground, but they led me past these to a far corner. There I saw a painting of a young woman in a shop with a hat in her hand; it was clearly Denise Laporte. She was unaware of the observer. Two straw hats on hat stands were in the foreground and she stood, turned to the left, examining a pretty hat with floppy ribbons on the front and a wispy feather on the back. Her head was tilted, as she concentrated on adjusting the ribbons until they were just right. She was completely preoccupied with her work.

Miss Cassatt translated as M. Degas began lecturing. "In the past, the subject of a painting has always been represented in poses which presuppose an audience. But my women are simple, honest creatures who are concerned with nothing beyond their physical occupations. It is as if you were looking through a keyhole." He gestured to the other paintings on the wall. "They also call me the painter of dancers, but they don't understand that the dancer has been for me only a pretext for painting pretty fabrics and for rendering movement."

Miss Cassatt asked him whether the girl in the picture was fixing the hat for herself or for a client. Was she dreaming of her young man, or seeing herself in the life of a wealthy woman who would wear the hat?

"Ah, it could be," he said. "A painting requires a little mystery, some vagueness, some fantasy. When you always make your meaning perfectly plain you end up boring people. Conversation in real life is full of half-finished sentences and overlapping talk. Why shouldn't painting be, too?"

I thought the picture captured the type of daydreaming that must have accompanied the dead girl's work of decorating hats for wealthy women who led lives she could only fantasize about. I asked if the painting was completed from a sketch actually done in the shop. Both painters laughed at my naïveté.

M. Degas was anxious to correct my assumptions. "No art is less spontaneous than mine. What I do is the result of reflection and the study of the great masters," he told me. "It is all very well to copy what one sees, but it is far better to draw what one now only sees in one's memory. That is a transformation in which imagination collaborates with memory. One visits the shop, the theater, the racetrack, but the work is staged in the studio. One must do the same subject over again ten times, a hundred times. In art, nothing must resemble an accident, not even movement. In painting you must give the idea of the true by means of the false. I frequently lock myself in my studio. I do not often see the people I love, and in the end I shall suffer for it. Painting is one's private life."

I wondered if the last comment was meant as an apology to Miss Cassatt, who'd been faithfully translating for me. They seemed as close as family in their relations, yet she'd told me that she hadn't seen him for months. She asked him more particularly about Denise Laporte and whether he knew she was with child when she died.

He looked shocked. "Strangled? The little one was strangled? How awful. No, I had no idea. The last time she came to me to model, it was some months ago. She was sad. Her lover was ill, she said. But, Denise, she always dreamed of a better future. She thought she would be taken care of by the man. I did not try to tell her differently. What does an old man know? In any case it was some American with lots of money, I think."

After translating, Miss Cassatt paused to tell him she had heard it was an Englishman. M. Degas didn't know. He wasn't interested in such details. He said categorically that the Americans were the ones with money, so it must have been an American. Miss Cassatt commented to me that he'd sold a number of paintings recently to American collectors, so he had a high opinion of them. He told us that the girl had been living with a man over the past winter. He had an address where he'd sent messages to her when he had modeling jobs. He promised to send it to Miss Cassatt.

TWENTY

Paul Durand-Ruel appeared at the door to tell Miss Cassatt that more visitors had come. As she turned to leave, there was an exchange with Degas that I did not understand. "He wants me to let him show a painting he did of me a while back," she explained with a shake of her head. "It is ugly, just ugly. I told him no. I told him no a thousand times." Another sharp exchange in French by the gesticulating M. Degas was followed by further explanation. "Ha! He says 'Women can never forgive me. They hate me, they feel that I am disarming them. I show them without their coquetry.' He just likes to needle me. Come, we must go greet some wealthy Americans. He'll like that. He can sell them some more of his pictures." She led us out and we climbed the steps back to her showing, where we found that the young ladies of the Johnstone party had arrived.

M. Durand-Ruel had preceded us and was ushering Mrs. Johnstone around the room, entertaining her with stories, by the time we entered. I wondered how successful he would be. I suspected her taste in art would be governed by the opinion of the official salons, but I had no way of knowing. She was dressed in a walking suit with a short yellow bolero jacket that stretched tight against her roly-poly figure and was edged with a fringe of little black balls that jiggled when she moved.

Lydia Johnstone and her two friends, dressed in the same suits they had worn at Notre Dame and each leaning on a parasol, were admiring the first picture by the door, of a woman and a child being rowed in a boat at the seashore. I noticed Miss Stuart had substituted a plain straw hat for the one she had returned to the milliner. They greeted Miss Cassatt and thanked her for the invitation. Their eyes were wide at the number and quality of the pictures hung around the room. Somehow all those plainly painted women doing ordinary tasks seemed more substantial than these artfully clothed young people. Miss Cassatt introduced them to the other American women.

"How wonderful," Lydia said. "We've been studying painting while we're here. I told my papa we had to have a teacher, but Mama wasn't sympathetic. She absolutely refused to let us have the paints and such in the house. So we found a nice young man with a studio we could go to in Montmartre." She named the artist who they studied with and Miss Cassatt blandly steered the conversation into what they'd chosen for the subjects of their paintings. It seemed, as beginners, they were sticking to flowers and inanimate objects. Miss Cassatt pointed out that Mrs. Choate Sears had chosen flowers as the subject of a painting of hers that hung in the Exposition. They were impressed.

Lydia spotted her mother with the art dealer and promptly began to nag her to purchase a painting. I wandered around taking in the pictures one at a time. Miss Stuart and Miss Brown stood before a scene of two women having tea. They commented on how familiar it seemed, and speculated on the conversation that might be going on.

Lydia joined us, annoyed at the rebuff from her mother. "Well, really, I don't see that it's any more expensive than a trip to Worth," she said. "I'm going to approach Papa. He would buy me a painting. I want one to take home with me."

Edith Stuart said, "I thought he told your mother to stop the buying spree. He might not be as easy to convince as you think."

That made Lydia angry. "Yes, well, some of us pay our bills when they come in and don't wait for a dunning letter. And if some of us have any more of those, Papa might really get upset and send someone home."

There was an uneasy silence that Grace Greenway Brown broke into. "Some people actually consider art an investment. I mean, they purchase a painting today, with the expectation that in a few years it will be worth even more."

"You got that from Mr. Palmer," Lydia said. "Honoré has visited some of the galleries with us," she told me.

"He mentioned to me that his parents had bought pictures in the past by newer painters who have already become quite well known," Grace added.

"Do you contemplate such a purchase?" I asked.

"No, not really. But I was interested to learn about it all the same."

Lydia was bored when the conversation veered from her concerns. "Lord James told me the art in his family goes back to the Renaissance. He said one of his ancestors had a portrait done by Holbein. The National Gallery wanted to buy it but they wouldn't let it go."

"You're very friendly with Lord James," I said. It was fairly easy to provoke an answer from her, as long as she was the topic of conversation and I was curious about the attachment, if it existed.

"Yes, we're getting very close. We've just been having a grand old time and I'm getting to know all about him, everything. You'd be surprised." I thought I *would* be surprised actually. "We even share our secrets."

"Secrets? Lord James?"

"Oh, yes. He can be very wicked about his relations. He says just the most terrible things about them. But I promised not to repeat them."

Miss Cassatt had joined us. "How are you proceeding with your classes? Will you return home with some finished pieces? Or, perhaps continue on here with your studies after the Exposition?"

"Oh, lord, no," Lydia said. "We've been really bad lately, with so many engagements and so much going on. And I don't think Mama would ever let me stay in Paris without her." She looked across the room to where M. Durand-Ruel appeared to be finally giving up on enticing Mrs. Johnstone to make a purchase. "But I might get Papa to agree." By the expression on her face, I assumed she was contemplating the advantages of staying in Paris without her parents. It seemed an unlikely scenario to me.

Miss Brown had no reservations about putting a pin in Lydia's inflated imaginings. "As with many things, we began with good intentions and we were serious at first. We attended classes twice a week and visited the studio to work one day in between. But then the Exposition opened and we got busy with all of those engagements. I'm afraid we haven't been back to our easels in several weeks." She had no illusions about their commitment to the work. They might be students in the art academy, but none of them had the stubborn dedication it would take to do what Miss Cassatt, and some of the other women artists in the room, had done.

Lydia looked around, oblivious to the conclusions the rest of us understood. "We'll go back to the studio tomorrow. You've inspired me. Someday I'll have a room full of pictures like this, too. Oh, no...I forgot...there's a reception tonight, and we said we'd do tea with the Barneys tomorrow. Next week, then. I'll send a message to the studio that we'll be coming. And I'll have to talk to Papa about staying on. Oh, Miss Cassatt, thank you so much for having us. I see my mother beckoning. She has yet another engagement for us. I'm sure she's disappointed M. Durand-Ruel by not buying a painting. But don't worry. I'll come back with Papa or Lord James. I'll get one of them to buy one for me."

Miss Cassatt assured her she was not in the least disappointed and the Johnstone party made their exit.

When they were gone, I found Miss Cassatt was quite acerbic in her views. "American women have been spoiled, treated and indulged like children. They must wake up to their duties. Women should be some*one* and not some*thing*." I thought of the young women in the Worth creations priming themselves to marry into the aristocracy so that they could become a duchess or countess. Those were the women she was thinking of. "Americans have a way of thinking work is nothing. 'Come out and play,' they say." She looked around the room full of her paintings, overflowing with her work. "I have not done all that I wanted to," she continued. "But I tried to make a good fight."

How very different her attitude was to that of the young women who had just left. But I realized that the others still in the room, looking at the work and conversing, shared her views.

Miss Cassatt told me that the artist Lydia and the others were studying with was known more for socializing with wealthy young women tourists than for his paintings. But his studio was in the area where Degas and other artists also worked.

"Could they have met Denise Laporte there?"

"An interesting question. I'll see what I can find out. Bertha is worried about her son, isn't she?" Miss Cassatt could be blunt.

"I'm afraid she is. All this talk about an American lover, I think she's afraid he was involved with the dead girl, even though that's highly unlikely, given his personality. He is too much of a gentleman."

"I am of two minds about whether to pursue this further," she said. "It might be possible to discover who the man was that she lived with, if Degas has the address. But who is to say he was the only one? And what good would it do our friend's son?"

I wasn't able to answer that question.

TWENTY-ONE

Miss Cassatt was as good as her word. She managed to get the address that M. Degas had used for Denise Laporte, and she sent it along in a note, which also contained an invitation for me and my family to visit her country house at Beaufresne.

"Beware," Bertha Palmer told me. "She'll want you to sit for her…you and your children."

The thought had not occurred to me. I remembered vividly the paintings I had seen at the Durand-Ruel gallery. "I hope she doesn't think we could afford a portrait."

"No, no. She'll just make you and the little ones sit and she'll do sketch after sketch before she ever paints. Then you'll be in one or more paintings that hang on some wealthy collector's walls."

I wasn't sure how I would feel about that, but we had too many engagements scheduled for me to accept the invitation, in any case. We continued to be very busy with an endless flurry of reports to write, seating charts to arrange, correspondence to answer, and all of the other tasks involved with Bertha's position as commissioner.

"The official reception at the American pavilion is coming up. We'll have a lot to do to prepare. Perhaps at the end of the summer you may be able to slip away before we sail home."

I thought it might be a good idea to consult Stephen before I agreed to sit for the artist. "I doubt my children would sit still long enough for her, in any case."

Bertha laughed. "Mary has quite a way with children. You'd be surprised. But what about this address? Can it help us to find the man?"

When I protested that my inability to speak French would prevent me from learning anything of use, she had a solution. "Lord James. You must get him to take you. His French is fluent, though heavily accented, and I know he'll be discreet." I hesitated but then decided not to point out that the Englishman might actually be the man we were looking for. She frowned. "I would prefer that Honoré not know we're looking into this. Yes, I'll speak to Lord James tonight."

When she was firm about her plans no one could cross her, so I wasn't surprised when I found myself engaged the next afternoon to visit the address for what had presumably been Denise Laporte's love nest.

Not that Lord James wasn't a bit hesitant about the outing. "You are quite sure about this?" he asked. "You wouldn't rather tour the galleries of the Louvre or even have tea on the rue Royale?"

"I'm afraid I am under orders from Mrs. Palmer."

"Well, in that case…" He helped me into a cab he'd hailed, then shouted the address to the driver and swung his lank figure up, landing beside me with his cane held like a conductor's baton. He entertained me by pointing out sights as we drove along.

Soon, we left the wide boulevards of central Paris for an older section of smaller streets, then we were traveling uphill in an area with vineyards and windmills.

"Montmartre," Lord James told me. "An area 'bohemian,' as we say." He had an exchange with the cabman. "He thinks he knows rue Burq, it's off rue des Abbesses. It's a place where some of the artists like to rent. Cheaper, don't you know. Bourgeois and working class." There were shops and cafés along the way, as well as older houses. Finally, we stopped in front of a three-story brick building and he helped me down. I was a bit uncomfortable as the cab trotted away. The neighborhood was not as respectable as the other ones I'd visited in Paris.

"It's all right. I told him to come back in half an hour."

I was thankful to have such an experienced guide. He knocked on the door with his silver-headed cane. The green paint was peeling a bit but it seemed an entirely respectable place nonetheless. A plump, middle-aged woman in an expansive apron opened the door, wiping flour from her hands. After an exchange, she let us into the foyer, which had a floor of black and white tiles and dark wood paneling. Lord James asked her about Denise Laporte.

They had quite a conversation, which, of course, I couldn't understand. She seemed to be willing to talk to him. That surprised me, but then he had a way of charming people.

"I told her you're an old friend of the girl's mother trying to get in touch with her. She says the girl was here, living with a man over the winter. But they gave up the place."

"Did I hear her say he was English?"

"*Anglais.* Actually she said he *spoke* English. I don't think she could distinguish between English and American." When he turned back, I thought she looked a bit coquettish when she spoke to him.

"Can she tell us his name?"

"M. Anglais—well, that's not a real name."

"Does she know where he went when he left? Didn't he leave a forwarding address?"

"Ah, no. She says he just left." The woman was shaking her head gloomily. There was nothing else she could tell us. She hadn't seen Denise or her paramour since the girl had gone back to her aunt and uncle.

I was disappointed, but then Lord James said, "Say, I have an idea. Lots of us staying here don't use a regular address. We get a box at the post office so, if we move around, we don't have to alert the folks at home. Let me ask her."

After more back and forth she told him that the man had, in fact, used a post office a few blocks away. We thanked the woman and Lord James asked her to send the cab after us when it returned. Taking my arm, he guided me down the street, which was steep, and around a corner. We were approaching the post office on the opposite side of the street when suddenly he stopped. I looked across just in time to see Honoré entering the doorway.

"No, let's not let him know we've seen him, shall we?" Lord James led me to a seat at a little café we'd just passed. "Oh, dear. And Mrs. Palmer particularly asked me not to let Honoré know about this little expedition. Tell you what, why don't we just position you here…" he said, as he held out a chair that would put my back to the post office, "and you just order a café." He motioned to a waiter and ordered in French. "And I'll trot along and see what he's up to." He stood in front of me, straightening his coat. "I can explain myself just wandering around this area and happening to run into him, don't you know. But I really couldn't explain being here with you." He looked at a loss.

"All right. But I'm not sure it's right to make this a secret. Perhaps we should just let him know what we're doing here."

"But Mrs. Palmer…"

"Oh, all right. You go. I'll drink the coffee." The waiter was slipping a tiny cup with a thick dark espresso coffee in front of me.

Impatiently, I kept my back to the area of interest and sipped the coffee, after loading it with sugar from the little pot in front of me. I worried the linen napkin with my gloved fingers, trying to imagine what was being said.

Finally, Lord James joined me, nodding to the waiter as he sat down opposite me. "It's all right. I'm pretty sure he believed that I just happened to be here visiting an artist I know."

"What was he doing here?"

"Picking up mail. As I said, it's common to have a postal address. I do it myself. Saves trouble if you change lodgings, don't you know."

"But why here?"

"It's a lively area—students, artists, working families. It's cheaper rent around here."

"But he's staying in rue Brignole with his family."

"Well, yes, but he arrived early, met his parents here later. He lived in a couple of different places before they arrived, you know. He'd been on tour, he told me. Rome and Switzerland, before meeting with them."

Of course, I'd known that, as Honoré had not come on the ship with us. I'd assumed he'd arrived a few days or weeks early to arrange for the house they were renting. But now it seemed he'd been in Europe some months before our arrival. If the police were aware of this, it was obvious that they would use it to support their suspicion that he'd been involved with the dead girl.

"Did you socialize with him before we arrived?"

"Well, yes. I met him at some parties and nightclubs. Around town. At the races. A few weeks before you all got here. By then he seemed quite at home in Paris." He sipped the coffee the waiter had brought. "But not like he'd been here for months!"

"Mrs. Palmer is worried that the police will try to accuse Honoré of being involved with the girl. But, surely, if he were seeing Denise Laporte you would have known about it. Have they asked you?" I remembered how she had come up to our carriage the first time we visited the House of Worth.

He looked uncomfortable. He had removed his hat to an empty chair and his long fingers were ruffling through his thatch of sandy hair. Now his pale face showed spots of red on his cheeks. "The inspector did ask something of the sort. I met the girl a few times at salon parties in this area. But that was before I knew Honoré. I never saw them together. Honestly." The sun streamed down on us and I noticed what long eyelashes he had, as he squinted at the bright light.

"But you're friends." I tried to hold his gaze in an attempt to force him to respond to me. "I can't believe he wouldn't confide in you about a romantic attachment." Surely Lord James did not suspect Honoré of being the girl's lover. He must know better than that and it was certain the police would continue to ask him about his friend.

He bit his lip. "He wouldn't exactly confide in me, don't you know. It's not like that with men. We keep our liaisons to ourselves. You don't go spouting off to your mates about a particular woman. One of them might get ideas and try his own luck...if you see what I mean."

It concerned me that he seemed to think Honoré could have been involved. "Hmmm. But you would have noticed something. You're together all the time."

"Not all the time. Listen, I do think he's got some kind of a thing. He has talked a little—in his cups, don't you know—about how hard it is if he likes someone his mother might not approve of. I mean to say, Mrs. Palmer is the tops, the cream of the crop, but she's a pretty imposing sort of person, don't you think? If Honoré was seeing someone she wouldn't approve of...well, if I were him, I'd keep it on the quiet. Wouldn't you?"

I could certainly understand the impulse to keep such an attachment from Bertha Palmer. I'd been a witness to her plan to link her son to Countess Olga's daughter but a milliner? "How would he have met a young shop girl like that? You said that you'd met her a few times at salon parties. Was he at those same parties?"

He eyed me, as if deciding whether I was worldly enough to hear the truth. I thought of Chicago's West Side, where I'd met all sorts of people from all sorts of backgrounds. He was mistaken if he thought he could shock me, but he didn't know that. He grimaced as if he'd bitten into something sour. "This area is known for the bohemian life. It's not controlled by social strictures that apply to the world inhabited by Mrs. Palmer—and by my relatives, for that matter, over in London. Of course, ladies like you and Mrs. Palmer aren't supposed to know anything about it. In France, it's accepted that men, even respectable, married men, not just artists, can spend time in this milieu. Look around you." He gestured with his long arm. "Here there are cafés, and cabarets. There are outdoor dances, and indoor performances by singers and dancers. The men come. The bourgeois and the artists, sometimes they bring their wives, but the upper-class men, they bring the little shop girls or the girls who sit for the artists as models. They have a good time. It's the way it is."

"I see. But Denise was living with a man. She moved out of her uncle's house and when she returned she was with child. That is not something that Honoré would do. He is American and, believe me, it would not be acceptable in Chicago."

His face froze. "With child? Dear god, I had no idea." He wiped his long fingers down his face. "Good lord. She must have told her lover and he abandoned her. What a sorry tale. But a not uncommon one. But see here, you're right. Honoré would never do that. He wouldn't, so it can't have been him."

At that moment our cab driver came clopping along, having found us, and I was grateful for the distraction. I certainly hoped, for all our sakes, that Lord James was right about Honoré.

TWENTY-TWO

Bertha Palmer was not satisfied with my report about the outing to Montmartre, since I had not discovered the name of the dead girl's lover. Lord James had pleaded with me not to mention sighting Honoré there. He claimed the post office had no information about the man who had rented on rue Burq and Honoré had a perfectly innocent reason for keeping a postal address. It was something the Englishman did himself. It left a sour taste in my mouth, but I promised to be discreet. If Honoré had resolved to keep secret some attachment of which his parents would disapprove, not even his dear mother—who was every bit as stubborn as he was— would be able to extract it from him. I actually feared for the effect such tension could have on the elder Mr. Palmer, who was looking rather frail.

So I confided in my husband but not in Bertha Palmer. Stephen agreed with my decision. I almost wished I could escape to Mary Cassatt's country house with my children. But Mrs. Palmer required my assistance in planning for the reception at the United States National Pavilion. It was located on the Quai d'Orsay on the left bank of the Seine. I had heard that dithering on the part of the United States Congress had delayed the appropriation of funds so, when they finally approved the money, space had to be taken from other countries to make room. As a result, the Americans were third in the row but on a crowded lot. First came an ornate Italian building, then a gorgeous but noisy Turkish pavilion with a full bazaar on the first floor. The white domed United States pavilion was next, nearly touching both the Moorish façade and the side of the Austrian pavilion just beyond. Some of the stodgier visitors complained of the noise from Turkish merchants hawking their wares.

Unlike many other national pavilions, the American one had no merchandise for sale. It was made up of a post office, rooms for reading and writing, and a large central reception area surrounded by four floors of balconies with broad arches on every floor letting in the light. There was even an elevator. Bertha Palmer had a small office on the second floor, along with the other commissioners, but it was nowhere near as spacious and elegant as her suite at rue Brignole, so we weren't often there. The third floor housed the high commissioner and the fourth was set aside as a place of repose for visiting ladies. There were ten exhibits from the United States scattered across the Exposition grounds, inside the various buildings for industry, arts, electricity, et cetera. But the national pavilion was reserved as a place where our countrymen could come to write and receive letters, or visit the American restaurant on the first floor.

It was a few days after my visit to Montmartre that I accompanied Bertha to the pavilion to oversee last minute preparations for a reception that evening. This was to be in honor of the dedication of a bronze equestrian statue of George Washington, which had been donated to the city of Paris by American women. There was a plaster copy of the statue mounted on the portico of the United States pavilion, but the original would be unveiled that afternoon at Place d'Iéna and the reception would follow. It was a sort of rehearsal for a much larger event that was planned for July 4th, when a statue of General Lafayette, given by all Americans, would be dedicated at the Louvre, followed by a procession to the United States pavilion, a reception, and then dinner.

These were the types of events that Bertha Palmer was famous for arranging back in Chicago. She was extremely competent and demanding. She was known for refusing to take on the task of organizing such occasions unless she was given complete control of all the arrangements, but she was also famous for the most spectacularly successful results. She always got her way in these matters at home.

Here in Paris, she had run into some headwinds. Mrs. Johnstone, for one, had objected to ceding all control to Mrs. Palmer. But since Bertha was the only woman commissioner, it was decided that arrangements for the reception of the women's gift rightly fell to her. I knew, even if Mrs. Johnstone did not, that the event would go off with such style and elegance they would realize that no one else would be able to match it in planning the July event, so they would have to ask Bertha to help with that as well. The queen of Chicago society took it as a challenge, and she attacked it head on. She would be greatly disappointed if anything was less than perfect. But I knew, based on the amount of effort she had put into this, it would be even better than she hoped.

When the ignorant Mrs. Johnstone appeared, uninvited, during our preparations, Bertha Palmer sent me out to the balcony overlooking the rue des Nations and the Seine to keep watch for Countess Olga. She had invited the Russian noblewoman to join us, in full knowledge that she would act as a charm to keep the rambunctious Mrs. Johnstone away. The woman had an unfortunate habit of treating the countess as if she were infected by the plague.

I was happy to walk out, past the plaster reproduction of George Washington on his horse on the second floor portico of the building. At the white balustrade that hung out over the walkway facing the river, I found Lord James idly watching the people strolling along the pavement. They were about two stories below us and we looked down on their heads. Beyond them, small boats and ferries full of visitors steamed up and down the river. It was a bright and cheerful view.

"Mrs. Chapman, how lovely to see you. I was just admiring your national building. It's quite... well...dignified, I guess you could say."

We could hear some noisy hawkers from the Turkish pavilion next door. "Yes, actually, when I first saw it, it reminded me very much of the administration building at the Columbian Exposition in Chicago in '93."

"Oh, yes. I didn't visit that fair myself, I'm sorry to say, but I heard very good things about it. It was called the White City, wasn't it? Rather like this in fact." He leaned out over the balustrade and craned his neck to look up at the outside of the building. "And that dome is quite impressive. Rather like the dome of your capitol building, isn't it?"

"I believe so. I heard it was suggested that we build a skyscraper, as a more strictly American type of structure. In fact, the Chicago architect Louis Sullivan wanted to design it, but that idea was rejected."

"Settled for something more dignified, eh? And with all those golden eagles it's practically imperial. There's a sculpture on the roof above us, isn't there? What's that all about?"

"Ah, that is *The Goddess of Liberty on the Chariot of Progress* by Mr. Phimister Proctor. He also did some wonderful animal sculptures for the Chicago exposition."

"Yes, well, the building really is quite decorous compared to the more ostentatious displays by some of the countries. And, more than that, it's quite comfortable inside, I must say. That is something I do admire in your countrymen. You certainly know how to make yourselves comfortable." I saw him glance suddenly downwards and followed his eye to see Lydia Johnstone and her two friends arguing, as they walked along the quay just below us.

Lydia abruptly turned her back and walked away from her friends and into the building.

With a regretful shake of her head, Grace followed her but Edith turned towards the river, folding her arms across her chest as if holding herself in. She looked quite small and alone with her back to us, the yellow ribbons that adorned her puckered white silk gown flapping in the breeze.

"I wonder what that was all about?" I said.

"Tut, tut," Lord James said. "It seems Miss Stuart has not been paying her bills. M. Worth himself finally paid a visit to Johnstone *père*, who was mortified and infuriated. He was so embarrassed he paid some portion of the debt, but then he called his daughter in and told her Miss Stuart would be on the next boat back to America, or she'd be out on the street."

"How awful. For all of them."

"Not pleasant by a long shot, although I do think it's just as well. Miss Stuart appears to be a rather desperate young woman. I don't know if she came on this trip with the intention of landing a husband but I must say, she must be very badly off to behave as she does." He gave me a guilty glance then quickly looked away. "You'd be appalled if you saw the way she flirted."

Poor young woman. It must be hard to be around a wealthy, spoiled girl like Lydia Johnstone if your own family didn't have comparable wealth. "I suppose a number of young American women must flirt with you, Lord James. So many do seem to be in search of a title. Surely you're not shocked by a little flirting? You must be used to it by now," I teased him.

"Oh, of course I am. I know what you mean. One feels absolutely hunted sometimes. But this was different. Quite brazen, don't you know. And not just me. She did it to Honoré, as well. I'm even a bit suspicious she may have been mad enough to try it on old Mr. Johnstone, himself."

"Oh, Lord James, please."

"I tell you, I wouldn't be surprised. That's what I mean by desperate."

"Surely you exaggerate and, in any case, I'm sure Miss Johnstone would not stand for anyone flirting with you now. She seems quite taken with you for herself." In fact, I wondered whether some pathetic attempt at flirtation with the Englishman might not have drawn down the wrath of young Lydia and perhaps she was the one who had caused her father to denounce Edith. On the other hand, I had seen Miss Stuart returning a hat to the milliner and I was sure she was cheating the woman. In any case, it was none of my business. "I must say, you, yourself, seem quite taken with Miss Johnstone." I could see his pale skin turning slightly pink at the suggestion.

"Well, yes. She's a jolly girl. And, if you must know, I actually am intrigued with the idea of Omaha. No, really. I mean, most of the young women I meet, and even more so their mothers, are mad to make a connection with London society and dream of a big London wedding. As you know, there's nothing I want to avoid more than that. I've escaped all that, so why would I ever want to return to that stuffy lot? Oh, no, that's not for me. So imagine my surprise to hear that dear Mrs. Johnstone has no dreams of a London society wedding. On the contrary, she absolutely insists that the weddings of her various children must be held in Nebraska. Imagine that, can you? Omaha, Nebraska. It's so fresh and simple. I can't tell you how attractive that is to me."

I looked at him with amazement. I knew he avoided his fellow Englishmen, but I wasn't at all sure his knowledge of geography was sufficient for him to have any idea how far from any center of culture Omaha, Nebraska was. For someone used to living in London and Paris, it would be quite a shock. But before I could question him more thoroughly regarding his expectations, I recognized another figure approaching from the bridge. "Isn't that Honoré?" I asked. "Do you know who that man is he's talking to?" I was sure I recognized the short mustachioed man I had seen with Paul Poiret.

Lord James squinted in the bright sunlight that was reflecting up from the river. "Ah, that's M. Kalash. He's involved with the racing." He glanced at me, as if to see if I disapproved. "Could be he's looking for payment, or paying out winnings."

"He takes bets? On horse races?"

"And other things. He's probably paid Mr. Palmer off for something he won. See, now he's leaving."

We were too far away and high above to hail the young Mr. Palmer but, as we watched, we saw him stopped by Miss Stuart, who even grabbed his sleeve. He looked embarrassed.

"Oh, dear. I hope she's not hitting him up for a loan. I'd better go down and rescue him before his good nature is imposed upon," Lord James said. Then he hurried away.

I watched as Honoré pulled away to enter the pavilion through the archway, followed by the tenacious young woman. Quite quickly after that, I saw Inspector Guillaume enter. He was walking briskly and, at the sight of the policeman, I knew I needed to go and find Mrs. Palmer. She wouldn't be happy to see him. In fact, she would be incensed if her plans for the reception were in any way interfered with. I needed to intercept him so I could temper her reaction if at all possible. It was going to be an irritating morning.

TWENTY-THREE

The inside of the pavilion was filled with light from the cupola. A round hall on the first floor, one level up from the street, was open all the way up to the dome, where a large flag of stars and stripes hung. Each of the three levels was edged by white painted wrought iron railings in a scrolling design and they were decorated with ornamental shields of red and blue. The archways on each level were hung with cherry-colored drapes but they were all pulled back to allow the light from the windows to stream in. In the center of the black and white tiled floor was a round sofa of red plush, and other soft seating was scattered around.

I came in from the porch on the second level and peered over the railing to see Inspector Guillaume striding purposely towards Honoré Palmer. At the movement, Bertha Palmer's head shot up from her perusal of a printed menu and she frowned when she recognized the policeman.

As I hurried down the steps to the converging group of Honoré, Edith, Bertha, and the inspector, I noticed Countess Olga entering from the street. Across the room Mrs. Johnstone was hectoring her daughter Lydia, but I saw her attention was excited by the sight of Inspector Guillaume, like a hound that has picked up a scent. When she noticed the countess, she glared at her.

"M. Palmer, you have not returned my calls," the large policeman was saying when I reached the group.

Mrs. Palmer answered, "I've had my son doing a number of errands for me, Inspector. You may not be aware of it but we are hosting a very important reception this evening."

He turned towards her slowly. "Yes, I know. It is for the statue that is to be unveiled today. We are very aware of the great honor the ladies of your nation are giving us. I apologize for interrupting. I have no wish to interfere with your preparations. But I must ask your son a few questions. Perhaps you are not aware that the thief has struck again, not once, but twice since the unfortunate affair at the opening of the Worth exhibit."

"No, I was not aware."

"It was at a reception at the Italian pavilion and a dinner at the home of the Canadian minister."

I knew that Bertha had been invited to both affairs but she had refused, instead attending a dinner at the house of an elderly French princess and then a salon of French writers and artists. I had been excused from both events and had picnicked in the Tuileries gardens with my family one night, and attended an outdoor dance with my husband and some of his friends from the Institut Pasteur the other.

"The young M. Palmer was present at both occasions, although he was one of a number of guests who departed before the thefts were discovered. So, I have a need to speak to him."

Bertha glared at her son and I could see Amelia Johnstone gliding towards us in the background, like a vulture investigating its prey.

"I escorted the Countess Olga and her daughter, Sonya," Honoré told him.

"Yes, M. Palmer very kindly took us," the countess said.

Meanwhile, Lord James had also joined the group. "Why, yes, we were all there...at both places," he said, waving his hand in the direction of the Johnstone party.

I noticed Edith Stuart slide up beside the Englishman. "Yes, we were all there. And so were the countess and her daughter, and the House of Worth people were there as well—in the ladies' retiring room. It's so helpful of them, don't you think, Lord James?" She put a gloved hand on the man's forearm. He regarded it with distaste and quickly shook it off. She batted her eyelashes at him in an all too obvious attempt at flirtation. I thought it very odd, but he had labeled her as desperate and that seemed only too true. I felt sorry for her, but the others ignored her.

Mrs. Johnstone boldly joined the group. "What is it, Inspector? Oh, dear, not another body? Have you found who killed that girl?"

Guillaume pursed his lips, but then he addressed her. "No, madame. It is nothing so grim. However, a very famous diamond worn by an English lady was stolen at the Italian embassy. And, at the Canadian minister's home, a bracelet of diamonds disappeared from the wrist of a Mlle Leonard of Boston."

"Oh, my goodness. That is unheard of where I come from. Who is doing this, and why haven't you caught them? My husband says we're not to wear anything but costume jewelry for the rest of our time here. Mrs. Palmer, you must warn the guests. Perhaps we should cancel the reception."

Bertha's eyes narrowed and she stiffened to her most regal pose. "Nonsense. We will do nothing of the sort. Perhaps there have been such incidents at the festivities you attended, Mrs. Johnstone, but I went to parties on the very same evenings where no such unfortunate occurrences took place and they will not happen here."

"Well, that's very optimistic of you, Mrs. Palmer, but I really do feel that we have a responsibility to alert our guests to the possibility of something like this. Forewarned is forearmed, as Mr. Johnstone always says. And you must admit that the fact a woman was found dead on one of these occasions cannot be ignored."

"No one is ignoring anything, Mrs. Johnstone. I will thank you to remember that I am in charge of these arrangements, not you." Mrs. Palmer turned from the angry little woman and addressed the policeman. "There will be Marines on guard at every exit and strategically placed on the first floor," she told him.

"An excellent precaution, Mme Palmer. I will also have men on guard or, if you permit, I will attend with my assistant and the other officers will be on call, in the event of any disturbance. It is true that we are still hunting the thief, but I promise you he will be found." He was looking straight at Honoré Palmer when he said this.

"There will be no disturbance, I assure you," Bertha told him. "And I, for one, will not hesitate to wear jewels. In fact, I would be most grateful if you would return my pearls, as they are really a necessary addition to my ensemble this evening. The gown was designed with the pearls in mind." She boldly looked the policeman in the eye.

"Indeed, madame," he said, after a pause. "You are very confident to want to risk your valuable pearls, which have been lost once already."

And returned in such a sensational manner, I couldn't help thinking, as I remembered the body of the little milliner lying at the foot of the mannequin who wore those very pearls. I had to restrain myself from a shiver and I had an ominous feeling about the reception that evening. But, apparently, Bertha did not.

"There will be no problems," she said. "And I would very much like to wear my pearls. Is there something I must do to get them back? Please let me know, and Mr. Palmer will have his lawyers attend to it at once."

"*Non,* madame. That will not be necessary. But perhaps the young M. Palmer here could accompany me to the prefecture. I could ask a few questions about the evening parties he attended and, after that, we could release the pearls to him to return to you. Unless you think that would not be wise?"

I realized what he was doing. It was a way to achieve his goal of interrogating Honoré but also—if Bertha herself had any doubt about the potential guilt of her son in the earlier disappearance of the pearls—she would expose her doubt if she wouldn't allow him to bring them back. She knew what the inspector was up to, as well.

"Yes, well, as you wish. But don't keep him too long. I need those pearls for this evening and I will need sufficient time to dress." With that, she strode away. I'd been holding my breath, for fear she would let loose one of her more sarcastic remarks, but now I could relax. Until the evening, at least.

I glanced around at the others and was disconcerted to see Edith smiling as she watched Honoré leaving with the police inspector. It seemed especially mean spirited of her to take satisfaction in his uncomfortable position. Perhaps she thought that here, at least, was one person whose lot was worse than her own. I noticed that Lord James was, in turn, frowning at her with disapproval. I hoped there would be no further cause for concern for Mrs. Palmer and knew I would be glad when the reception was over.

TWENTY-FOUR

The evening finally came. Marines were posted as extra security to prevent any catastrophes, such as the one at the Textiles Building. I shivered at the thought. Mrs. Palmer had insisted on extending invitations to M. Worth, his brother, daughter, soon to be son-in-law, and the young M. Poiret. She'd even asked for Mlle Arquette and staff from the House of Worth to set up a cloakroom on the fourth floor in the ladies' area. It was as if she were either tempting fate or showing the locals how to do it. In either case, I knew I would be relieved when the evening came to an end.

Of course, it was a perfect occasion for her to knock heads once again with Mrs. Johnstone in the contest of who had claim to superior considerations. There were two separate receiving lines, one featuring the ambassador, with Mrs. Johnstone and her husband at the end. On the opposite side of the room, Mrs. Palmer had arranged the members of the United States commission for the Exposition, including some of the wealthiest men in the country. Her line also had the enviable merit of finishing just at the start of the cold buffet. Mrs. Palmer herself was unruffled in her magnificent gown, adorned with the cornstalk pattern, and she wore the pearl choker, as she'd said she would. Mr. Palmer had declined to stand in the receiving line, and instead sat comfortably sipping his champagne and admiring his wife. I thought I saw Mr. Johnstone shooting him an envious glance from across the room.

I stood near the door. It was a hot evening, and the air was heavy and still. It made you want to move, just to keep your clothing from sticking to your skin, and to create your own little breeze, however fleeting. But we soldiered on. My husband was ensconced with Potter Palmer on the round red plush seats in the middle of the room. Stephen looked unbothered by the heat as he sipped champagne from a crystal flute, while keeping an eye on the older man. I caught my breath at the sight of him, content to know he was there, my rock in this sea of shifting figures.

But I wasn't comfortable, especially with the elbow-length kid gloves that encased my hands and arms. I was glad I'd worn my old pink silk gown, as I feared it would suffer from the sweltering conditions and I would have hated to damage the borrowed Worth gown. The air held the threat of a thunderstorm.

"Mme Chapman, it is a pleasure to see you again." M. Jean-Philippe Worth took my gloved right hand and raised it to his lips. I had to restrain myself from pulling away, I was so unused to that custom. At once I regretted not wearing the Worth gown as I saw his eye run over my figure. How intimidating to stand before a man whose business it was to clothe the wealthiest and most beautiful women in the world.

I greeted him and asked after his daughter. He snatched two glasses of champagne from a passing waiter and turned to offer me one. "She visits Mlle Arquette on the upper floor to ready herself with last minute adjustments. I await her. And M. Cartier, likewise." That young man stood a few steps away conversing with M. Worth's brother, Gaston, in French. M. Poiret entered and made a formal bow to us, but M. Worth chose to ignore him, and the younger man proceeded to the reception line without stopping. M. Poiret quickly took in the situation and chose Mrs. Palmer's line.

"M. Poiret is a talented young man, from what I've heard," I said.

M. Worth frowned. "Perhaps, but he is too much for the informal. He has not the taste for the grand style. And he has the other faults of the young man."

"What faults are those?"

"The women…the parties…the horses." He waved a hand. "It is the way with all the young men. They want to try their luck."

"Does M. Poiret gamble, then?"

"Of course, as with all the men. He boasts of his winnings." He leaned towards me. "But he is quiet about his losses, eh?"

"I see." I would have questioned him further, but at that moment there was a disturbance behind us that was too loud to ignore.

"I don't know what you think you're going to do." It was Lydia Johnstone in a strident voice. Both M. Worth and I turned instinctively at the sound. She wore a black satin gown with a design of raised velvet. The neckline dipped dramatically and it had bell sleeves that came down almost to her elbow-length black kid gloves. She had a lacy black fan open in one hand and a black plume ran across her head, from one ear almost to the other. Despite her mother's protests, she wore a heavy gold and silver necklace with matching drop earrings. The gown was luscious, but her face was an ugly red, and she seemed to sneer at Edith Stuart who was pulling away from the clasp of her hand. Edith wore a gauzy purple chiffon gown with silver satin ribbons, and a corsage of white camellias at one shoulder. Her eyes were closed to a slit and her teeth were bared.

"Oh, you won't get rid of me that easily," she said, in an unpleasantly raspy voice.

"Please, Edith, Lydia." Grace Greenway Brown seemed to be the only one of the group to be aware of all the eyes turning in their direction. She wore a white silk gown with pink and gray trim in the shape of twining vines around the hem and a closely embroidered pattern on the bodice. It had been pointed out to me as a Jeanne Paquin design. Edith reached out a gloved hand to clutch at her.

"Grace is going to move out and get a place with me. On rue Royale, aren't you?" She turned back to smirk at Lydia.

"Nonsense, she's got barely more money than you do," Lydia said.

I turned away in an attempt not to overhear any more.

"Don't be so sure of that. You'll see what I can do," I heard Edith say.

I looked around, surprised not to see Lord James, given his earlier comments about Lydia Johnstone and Omaha. I'd seen him earlier but he'd since disappeared. Luckily, Countess Olga and her daughter entered just then and greeted me warmly. The countess looked more aristocratic than I had ever seen her. She wore a dress of ivory satin and lace, heavily beaded with pearls, and embroidered with sequins and gold thread. She also wore more jewels than I had ever seen on her before—a tiara, necklace, earrings, and a matching bracelet, all of diamonds set in platinum.

"Magnificent," M. Worth said, when she and Sonya, who wore her champagne-colored Worth gown with the garlands of pink fabric roses, had passed on to Mrs. Palmer's reception line. "They are the family jewels, you know…the husband's family in Russia."

"Apparently she has joined Mrs. Palmer in refusing to be intimidated by the jewel thief," I said. "We heard there were two more robberies."

"It is true." He nearly clapped his hands. "It is good, you see. It is not only at the functions of the House of Worth that these things happen. We were there, too, when they had the most recent robberies. But my poor Andrée, she had already lost her only precious stone. It was not she who was robbed."

As if in response to her name, M. Worth's daughter arrived from the elevator and they proceeded in. I greeted a few more newcomers and helped them determine which line to join. The crowd thinned a bit as people spread out to adjacent rooms or up the metal stairs to the upper floors. Sometime later, the air was still heavy, and I was about to gather my limp skirts and abandon my post by the door to find my husband, when I noticed Countess Olga making her way through the brightly colored throng of people. She looked quietly distressed and headed for Inspector Guillaume who stood in evening dress near the doorway. Something was wrong with the countess, but before I could determine what it was I thought I heard a scream. There was a rustle through the crowd, like a breeze through leaves. People stopped, listened, then began to talk again, as if to ignore and blot out some slight embarrassment. But suddenly there was another scream from the second floor.

With the instinct of a mother who hears the tone of her child's cry and knows it is serious, I picked up my skirts and hurried up the curving metal staircase and out through the arches to the balcony where I'd stood with Lord James that morning. Honoré Palmer was there, leaning over the railing. Beside him, Sonya Zugenev gulped sobs and clutched the stone balustrade as she shivered, her hair falling across her face.

"What is it?" I asked, but by then I, too, was looking over the balustrade, and I could see a body lying on the stones below. "Oh, no."

"No, no, no," Honoré groaned. An expression of deep anguish spread across his face. He jumped back and ran to the steps, pushing his way through the confused people heading in our direction.

I followed, calling out to my husband as I descended. By the time I was out on the rue des Nations, Bertha Palmer, her husband, and Inspector Guillaume had reached the prone figure. Honoré was on his knees, his hand on the woman's shoulder, lifting it so he could see the ruined face. My husband pushed through and bent down to examine the smashed and bloody form.

"She's gone," he said. He looked up at me. "Who is she?"

"Edith Stuart," I said. The dead woman's limp hand seemed to reach out towards me on the gray stone walkway. I saw a bright reflection winking in a little pool of water, just beyond the reach of her fingers. It came from a bracelet of tiny diamonds. What had she been doing with that?

Inspector Guillaume waved an arm and had men surround the little tableau, pushing the curious guests back. "Return to the pavilion, please. All of you," he directed. The policemen began to herd people away. The inspector studied the figures before him. "M. Palmer, you will come with me, please." Guillaume motioned to two of the uniformed officers, who stepped up to Honoré and took his arms as he rose from Edith's body. When he tried to shake them off one of them twisted his arm. Reaching into Honoré's pocket, he pulled out a shiny string, whipping it away from the young man. "*Regardez!*" he yelled. It was a string of diamonds…a necklace. I remembered Countess Olga talking to the inspector just before we'd heard the screams. Not another theft, surely?

"No, wait." Bertha Palmer was avoiding the officer who was attempting to direct her back inside. "You can't take him. Honoré, what happened?"

"I don't know."

"Madame, it will be necessary for you to go inside. I must talk to your son."

"No." This time it was Potter Palmer who stepped forward unsteadily. "Enough of this, there will be no more, there will—" He stumbled. I watched with growing horror, as I saw him fumble and reach out, as if to grasp something. His eyes rolled up in his head and he fell heavily, but Stephen lunged forward and caught him before he could hit the hard stones of the street. He crumpled in my husband's arms and Bertha Palmer ran to them.

"He's ill." Stephen lowered him gently and loosened his collar. "We must get him to a hospital immediately." He looked over Bertha's trembling shoulders to Inspector Guillaume.

The inspector called out to his men and, in a moment, a carriage pulled up. They lifted Mr. Palmer into it and Stephen joined him. Bertha began to follow them but she saw that Honoré was being held back by two policemen. "Mother," he called.

"Let him go," she said.

"No, madame, I am sorry, but he must stay," the inspector said.

Her face was a picture of agony. "Go," I told her, stepping forward. I exchanged a glance with Stephen over her shoulder. He looked grave, so I feared for Potter. "I'll stay. I'll watch over Honoré. Go."

Suddenly, Lord James was at my side. "Don't worry, Mrs. Palmer, we'll take care of Honoré. You go with Mr. Palmer."

She was pulled into the carriage, where she collapsed in tears. As they galloped away I turned back to follow the officers who were dragging the squirming Honoré into the pavilion. For once, Bertha Palmer's plans had all fallen apart in a manner that could never have been predicted. Incongruously, I thought of one of my children's favorite rhymes—"Humpty Dumpty fell off a wall, Humpty Dumpty had a great fall. All the king's horses and all the king's men couldn't put Humpty together again."

TWENTY-FIVE

In the end, we weren't able to fulfill our promise to Mrs. Palmer. After a lengthy interrogation, Honoré was arrested for the murder of Edith Stuart and there was nothing either Lord James or I could do to prevent it. At least Inspector Guillaume was willing to let the two of us remain with Honoré during the ordeal.

We ended up staying for hours at the pavilion, as all of the guests were questioned. Eventually, most were allowed to leave. Honoré claimed that he had heard the first scream and mounted the steps, where he found the balcony empty, until he looked over the railing and saw the body below. Sonya had followed him up the stairs and, when she saw the body, hers had been the second scream.

What he did not explain was why he'd been headed towards the balcony at that moment, or why the diamond necklace—which had been stolen from Countess Olga—had been in his pocket. I suspected he'd been on his way to meet someone on the balcony but he denied it. And why had he been so tragically struck by the sight of the body? Inspector Guillaume had not seen his face on that balcony but I had. It was as if he were struck by a great personal loss. Could it be that Edith Stuart meant more to him than any of us had realized? I was never able to ask him, myself, as we were not allowed any private moments together. From some uneasy glances exchanged between the young men I wondered if Lord James knew something about a rendezvous but when I asked him later he denied it.

Inspector Guillaume theorized that Honoré was the thief, and that Edith Stuart had either been a confederate or that she had seen him steal the jewelry. He further suggested that she had threatened to tell the police about him and that he had thrown her over the railing to her death in order to prevent that. Honoré denied everything and that was all he would say. He seemed to be frozen in some sort of inner contemplation. Perhaps the collapse of his beloved father, and the destruction of his mother's world, had shocked him that much. I could not tell. He looked blankly at the inspector when he was asked why he had been where he was, if he had *not* stolen the jewels. His stubbornness in not replying was so robust it reminded me of his mother.

In the end, Inspector Guillaume took him away under arrest. When they were gone I disgraced myself by bursting into tears. Poor Bertha. All her advantages in life were suddenly seized and ripped from her. That her reception and reputation were in ruins was a minor matter. That her son was thrust into prison, accused of theft and murder, was devastating. But on top of all of that, her beloved husband had collapsed at the very moment that her world fell apart. I could not face returning to the house on rue Brignole. I was afraid of what I would find there. My tears were merely a manifestation of my cowardice.

Lord James was obviously embarrassed by my display of emotion but, to his credit, he did not abandon me. He stood by awkwardly and, in the end, found a carriage to deliver me home. Stephen and Bertha were still at the hospital and I spent the rest of the night in my children's room watching them breathe.

The next few days were painful. The weather remained stifling, with an overcast sky that periodically opened up to downpours of heavy rain. Confined indoors, my children became cranky and fractious. The atmosphere of the house had changed from one of festivity to gloom. Bertha was consumed by caring for her ailing husband, traveling to be at his side at the hospital at all hours. When she was in residence, various legal and political figures came and went. I was not invited to their meetings, and my services as her social secretary were not required. I learned more from my husband than my employer.

Stephen told me that Potter Palmer had suffered a setback but would recover. Because of the attack he'd suffered in Rome the previous year, both he and his wife were extremely frightened by his sudden collapse. Bertha insisted her husband needed complete rest and quiet, so when plans were made to bring him home to rue Brignole, Stephen suggested I take Mary Cassatt up on her offer of a visit to her country estate. It made perfect sense as a way to get our noisy toddlers out of the way until Mr. Palmer was feeling better. Although, truthfully, I didn't believe that would happen so long as his son was in a French jail.

"But wouldn't it be disloyal to desert Mrs. Palmer at this time?" I asked him.

He shook his head. "I don't think so, Emily. I don't think she has any use for you at the moment, and I'm afraid your presence even acts as a rebuke. You can't help but remind her of what an awful disaster her last social engagement turned out to be. And she's not capable, at the moment, of trying to deal with the likes of Amelia Johnstone, or any of the other society matrons who are only too anxious to gloat."

"It's true. But I feel like I've failed her. If I'd managed to find out who was stealing the jewels, those two women might still be dead, but at least Honoré would not stand accused of murdering them. The police are saying they discovered he was the thief and that's why he killed them. But he never would have stolen like that, much less kill two young women. I'm very certain that he's completely innocent, but I'm at a loss how to prove that to the police. They don't know him like we…and his family…do. Oh, how did we ever get to such a terrible place?"

He came over and put his arms around me. "It's not your fault, Emily. There's nothing you could have done. You said it yourself, it's not the same as back in Chicago where you have Whitbread to depend on. You were right. Mrs. Palmer and I were wrong to think you could do anything in a foreign city where you don't even know the language." He kissed my head and pulled me close. "Take the children to Miss Cassatt's. I want you all away from this."

I resented the fact that I was so helpless, but I had no reason not to give in. Perhaps it was the only favor I could do for Bertha Palmer at the moment. I couldn't alleviate her suffering, but at least I could remove our rambunctious young children from her home, in order to provide a more peaceful setting for Mr. Palmer.

So it was arranged that Delia and I would take the children, and Stephen would remain. He, at least, could ease her mind by providing medical advice and constant supervision of the patient.

Miss Cassatt was delighted with the plan, even more so as she understood she would be doing Mrs. Palmer a service by providing an alternative home for our young children. We all regretted that there was nothing we could do to relieve Bertha's mind about her son's situation, but Lord James assured me that he would not rest until his friend was cleared of all charges. It did not help that there had been no additional jewel thefts since Honoré's incarceration. Inspector Guillaume readily gave me permission to leave Paris, once he was reassured that I could be requested to return at any time.

TWENTY-SIX

The children and I traveled by train, and then pony cart, from Paris to Beaufresne, Miss Cassatt's home in the countryside north of Paris. It was a large old mansion that she had spent much time modernizing and, as her Philadelphia relatives chose to remain in Paris, there was plenty of room. Her very competent French housekeeper, Mathilde, soon had us all sorted and settled, and my children were excited to ramble around the large garden where there was a small pond with a bridge and a little house. After the rigors of the meetings and formal receptions in Paris, it was wonderfully relaxing for me, too. I rose early with the children, who were welcomed by the cook in the big old-fashioned kitchen. Then they scrambled out to explore the garden. Jack was soon adopted by the gardener, M. Giroux, who taught him to fish. Tommy was still small enough to cling to Delia's skirts but he had a fine time tripping around the garden chasing butterflies.

Four-year-old Lizzie took an interest in Miss Cassatt and was drawn to watch when the artist took out a pad and pencils or pastels to sketch. This was very much to Miss Cassatt's taste, as there was an eager glint in her eyes when she watched me and Lizzie.

"What's she doing?" Lizzie asked. My daughter was already impertinent and unconsciously rude.

"Miss Cassatt is an artist, Lizzie. She makes very beautiful paintings that people like very much. And she has been nice enough to let us come and visit her. Have you said thank you to Miss Cassatt for having us?" I was sitting on a long screened-in porch that had been added to the back of the house. I had donned a light apron over my frock and borrowed a sewing box from Mathilde. I finally had time to repair some of the rips and tears in the children's clothes. I was no great seamstress but it seemed a restful and pleasant task as I sat looking out over the green of the garden. Lizzie wore a white muslin dress that she had not yet managed to ruin with grass stains. She roamed the room, stopping to look over Miss Cassatt's shoulder as the artist furiously sketched away, as if desperate to capture a moment. Lizzie swung her hands back and forth considering the artist's work, impressed by her complete attention to the task. Determined to get attention from someone, my daughter sauntered over to me and leaned against my knee, propping her face in her little hands to study Miss Cassatt.

"Lizzie." I jiggled my knee to get her attention. "What do you say to Miss Cassatt?"

She stood up and gave a big sigh, as if I had asked for some great feat from her. "Thank you for having us, Miss Cassatt. I really like your garden and your doggie." After this pronouncement my daughter collapsed against me again and stared at Miss Cassatt, as if challenging her.

The artist looked up and grinned. "You are very welcome, Miss Lizzie. We are very happy to have you. Now, can you just stay as you are on your mother's knee for a few more moments?" She flipped the sheet on her pad to a new one. "I'd just like to get a sketch of you like that."

I groaned inwardly. It was my experience with my children that this kind of request—that they remain still—would inevitably provoke motion and the opposite of what was requested. But whether that reaction was reserved for parents, or whether the artist had much more experience in getting children to cooperate, I was amazed to see my daughter remain comparatively still as she continued to gaze at Miss Cassatt. They carried on a discussion about the probable age of the artist's dog and his various likes and dislikes. I surrendered to the wonder of it, shaking my head in disbelief as I continued to patch rips on the knees and elbows of my children's clothes.

Eventually Lizzie tired of us and ran out to help Tommy chase butterflies. I despaired of the white dress but I knew Delia was handy at getting out stains. Miss Cassatt sat back to look at her work. I had discussed the possibility of our becoming models with my husband before we left Paris. He had laughed and proclaimed himself ready and willing to see an image of his offspring hanging on the wall of some wealthy collector. Like me, he was intensely skeptical about the possibility that any of our children could be made to sit long enough for someone to capture their likeness.

Miss Cassatt swiveled her sketchpad on her knee and I gasped. It was Lizzie as in life. You could feel her weight against the knee of the barely sketched woman, who was me. She leaned her face on her hands and looked straight at you, with curiosity and skepticism.

"You won't mind if I use it for a painting?"

"Of course not. It's quite wonderful."

"Thank you. Tell me, have you heard anything from Paris?" she asked. Busy sketching on a new sheet of her pad, she was swiftly looking up and down, up and down. I supposed she was catching my likeness and I tried not to notice, as I picked up a little pinafore of Lizzie's to repair.

"No, I haven't." We'd been at Beaufresne for a week. I'd written to Stephen twice but, so far, I'd received no response. I suspected there was no good news and it was like him to not want to spoil our visit with bad news. But it was frustrating.

"The young Mr. Palmer must be still under arrest, then. They must believe he pushed that woman to her death."

"I'm sure he would never have done such a thing. It's impossible," I protested.

She flipped to another sheet on the pad. "What about the young woman who was killed? What was she like?"

"Edith Stuart was a young American woman who attended the art academy in Philadelphia with Miss Johnstone. I understand that you also studied there."

"That's right."

"She traveled to France with the Johnstones and was living in Paris with them."

"Do the police think that she and Denise Laporte were involved with the jewel robberies?"

I sighed. "The police seem to believe that both they and young Mr. Palmer were involved. Denise was often present in the ladies' parlors of the gatherings where the thefts took place, helping the staff from the House of Worth. The theory the inspector seems to have come up with is that she not only had a liaison with Honoré but that she also helped him with the thefts. They think she was so desperate for money to help care for herself and her unborn child that she threatened to expose Honoré. So, following along in that theory, they think he killed her to prevent her from revealing that he was the father of her child.

"All of which makes no sense, whatsoever. The actions they're suggesting are all totally out of character for him. I have only ever seen him be a kind and thoughtful person with impeccable manners. He cares deeply for his parents and would never do anything to bring them such grief. And, if he had taken the pearl choker for some reason, it's ridiculous to think he'd return it by putting it on the mannequin. He had plenty of opportunities to return it to his mother's jewelry case, with no one being any the wiser."

"And Miss Stuart?"

"Inspector Guillaume theorizes that either she was part of the group that did the thefts, or that she saw something that could link Honoré to them and also tried to blackmail him. She, too, was very desperate for money. She couldn't pay her bills, and Mr. Johnstone had threatened to throw her out of his house. They've charged Honoré with pushing her from the balcony to her death."

There was no sound but the scratching of her chalk on the paper for a few minutes. "Was he seen to do these terrible acts, then?"

"No, of course not. Sonya, Countess Olga's daughter, saw him on the balcony. Exactly how much she saw, I don't know. She was hysterical. But I saw the look of horror on his face when he looked over the railing. It was not the shock of seeing a mere acquaintance dashed on the ground below you. It was much more than that, somehow."

The scratching of the chalk stopped but I kept my eyes on my sewing, biting my lower lip as I remembered the look on Honoré's face. It was as if the floor had fallen away from under his feet.

"You think he was horrified by what he'd just done?"

"No, not that. Why would he ever do such a thing? If Edith Stuart wanted money, surely he could've given it to her. What could make him push her to her death? It makes no sense."

"Perhaps money was not enough for her. If she was going to expose him for the thefts…if she wouldn't take money but wanted revenge instead, a young man might feel he had no way to stop her."

"But what wrong could he have done to her for such bitter revenge? No, I don't believe it. It seems to me that Edith Stuart was one of those young women who just do not know how to live if they don't have the resources to pay for the lifestyle of their peers. She wasn't really pursuing art as a vocation, as you do. Her only vocation was to marry, and only by marrying a wealthy man could she continue to live in the only manner she had ever known."

Mary Cassatt shook her head. "And the only way to meet men wealthy enough to sustain that way of life, is to wear expensive clothes and follow the pursuits of the wealthy society those men frequent. It was the same when I was young. When will these women have the sense to arm themselves with skills and pursuits that will allow them to stand on their own? If her family lacked the money to support such a lifestyle, why did she insist on pursuing it? The expense is ruinous and the outcome is bound to be disgrace."

"From what I could learn, her extravagance had already brought her to the brink of ruin." I looked across at the artist. She laid her sketchpad on her lap. "I even wondered if it drove her to the final extreme."

"You think she flung herself from that balcony to the pavement stones below?" She shivered and her words had conjured up a view of the dismal sight for me as well. "You truly do not believe Bertha's son did this?"

"No, I don't. But I don't know how to prove it. And he refused to reveal where he was the afternoon Denise Laporte was strangled. He's hiding something, but I don't believe he's a thief, and I cannot believe he killed those women. And I am so terribly sorry that I've failed Mrs. Palmer in this. She asked me to help find the real culprit in the jewel thefts." I explained that Bertha had asked me to help, based on my work with the police back in Chicago.

"But there's not much you can do if the police are in charge."

"That's what my husband said, too. But I feel I've failed Mrs. Palmer after all she's done for me and my family. And the way this has hit Mr. Palmer...the shock made him collapse. It's unbearable. In the events of one night she almost lost her husband and her son. She needs them back. My husband will do all that is possible, medically, to help Mr. Palmer, but if their son is imprisoned I fear neither of them will ever recover." I thought of the bright and elegant house on rue Brignole, busy with activity and the excitement of visiting Paris, and I doubted I would ever see it that way again, or even be able to remember it as it was before all of this.

Miss Cassatt grasped the sketchpad on her knees and frowned. "I, too, wish there was something I could do for them." She shrugged. "I can only draw and paint. It's all I'm good for. But if you wish to return to the city, if you think there's anything your presence could do to help the young man's case, you must feel free to go. I know getting the children out from under everyone's feet is desired, but there's no reason not to leave them here. No, really, I'm quite serious. Between Delia and Mathilde there is no difficulty caring for them and, as you can see, I'm delighted to use them as models. It's entirely selfish of me to want them to stay. So you can return to Paris if you feel you should. Just say the word and Mathilde will make the arrangements."

My heart rose at the thought. I looked out the screened windows and saw Tommy take an unsteady step and then plop down to the ground with a surprised look on his face. Delia stood smiling at him on the shaded green lawn while Jack chased Lizzie, who had somehow latched onto his fishing rod. The gardener looked up from trimming a hedge to watch them, and Mathilde appeared with a tray of lemonade and sweets that she put down on a rustic wooden table under a huge beech tree. Pink and white blossoms nodded gracefully against the background of different shades of green from grass, leaves, and fernlike water plants around the pond.

I could have left them, as Miss Cassatt said. But what good would it do? What could I do to relieve the pain of my friends back in Paris? Even if I could convince Inspector Guillaume that I was competent to help, what could I do, really? The only role I could see for myself would be as a hindrance, a useless busybody merely irritating the authorities or provoking embarrassment in the small American community of Paris. I deeply regretted my lack of ability, but I had to tell Miss Cassatt that, as much as I thanked her for the offer, I could see no advantage to my return.

TWENTY-SEVEN

Two days later I had still received no response to my letters, so I asked to accompany Miss Cassatt's gardener, M. Giroux, on his trip via motorcar to the nearby town of Beauvais, which was on the Thérain River. There was a post office there, with a telegraph wire, and I thought that if I sent a telegraph to Stephen he would have to respond.

M. Giroux left me at the post office, with instructions to meet him in two hours and the suggestion that I lunch at a café along the river. The arrangement suited me and, after sending my plea for information, I shrugged off a pang of guilt for being so insistent and strolled down towards a stone bridge over the river.

The countryside around the village was flat, surrounded as it was by fields of farmland. The river was tranquil, with a few small barges coming from Paris and a scattering of small boats filled with picnickers or leisurely tourists. I noticed one just pulling up to a dock below me. A tall man wearing a white linen suit and a straw hat stood, using a long paddle to skim the boat alongside the wooden dock. When he jumped lightly off and secured a line, I recognized him. It was Lord James. He handed a woman, who was wearing a white lawn dress with a simple straw hat and carrying a lacy parasol, onto the dock. I was shocked to see it was Countess Olga. I had been mulling over the situation in Paris, but I had never thought to see some of the players in that drama here. It was so incongruous that I stood stupidly watching as they approached, and they were the ones to greet me before I could say anything.

They both appeared only too delighted to see me. They were aware of my visit to Miss Cassatt and they asked after her. I told them that she was not with me and that I was anxious for news from Paris. I was a little shocked that they seemed so unconcerned, while I was so terribly worried about the Palmers. It vexed me that I didn't know anything, so I quickly begged them for any information about the situation. They looked shocked.

"Oh, my goodness, Mrs. Chapman. You haven't heard," Lord James said. "Honoré's been released. They had to let him go. Sonya told them they were all wrong about what they assumed and they had to release him. You didn't know that? They didn't tell you?"

I mumbled something about how they were sure to be terribly busy with so many things happening, but it stung me. Neither Stephen nor Bertha Palmer had thought to let me know about such an important development.

"And the senior Mr. Palmer is recovering well at home," he continued. "He's still on complete bed rest and they're not seeing anyone, but it's sure to help him that his son's been released."

I'd been so worried, and now it seemed the situation had vastly improved. How could they not let me know? For the whole week, I had waited for news but none had come. It occurred to me that perhaps they hadn't told me because they didn't want me to return to Paris. But why?

I tried to put aside my questions in order to respond to their inquiries. When I explained that I had a couple of hours before I would return to Beaufresne they insisted I join them at a nearby hotel for lunch. It had a good cook and a lovely patio overlooking the river, they told me. So, taking me by the arms, one on each side, they led me to a three-storied stone building only a few steps away.

At the doorway, Countess Olga excused herself to leave her things in a room and Lord James led me through a cool, dark drawing room and a small dining room set with linens and crystal. We continued out onto an open patio, which was under the shade of several tall elm trees and overlooked the water running serenely about ten feet below.

He nodded to the waiter and held out a chair for me.

"Whatever brings the two of you here?" I asked, still bewildered by the chance meeting.

"It's the countess," he said. "The count is in Paris, you see. He's visiting his daughter and, when that happens, Mme Olga likes to get out of town. It's quite awkward. He only makes the trip a few times a year and, of course, she has to let him see Sonya. Usually the countess visits friends in the south but this time his visit was unexpected, so she was at a loss. I know this place. I've been here many times over the years, so I suggested we come out for the day. Here she comes. Don't let her know I told you." He stood to hold a chair out for her and she came across the room, leaning on her silver-headed cane. When she was seated, he sat back down again.

Finally, I could ask for more details about what had been happening in Paris and how it was that Honoré had been released.

"My poor Sonya," Countess Olga told me. "She was so hysterical that night she was unable to give the police a statement. And then they found my necklace in Honoré's pocket. Of course, he was not responsible for Mlle Stuart's death. There was someone else. Sonya and Honoré were together the whole time.

"You see, it must have been when Sonya took me to the ladies' parlor on the fourth floor to fix my hair arrangement that it happened. I remember that Miss Johnstone and her friends were already there. They were arguing. We tried to ignore them and Mlle Arquette helped us. I removed the necklace, and earrings, and the bracelet that had caught on the lace of my gown. There did not seem to be any risk of theft, as Sonya and I were both right there. She and mademoiselle attended to my hair but the argument was distracting. When the young women finally left we hurried to get back to the dancing. Sonya suddenly realized that we had forgotten the jewels. We returned to the parlor to search for them, and Mlle Arquette assisted us. She was distressed. I decided I needed to tell Inspector Guillaume at once, even though I knew it would be a great tragedy for Mrs. Palmer. I was telling him when we heard the screams. I went to the balcony and found Sonya had fainted.

"When we heard that Miss Stuart had died, Sonya was inconsolable. The inspector insisted on talking to her but she was weeping too hard. Finally, I took her home and the doctor put her to sleep for two days. It was only when she awoke that I was able to get the true story from her. She says that she was with M. Honoré when they heard the scream and they rushed to the balcony together. There they found the necklace on the railing. He picked it up, and then they looked over the railing and saw that poor woman. Of course they were shocked. Sonya screamed. M. Honoré ran down below. They neither one of them knew who it was—at least not then—or who had hurt her." She told me all of this with breathless excitement. "Of course, I went to Mme Palmer as soon as I got Sonya to tell me, then we went to the inspector…with Mr. Palmer's lawyers, you understand. Guillaume insisted on coming to talk to my poor Sonya, but she was very brave and she told him everything, and then they had to let M. Honoré go." She clapped her hands. "We are all so very happy with this. Sonya and M. Honoré are together all the time now…they are so very happy."

"Too true," Lord James told me. "I think they're only waiting for Honoré's father to recover before there's an announcement. It's true, isn't it, Countess? You would know."

She looked down meekly and, at that moment, the waiter arrived with a steaming bowl of chicken in a broth with potatoes and green beans. He ladled some onto each of our plates and uncorked a bottle of wine. He filled our glasses, then swept away to attend to another table where an older couple sat waiting.

"I am not free to confide in you, Lord James. But I can tell Mrs. Chapman that Sonya's father has made a special trip from Saint Petersburg to meet the Palmers. He is visiting now."

I managed to look pleased while tasting my food and taking a sip of my wine. At least this plan of Mrs. Palmer's was coming to pass. It seemed she would indeed return to Chicago with a son engaged to foreign nobility, if and when the French police allowed him to go. I hoped the young people would be happy, but I was certain it would never make up for the distress the incident had caused the Palmers.

Countess Olga smiled in a way that made her look a bit younger than the fine lines around her eyes usually suggested. She turned to Lord James to tease him. "But you must share your news, Lord James. Do not be shy. Tell Mrs. Chapman." She lifted her glass and sipped, watching him over the rim.

"Yes, well." He turned to me. "I dare say it won't come as a complete surprise to you, Mrs. Chapman, when I tell you I've proposed marriage to Miss Johnstone and she's accepted." His face was tinged with pink by the end of this announcement. It seemed he was serious about his desire to see Omaha, Nebraska.

"Congratulations, Lord James. But I hope you don't mind my asking, if you have so recently announced your engagement, why are you here and not in Paris with your betrothed?"

He picked up his glass and gulped a couple of mouthfuls of the tangy white wine, then beckoned to the waiter to refill our glasses. "Yes, well, as you might imagine, the ladies are quite occupied with the construction of the trousseau and, while I'm all for the occasional visit to M. Worth's establishment, I do draw the line at spending a full week there. As it happens, I know the proprietor of this hotel and I've spent quite a few pleasant visits here. When the countess was looking for a place to visit, I volunteered to take her, don't you know."

"He was so adamant in recommending it, I had to agree," she added.

"Yes...so I thought I'd remove myself and let the ladies get on with it by accompanying the countess." He waved the air with a long fingered hand. "They're better off without me."

Countess Olga turned to me confidingly. "And, besides, I hear there is an especially large contingent of the English in town this week. Perhaps even some relatives a certain young man may wish to avoid."

"Yes, well, never a time like the present for getting out of town when the Lawford tribe descends. One's obnoxious relatives are not to be afflicted on one's affianced," he said. "Not if one plans to stay affianced, anyhow. No, really, you've no idea how hideous the relatives can be to someone not of the fold. Especially when marriage is contemplated. I consider myself a lucky man that my soon to be in-laws are blissfully unacquainted with the rankings of English society and they will be much happier the less contact they have with that group. Believe me, the rest of the European aristocracy, like the countess here, have a good appreciation for the great—I may say very great—merits of an American mate. But in this, as in many things, the British Isles are just plain backward. I really won't take the chance of having my future family insulted by my wayward past."

Both the Countess Olga and I expressed some doubt about the wisdom of this course of action, but the Englishman was adamant. I soon noticed the time and thanked them for their company. Lord James walked me back to meet M. Giroux, entertaining me with stories about the town. I was inattentive, as I was distracted by all I'd learned and, more than ever, I wondered why I'd been left in the dark about developments. I noticed, as I said goodbye to each of them, that both Lord James and the countess assumed I would soon be returning to the house on rue Brignole.

TWENTY-EIGHT

I decided to take Mary Cassatt up on her offer. I would leave the
children in the care of Delia and Mathilde and return to Paris
to uncover what was truly happening. The artist had taken to
retreating to the little house at the end of the pond for most of each
day. She'd set up a print shop there, and a man who was a skilled
technician came out from the city to work with her. It seemed to
me that it would be better to leave both her and the children to their
occupations while I returned to Paris. Inactivity was making me fret.

Mathilde made all the arrangements and, since the inhabitants
of rue Brignole had failed to enlighten me about all of the events
I'd missed, I felt no compulsion to warn them of my arrival. What
did they think I would do if they continued their ominous silence?
And why, oh, why had they failed to share the encouraging news
of Honoré's release?

When I reached the house on rue Brignole I had to wait restlessly
in our rooms for Stephen to return from a visit to the Institut
Pasteur. He found me curled up with a book on a couch overlooking
the luscious garden. But my attention was wandering. It seemed
unnaturally quiet without our children.

I expected some guilty apology from him for his lack of
communication but, instead, he expressed only a vast sense of

relief. Perhaps his silence had been meant to provoke my action. He knew me well enough to do that.

"I didn't write because I wasn't sure what to tell you," he said.

"What do you mean, you didn't know what to tell me? Surely you could have told me that Honoré had been released. I can understand if you and Mrs. Palmer still didn't want the children underfoot. But I'm not a child. You could, at least, have let me know the good news. I was so worried."

He stood before me, blocking the light, like a sorry schoolboy. "The thing is, Emily, I'm not sure it *is* good news." Abruptly he sat down beside me, and gave me a hug. I hugged him back but then pulled away to look at him.

"Tell me what happened."

He brushed the hair away from his forehead with one hand. "When you left, Honoré was in custody of the police and Potter was about to come home from the hospital. It had been a great scare for Mrs. Palmer, especially after the attack he had in Rome last year. She stayed at his bedside most of the time. She was grateful to you for taking the children away. It was one less thing to worry her. Then, one day, Countess Olga showed up."

"I saw the countess and Lord James in the country. They were the ones who told me Honoré had been released. They said Sonya had finally recovered enough to tell the police that Honoré couldn't have pushed Edith Stuart from that balcony because he was with her."

Stephen frowned. "That's the story she tells now. But that day the countess and Mrs. Palmer were closeted together for several hours. When I came back from my work at the Institut, Bertha was back at Potter's bedside and Honoré was with them."

"Surely his release was a good thing, wasn't it? Why do you seem so reluctant to tell me about it?"

"It was a good thing for Potter. He was still restricted to his bed at that point but when he saw his son you could see him relax. It was very good for his recovery and within a few days they allowed him to get up. He still needs to take it easy and Bertha has absolved him from attending any events. It wasn't as serious as we thought but it gave her quite a scare."

"And I'm sure it eases her mind to have you available to keep an eye on him."

"It's my pleasure, after all they've done for us. But I have to tell you, Emily, things are not as happy here as you might think. Bertha and Honoré both behave as if they're at odds with each other. They go through the motions of living their lives but, behind that front, they're on edge. I don't know why, and I cannot get either one of them to confide in me. Perhaps you can. I wanted to call you back, but Mrs. Palmer asked me not to."

I was hurt to think she specifically asked him not to tell me about Honoré's release. Perhaps she would be unhappy to learn of my return. I thought it was a good thing I hadn't told them I was coming. If she had asked me to stay away, I would have had no choice but to obey. But, now that I was here, it would be difficult to persuade me to leave again. I could see that Stephen was concerned, and that made me determined to stay in Paris and uncover the source of this vague worry.

"Have you talked to Honoré?" I asked Stephen.

"Very little. Ever since his release, he's been squiring Sonya around. Her father came to town, apparently to meet him. There's reason to believe an engagement will happen very soon."

"That's what the countess and Lord James hinted at. At least that must make Mrs. Palmer happy. It was her plan to get them together."

He sat back against the cushions, one arm extended along the couch. "You would think that. But it's my impression that Mrs. Palmer is still under some kind of strain. She hides it from Potter, which is understandable. She keeps the countess by her side all of the time, when she's in town. I suspect that she and Olga may want that match more than Honoré does. I think at this point he's willing to do anything to please his mother and he's going through with the marriage in order to make up for the embarrassment caused by his arrest. Apparently, Countess Olga escaped to the countryside while her husband was here—that must have been when you saw her—but she's returned. I don't know whether that constant attendance is to protect her from harm or something else. There's something not right, Emily. I just don't know what it is."

"What about the police? Has Inspector Guillaume arrested anyone in connection with the deaths of Denise Laporte and Edith Stuart?"

"Not that we've heard. The most likely theory is that Edith's death was a suicide. I don't know if the inspector accepts that or doubts it."

"Do you? Doubt it?"

"I don't know what to think. I didn't know the young woman. Do you think she might have killed herself?"

"I don't know. But I do know that she was in debt—her friend Lydia had turned against her and Mr. Johnstone was throwing her out of his house. She seemed a young woman with many problems but to take her own life? I don't know. And what of the jewel thefts? Have they continued?"

He looked confused. "Jewel thefts? Oh, yes, of course. I confess, I have no idea. I haven't had time to think of them." Like Bertha and I, he'd never believed Honoré could be involved with the thefts. Unfortunately, the police did not see it that way. "Emily, it's not the thefts that I worry about, it's Honoré's expected engagement to Sonya. I can't help wondering if it's only happening because without it, and Sonya's claim that she was with him on the balcony, Honoré might be convicted of murdering Edith... or even both her *and* the milliner."

"Why ever would he have murdered either one of them? But, regardless, you don't believe the young people are really in love?"

"I can't help suspecting that the marriage is more the result of an agreement between the mothers than feelings between the two young people. It's not that they aren't fond of each other, or that the marriage would be unsuitable, but the wills of the mothers just seem much more the driving force in this. They're like two tigresses protecting their young."

I presented myself to Mrs. Palmer later in the day and found her accompanied by Countess Olga, who had taken my place as her constant companion. The countess seemed quite happy to see me and was warm in her greeting. She was hugely sympathetic to Mrs. Palmer's concerns about her husband.

Bertha was cordial, but distant, appearing preoccupied. With her husband still recovering, she had decided to curtail her participation in the social activities of the Exposition for a short time. So she very kindly released me from my duties and suggested I take the opportunity to visit it as a tourist. I assured her the children were enjoying the country too much to need to return, and that seemed to relieve her. With the countess present, I didn't feel that I could ask Mrs. Palmer about the release of her son, or the jewel thefts, so I asked for a few minutes in private. Mrs. Palmer seemed reluctant, but I followed her to her suite of rooms and bid the countess goodbye as I closed the door.

"I was so very happy to hear that Mr. Palmer's health has improved so much," I told her. "I was also so pleased to hear of Honoré's release. That must have been a huge relief for you. I met Lord James and the countess in the country, otherwise I might not have known about it. I know you were all very busy with the situation here, but I was disappointed no one had informed me."

She headed for her elegant desk, which was covered with several untidy stacks of paper. She wore a tea gown that was unusually wrinkled for her. That, as much as anything, worried me. "It's been a great strain, worrying about Mr. Palmer and Honoré at the same time. I can't tell you how grateful I am for your husband's care and advice."

"I heard that Sonya Zugenev was able to clear Honoré with the police."

She grunted. She was shuffling papers, not looking up at me. "She didn't clear him so much as to make it impossible for them to justify keeping him in custody. But I had to enlist the aid of several lawyers, and some of the local officials, to force them to release him. Your Inspector Guillaume fought it at every step. He's not convinced of Honoré's innocence and he's in a position to do a great deal of harm." She looked up at me with a glare. I wanted to deny that I had any influence with the French inspector but I was leery of starting an argument.

"Mr. Palmer's health only really started to improve when he saw Honoré in the room and out of police custody. And it was only with the help of the countess and her daughter that Honoré was released."

"I hear that he and Sonya are to become engaged."

She lowered her head and continued to sort through her papers, without responding.

"You must be happy about that."

"The young people are fond of each other," she said. "The count visited from Saint Petersburg last week. I couldn't let him speak to Potter, he was still too weak, so I talked to him myself. He seems satisfied with Honoré." She raised her head and stared across the room for a moment. "There is still a great deal of acrimony in that family. He warned me that his wife came from Gypsy stock, as if that would matter. He wants her to accompany Sonya to America. He offered a modest dowry. I suspect he's looking forward to relief from supporting his wife, although the family is supposed to be wealthy. He wasn't a very pleasant man. He didn't like it when I told him there could be no real engagement until Mr. Palmer is completely recovered. I had to insist."

I was sure she'd been firm. She would never endanger her husband's health, even if he was really better than expected. It made me wonder why there was a need to proceed with the engagement at this time, unless Stephen was right and it was required in order for Sonya to provide Honoré with proof of his innocence. "Are you sure that Honoré is truly enamored with her? Surely there's no need to rush into it." I remembered her plans for his political career back in Chicago but, with all of the upsets of the summer, I couldn't believe she would want to execute those plans if she thought her husband still needed more rest.

She was not happy with my daring to question her. "It's time for Honoré to give up his entertainments and get down to business. He has agreed to the engagement and it will be announced just as soon as Potter is strong enough. He knows how devastating it was for his father when he was taken by the police." She shivered. "That cannot happen again, and it is his responsibility to see that it doesn't. The engagement will make it clear that Sonya's story is unshakeable and that she trusts him completely. As he trusts her. There is no question the marriage will follow but in Chicago, not here."

I could tell this was the end of the conversation as far as she was concerned. I wanted to question the wisdom of a rush into marriage, and she knew it, but she dismissed me before I could comment further. As the tall door closed behind me I wondered what I would do in her place, if Jack or Tommy were involved in such a situation. The one thing I was sure of was that I would never encourage them, or their sister, to seek an aristocratic title in their mate. What a fool's errand that seemed to be for all the young people I had met in Paris. How much more satisfactory to seek the deep contentment and companionship Stephen and I had found with each other. Or a passion such as the one Miss Cassatt had for her work, even if it meant she had not married.

At dinner, only Honoré joined the countess, her daughter, Stephen, and myself. He performed his duties as host quite capably, but he seemed distracted by his concern for his father. He was attentive to Sonya but no more so than to the rest of us. He seemed quite different from the last time I'd seen him, when he was taken away from the scene of Edith's death. I longed to ask him about that moment on the balcony, when he had seemed so stricken by tragedy…as he looked down at the body on the ground below. I couldn't help wondering if there hadn't been something between him and Miss Stuart. But there was no opportunity to bring up so sensitive a topic. The most I could do was to congratulate him on his release from custody.

"Yes. That was pretty awful. I certainly learned something about the French justice system. But Sonya was able to set it all straight, and that was a great relief to my father. As soon as he saw I was out, he began to improve. We're all very grateful to her for saving me."

After that graceful admission, he excused himself to join his mother in her sitting room. The countess and her daughter soon left, and I sat for a long time in our rooms, musing on the state of things. I couldn't let it go. Stephen was right. There was a part of the situation that didn't make sense, and I decided I needed to find out for myself exactly what it was. I had not a breath of suspicion that Honoré could have been involved in the deaths of Denise Laporte or Edith Stuart. But there was something he was hiding, and I suspected it had to do with the robberies. Mrs. Palmer had originally asked me to investigate the thefts, but I had failed her. Now I was determined to try again. The deaths might be in some way connected to each other but I couldn't see how. In any case, they were beyond my skill to unravel. But the thefts ought to be explained and I thought it was time for me to try to do so.

TWENTY-NINE

When I went to visit him the next day, Inspector Guillaume seemed less interested in the thefts. "*Non*, there have been no more thefts. Not since the young M. Potter was taken into custody. Of course, now he is released, so we shall see." Inspector Guillaume shrugged. It had taken a lot of persistence before I was finally allowed to see him in his office, with the miniature guillotine on the corner of his desk. But I was stubborn. I wouldn't go away, so, finally, one of the young police officers had thrown up his hands and led me to the man.

"And the death of Miss Stuart, what have you determined about that?"

Another shrug and a raised eyebrow. "Apparently, from the testimony of the lovely Mlle Sonya, M. Honoré Palmer could not have been responsible, so the only conclusion we can come to is that the woman threw herself from the balcony."

"Suicide. But you don't believe that?"

"I think the daughter of the countess will soon be engaged to the son of the American millionaire. Presumably it is young love, and they will live happily ever after, as you say. Unfortunately, the Mlle Stuart will not live happily, or unhappily, anymore." He frowned at me. "But for the young M. Palmer now the debts are all cleared, you understand? We have investigated and it would seem all of his obligations have been paid off."

"But his mother may have done that, you know."

"Perhaps."

"You can't think he sold the stolen jewelry to pay them off? I can find out from Mrs. Palmer if she gave him the money."

"But, of course, what will the loving mother of the son say in that instance? *Non.* We will not know. M. Palmer, he is very lucky in his marital arrangements. The poor Mlle Stuart and the little milliner, Denise Laporte, they are not so lucky."

He was very cynical. Considering me closely across the desk, he apparently decided to test my mettle. "But you have worked with the police in your city of Chicago, no? What would your policeman there think? There is a young woman, a milliner. She sees the life of the wealthy women for whom she makes the hats. She wishes to also have nice things, so she becomes a model for artists, lives the bohemian life, and she meets men who admire her. She becomes infatuated with a foreigner. Moving out of her uncle's house, she lives with the man. But something happens—perhaps the man's relatives come to town and he must get rid of his mistress—and she must return to her uncle's house. She finds she is going to have a child. The man, he has paid her off but now he has run up the debts, which he also must hide from his parents, lest they cut off his funds completely."

I knew he was speaking of Honoré. I thought the young man was keeping a secret from his parents but I could not believe this story was the explanation. He would never have acted in that manner. I knew that, and his mother knew that, but the French police had their own way of looking at things. Guillaume continued relentlessly.

"He must correct his problems, quickly, to keep them from his parents. Either he hears of the jewel thefts from the earlier exposition, or he is recruited by the Pied Piper of that time. It could be either. We do not know because the earlier crimes were never entirely solved. We may have arrested members of the gang, but we never found the mastermind behind it all. So, this man, he uses the little milliner and he convinces others to help him. Then he begins to pay off his debts by stealing the jewels. But, for Denise Laporte, it is not enough, she wants him to acknowledge her and marry her and claim the child. This he cannot do. His own mother's pearls are stolen.

"When the Pied Piper worked in the last exposition, we found that he arranged for stolen jewels to be passed to the fence by placing them in plain sight in one of the exhibits. Once again this method is to be used to pass the jewels on for sale. M. Palmer gets the young Laporte girl to let him into the exhibit. She is working on the hats, you understand. But Denise has heard of his mother's plans to marry him to the daughter of the countess. She sees him, she waits till they are alone, she argues with him, but he cannot have her destroy all of his plans, so he strangles her, and leaves her and the pearls there for his fence." He looked across at me. "If not for your curiosity, it might have been some days before the body was found. We believe the pearls would have been gone by then, that very evening no doubt."

"I assure you, Mr. Palmer would never behave in this manner. He would never have treated Miss Laporte that way and he is wealthy. He has no need to steal jewelry."

He shrugged at my protests.

"And what about Miss Stuart?" I asked.

"Ah, another young person with debts. Miss Stuart, either she saw something, or she was a part of the robberies. The pattern of the Pied Piper was to recruit young people like Miss Stuart. She was becoming desperate about money. When M. Palmer was found with the stolen necklace in his pocket we assumed perhaps she had discovered him in the midst of the theft, threatened him, and he had pushed her over. But, of course, Mlle Sonya now says he was with her and the necklace was on the railing. He picked it up, they looked over the side together, and saw the body. So we are to believe the young woman was so distraught that she threw herself from the balcony. But, if so, we ask where did the necklace come from? And the other jewelry in the hand of the dead woman, how did it get there? If she stole it, as the countess would have us believe, it must solve her financial difficulties, is it not so? So why jump? If she did not steal it, then who was there with her, and did they push her or did she jump? These are the riddles we deal with. But M. Palmer, he has been removed from the calculations by Mlle Sonya. He is a lucky man, is he not?"

I could see that the police thought all of the pieces of this puzzle fit together if they had Honoré as their chief suspect. They wanted to cast him as the Pied Piper who had recruited Edith Stuart to steal for him. But, to me, it was like trying to fit a round puzzle piece into a space that was jagged. I could not imagine the young man I knew—the son of Bertha and Potter Palmer—engineering the thefts of jewels and undertaking the cold-blooded murders of two young women. But I also didn't believe the story Sonya told so conveniently after a few days, either. I had seen the reaction on Honoré's face with my own eyes. I didn't believe he'd been with the young Russian aristocrat and that they'd come upon the scene together, as she now claimed. He knew, or thought he knew, the woman on the pavement below, and her death had pierced him to the core.

But this was not something I wanted to share with the inspector, so I bid him goodbye. I left with a conviction that the police would never look beyond Honoré Palmer for a suspect, unless I was able to provide evidence that pointed clearly to another culprit. If things remained as they were—unresolved—it would leave a deep shadow on my friends the Palmers. Whatever secret Honoré was keeping, however painful it was, until it was revealed I feared for the welfare and safety of the family that had been so generous to my own. And, besides that, I could not remain in this state of suspense. I wanted to know what had really happened. To do that, I needed to know the truth about Edith Stuart, a young woman who had been so alive, even if unhappy and strained, in the afternoon, and so very dead by the end of the night. Although, what I would do with the knowledge, once I had it, was a different question.

To unravel this entire ball of misery was beyond my ability at the moment. But I felt more confident that I could at least identify the person, or persons, responsible for the jewel thefts. Surely I ought to be able to do that.

THIRTY

Once more I stood before the blue door on the rue de la Paix. Despite the recent tragic death of her friend, Lydia Johnstone was celebrating her engagement to Lord James by assembling a trousseau that would be the envy of every single woman and matron back in Omaha. This I had learned by some strategic visits to wives of the United States Commission members. They were slightly scandalized by my lack of tact, but none of them had known Edith, so they forgave the haste with which she was seemingly forgotten by her dear friends. All their sympathy was reserved for Mr. Johnstone, who had the sorry task of arranging to have her body transported back to Philadelphia as soon as possible. It was a gruesome subject that offered a chance to shiver at the thought of what might be involved. In the course of these discussions I learned that the Johnstone women spent the better part of every day at the various houses of couture in Paris. I thought that if I could talk to them I might be able to learn whether it was possible that Edith had been involved with the robberies and whether she could have been so desperate as to take her own life. Surely they would have noticed if Edith and Honoré had formed some kind of connection.

As it happened, while I'd been visiting Miss Cassatt several messages had come from the House of Worth, inviting me to return for the final fitting of my walking suit. It was simple to arrange an appointment when the Johnstone party would be there. So I entered the blue door, held open by the uniformed doorman, and followed a young vendeuse up the grand staircase and through the rooms of fabric. Once again I was impressed by the high ceilings, the sculptured cornices, the hanging chandeliers, and the gold trim on the ivory tinted woodwork. Light streamed in from the tall windows on one side as we entered the main room. There were several gatherings of elegant chairs and spindly tables, but I purposely approached the grouping in the middle, which included Mrs. Johnstone, her daughter, and several other women of the American delegation. Grace Brown was with them and she appeared to be the only one of the group who was wearing mourning.

All of their attention was on the figure of a model, who stood before them wearing a magnificent wedding gown. Mlle Arquette was not present but another saleswoman stood, poised, her hand extended like a magician demonstrating the results of a feat of magic. The gown had a high neck, then a trim of small satin roses around the shoulders from which flowed a graceful length of white and cream tulle accented with delicate lace. Tulle sleeves billowed out and were gathered at the wrist and trimmed with more lace. The narrow waist was cinched in with a cluster of wax orange blossoms attached at one side, while the skirts fell in layers of white satin and taffeta, with a topping of tulle trimmed in frothy lace at the bottom and spilling out to a generous train in the back. The model was tall, like Lydia, so one could imagine how striking she would appear at the altar. Omaha was going to get quite a display of opulence with this wedding. No one could not be amazed by the effect. And even I, with as little expertise in fashion as I had, could not help but be impressed.

"How very beautiful," I said, boldly stepping up to the Johnstone group. I had wanted a reason to approach them, and the gown was a perfect pretext.

Mrs. Johnstone was pleased by the impression the gown made. "Mrs. Chapman, isn't it lovely? We were just discussing whether to add another cluster of orange blossoms at the neck. What do you think? Mlle Langlois is helping us. I guess M. Worth is too busy today." She sniffed.

"Pardon, madame. As I told you, something most unexpected has come up for M. Worth. But, as you can see, he has put all of his artistry into the design of this gown. It is good, yes? We can proceed to alter it a little here and there when we try it on the mademoiselle." Mlle Langlois smiled at Lydia, who was sipping champagne. I noted the change in attitude towards wine in the showroom for this party. I assumed that, having landed the marital catch that was so welcome to her mother, the daughter now had the final say on both the drink and the dresses. She looked like she was enjoying her change of position.

"I won't be able to try it on today," she announced. "We still have to make some decisions about the two ball gowns and the going away suit." She was obviously enjoying her newfound importance. I imagined she would return as often as possible to continue to receive the unfamiliar deference from the staff and, more importantly, from her mother. She was reveling in it. She deigned to acknowledge me, as Mlle Langlois sent someone for another sprig of the wax orange blossoms. "Mrs. Chapman, how nice to see you. I don't believe we've seen you since the announcement of my engagement to Lord James."

"Congratulations. I hope you're very happy in your marriage. I understand Lord James is quite enthusiastic about going to Nebraska. He's mentioned it to me several times."

"Oh, yes, we've told him all about it and he's excited to come," Mrs. Johnstone told me.

But Lydia made a moue of discontent. "Yes, I suppose. The wedding will be back there and you can be sure they've never seen anything like this before." She gestured to the gown. "And nothing like Jimmy, either." She was enjoying her sense of proprietorship regarding the English aristocrat. "Oh, do join us, Mrs. Chapman. There's plenty of room." When I explained

I was there for a final fitting before delivery of my walking suit, Lydia insisted on seeing me in it.

While they moved on to some of the other outfits for her trousseau, I was led away to try on the suit. Sure enough, it was on a dressmaker's dummy, so I could consider myself immortalized in the attics of the House of Worth. I doubted I would ever have the resources to order more from them, but they knew their business. A seamstress, in a white shirtwaist, with billowing sleeves and a workmanlike pin cushion hanging from her waist, helped me into the skirt, blouse, and jacket, arranging the chains of decorative charms at the waist, pinching and pulling to get each seam in precise alignment, and finally perching the plush velvet hat on my head. When I saw myself in the standing mirror, I was transformed from an ordinary nondescript woman in a gray skirt and jacket into a vision of academic chic.

The soft gold of the skirt and jacket was decorated with a wide deep brown satin ribbon trim at the waist, the elbows, and dropping from the high neck. That touch had been added since my last fitting and it was just right, complementing the deep brown color and large fluffy feather of the toque. As far as I could see, it fit me perfectly.

The effect was even more pronounced when I walked out into the light of the main room and modeled the outfit for the Johnstone party. Mlle Langlois looked quite pleased, and I thought Mrs. Johnstone was somewhat appeased to see that M. Worth also did not appear for a protégé of Mrs. Palmer, on a day when he had avoided her. They all exclaimed at the aptness of the suit for me, with my academic aspirations. It was obvious the style would not suit Lydia, but she was happy to praise it as a style for me. She was so confident in her own opinions that day, that she even made some suggestions that I acknowledged with a smile, and promptly ignored.

Meanwhile, a model had come out wearing another outfit for the trousseau. I was at a loss for words when I realized it was an almost exact copy of the billowing white silk with bright yellow ribbons and yellow jacket, gloves, and boots that Edith had worn. I heard a faint gasp from Miss Brown, as well.

The sight gave me a perfect opportunity to introduce the topic of the dead girl. I had to swallow my distaste to speak. "Oh, dear, that is lovely. But it does remind me of poor Miss Stuart. I've been out of town. I was glad to find, when I returned, that young Mr. Palmer had been released by the police. But still, her death must be a great burden for all of you. It was so sad…so tragic…she was so young."

I heard Mrs. Johnstone sniff at this, but Lydia was perfectly willing to discuss it. She shook her head. "What a complete waste. We're all sorry about Edith, of course. But Papa has had the most awful time with the authorities and cabling home to her family. Just getting them to foot the bill to transport her home was a big struggle. Really, can you imagine? But I decided I won't let it blight the news of my engagement. I know Edith wouldn't want me to do that. I mean, we were a bit at odds at the end, but really it was her own fault. And, personally, I think it's a terrible way to thank us for all we did for her, jumping off the balcony like that. If she really felt that way, I don't know why she couldn't have waited until she went home to her own people. I'm sure if that's what she really wanted she would have had plenty of opportunities there."

"Oh, Lydia." Grace tried to stop her when she saw that Mrs. Johnstone had no intention of doing so.

"No, Grace, it's true. I think it was very petty of her. Very. She got herself into debt, you know, so she had only herself to blame. She was just jealous. She knew where it was going with Jimmy. Why, she even tried to get money from me. She threatened to tell a secret. As if it was that important."

"Lydia, please," Miss Brown interrupted.

"It's true. She knew I had promised him not to tell anyone he was afraid of heights and she threatened to gossip about it.

She said she'd tell everyone he refused to ride the Ferris wheel with me, and she and I went up together instead. As if anyone would believe that Jimmy had anything to do with that dead hat girl. She tried to say he could have killed the girl. I mean to say, how ridiculous is that? But I told her I didn't intend to give her a penny. She could tell the world for all I cared but if she did, I'd get Papa to take back the boat ticket to get her home. Then where would she be?" She seemed to notice that she was making the group uncomfortable. Shifting in her seat, she rearranged the skirts of her pink linen outfit. "Anyhow, she had no reason to jump from a balcony. Nobody would have let her starve, for heaven's sake."

She and her mother abruptly began a conversation with Mlle Langlois about the yellow ensemble, so I returned to the fitting room to change back into my own clothes and arrange for the suit to be delivered. It was apparent that the Johnstones believed Edith Stuart had killed herself. Despite their dislike for the Palmers, they had no suspicion that Honoré might have caused the young woman to fall to her death. Lydia's story confirmed that Edith *had* resorted to blackmail, but perhaps the reason for the blackmail was untrue. Lord James's secret did sound rather slight. Perhaps the real threat had to do with the Johnstones and not the English lord.

In the back of my mind I wondered about Mrs. Johnstone and her group. She and her husband had been at the earlier exposition. Their children would have met other young people there and could have recruited them. They were present at the jewel thefts. What if Edith Stuart knew about the thefts and even participated in them? Could that be the real reason for blackmail? Perhaps they had tried to get rid of the threat by sending her home. If that was the plan, it sounded like she had not cooperated. Did her plans to remain in Paris, even if not in their household, result in too dangerous a situation, so they had to deal with her? Unlike the Palmers, who had fallen from grace and were effectively expelled from society at the moment, the Johnstone family appeared to be at the top of the heap. They were enjoying the notoriety of their daughter's engagement, and certainly the gorgeous gowns, and no doubt the many planned receptions and balls would display Lydia as ripe and beautiful to the outside world. But I had the sense that something internal was rotten in that circumscribed little world. I just didn't know what it was yet. On the other hand, perhaps I was allowing my concern for the Palmers to prejudice me against them. Certainly Lord James must be close to them now and he had never spoken of any suspicions. But then he was a young man intent on marriage. He could be blind to any hints of wrongdoing.

I bade them goodbye on my way out, and Mrs. Johnstone urged me to attend the upcoming Fourth of July celebration, when the statue of Lafayette would be installed at the Louvre followed by a procession to the United States pavilion and then a reception. It amazed me that they would not be haunted by the memory of Edith Stuart on such an occasion, but both the mother and daughter seemed impervious.

"You must come," Mrs. Johnstone said. "I'm in charge of all of the arrangements this time. There will be no disturbances, you can count on it. And you should feel perfectly fine about wearing real jewels. We have complete assurances from Inspector Guillaume that there will be no thefts this time. I'm sure I'm sorry if the Palmers are too indisposed to attend, but everyone understands." She was quite an awful woman, but I smiled and walked away.

THIRTY-ONE

I was following one of the saleswomen, wending my way out through the display rooms, when I heard my name called faintly from behind. I stopped in the black and white room, surrounded by glass cases full of ornamental snuffboxes and fans, and Grace Greenway Brown caught up with me. She wore a modest black outfit with a plain black straw hat. It seemed to me she was Edith Stuart's only mourner.

"Excuse me, Mrs. Chapman, but may I speak with you before you leave?"

"Certainly." I thanked the saleswoman and told her I would find my way out, then turned back to Grace.

"I wanted to ask about Mr. Palmer. Can you tell me how he is?"

She was certainly politer than her companions, who had never asked after the sick man. "He's improving, thank you for asking. He's back at the house on rue Brignole, where Mrs. Palmer and my husband are keeping an eye on him. I've only just returned from the country and I haven't seen him myself. He's up and about but not well enough yet for outside activities." I wanted to know what Miss Brown thought of the death of her friend. This was an opportunity to sound her out away from the Johnstone family. "We're all very sorry about Miss Stuart. She was so young to meet such a tragic end."

She closed her eyes. "It was awful. And I'm sure you must find the callous attitude of Lydia and her mother quite shocking.

I can only say that Edith was not herself in those last days. She was acting very strangely." She looked at me as if asking me to forgive the dead girl.

"Lydia indicated that Edith tried to extort money from her. She must have been quite desperate." I was reminded that Lord James had said Edith had acted as if she were trying to seduce him. I wondered what Grace thought of that. She must have been a witness to the behavior, if it really happened.

She seemed to guess my thoughts. "She was very desperate and very unhappy. When Mr. Johnstone found out about her debts and planned to send her home, she did some deplorable things. But all she accomplished was to diminish herself in everyone's eyes. It was a very sad thing to see."

"Do you think she was really desperate enough to jump from that balcony?"

She moved to one of the tall windows before she replied. I stepped beside her and looked down to see people strolling below us on the rue de la Paix. It might have been just the height that Edith Stuart had fallen from on the Quai d'Orsay. The thought made me feel a touch like ice down my spine.

"Oh, I hate to think that she was that desperate. But she must have been, mustn't she? I know the police thought Honoré…the younger Mr. Palmer…was involved, but that couldn't be. He wouldn't do such a thing. Mrs. Chapman, can you tell me, has he really been released by the police? Are they convinced he had nothing to do with Edith's death? Is he clear now? I heard that Sonya Zugenev was able to tell the police that she was with him the whole time and so now he's safe. Is it true?" Her cheeks had reddened, and the blush spread to the tips of her ears, above small gold and pearl earrings. Her breath came fast.

I hastened to reassure her. "Yes, he was released. He's home now. Miss Zugenev told them that he was with her right before Edith fell to her death." She took a big breath at that, but then she bit her lip, as if keeping something back. I couldn't resist telling her more. "I believe Honoré and Sonya have been in each other's company almost constantly since his release. I've been told that an engagement may be pending, that they are only waiting for the elder Mr. Palmer to recover. The count, Sonya's father, has even come to Paris to meet the Palmers."

She let her breath out and looked down at a horse-drawn carriage in the street. A man jumped down and turned to help a woman, who balanced her parasol with one gloved hand and took his hand with the other. As she stepped down he tipped his head to avoid her wide hat, heavy with ribbons and floppy fabric flowers. When she was safely on the ground, he pulled her arm into his and bent to whisper in her ear. I couldn't see the woman's face, as it was shaded by the large hat, but she grasped his arm and leaned towards him as they stepped away.

Suddenly it occurred to me that there might also have been something between Miss Brown and Honoré. She smiled faintly and turned back to me. "Mrs. Chapman, there is something I should tell you. Edith was also attempting to get money from me. She threatened to tell Mrs. Palmer that her son and I had been meeting secretly. That afternoon—when the young milliner was killed—I was not at the Ferris wheel with Lydia and Edith, I was with Honoré. We were strolling through the gardens while the others rode the wheel." She clasped her hands at her waist. "You see, we met before Honoré's parents arrived in Paris. We have much in common. I assure you it was all very proper but, once Mrs. Palmer arrived, there was such animosity between her and Mrs. Johnstone we decided to be discreet." She crossed her arms and shook her head. "And then Mrs. Palmer got it into her head to pair Honoré with Sonya Zugenev. He didn't want to disappoint her. I told him it wasn't right, that he should introduce me to them properly. But he insisted it was only part of the flurry of activity having to do with the Exposition and his mother's duties as a commissioner. He assured me that she and his father would eventually be happy to receive me, but he wanted to wait until the Exposition was over to introduce me. He said that when we were all back home none of these European aristocrats would mean anything. He almost treated it as a little joke." She raised a gloved hand to her forehead as if it hurt. "We were foolish. But I suppose it was attractive to have a secret rendezvous here, in Paris, the most romantic city in the world. And when we could slip away, it was only the two of us. We did nothing wrong, I promise you. We talked and talked. He bought me flowers. We had coffee at cafés. We were lost in our own world and escaped to it whenever we could."

How simple that would be, with all the excitement of the Paris Exposition. With so much going on, a young couple could easily slip away and walk the streets together and no one would miss them, as long as they showed up at the functions they were expected to attend. Looking out at the bright sunshine on the street full of strolling people and the cafés under gently flapping awnings, I could see how the secretiveness of their actions might be seductive as well.

She looked at me earnestly. "After they found that milliner in the Worth exhibit, I told him we needed to admit we'd been together that afternoon. But he pleaded with me. He said there was no connection between him and the girl, so there was no reason to expose ourselves. By then he was sure his mother would be angry to have her marriage plans for him disrupted. He insisted that when he finally told her, she would be angry but would get over it, and he was sure he could depend on his father to support him. He was afraid that a revelation now would spoil his mother's plans and her enjoyment of her time as a commissioner for the Exposition, especially since I was traveling under the protection of the Johnstones. They are such rivals, Mrs. Johnstone and Mrs. Palmer." She shook her head again. I could tell from the way the words were spilling from her that she had been bottling all of this up inside for quite some time. She must have been worrying it all week, unable to confide in Lydia or Mrs. Johnstone.

She walked away, to the middle of the room, her heels clicking on the gleaming wooden floors. Turning back to me she said, "I never should have gone along with him. But he was so sure of himself. After the Worth reception, he got word to me that he was being followed by the police, so we could not meet. I had hoped to talk to him at the reception in the United States pavilion that night. I arranged to meet him in one of the side rooms. By then, Edith was threatening to expose our attachment. Honestly." She raised her hands as if surrendering. "I wanted to tell him that the secret meetings had to end. If he cared for me, he needed to tell his mother about me. I was going to tell him I was breaking it off unless he was honest with her." She took another large breath, lowering her hands to clutch them at her waist. "But then he arrived at the reception with Sonya on his arm…and when I went to the room where we were to have met, he never came."

She paused, as if overcome with emotion. But she raised her head and swallowed, then continued in a rush of sentences. "The Countess Olga came instead. She explained to me that Honoré would not be meeting me. She suggested that his regard for me, while real, was by no means exclusive. She said that, for a wealthy young man like him, one had to expect that he would have many experiences on his grand tour and that it would be wrong to assume an attachment." She paused and looked up to stare directly into my eyes. "She said the police believe he had a relationship with Miss Laporte before she died. I told her that was just ridiculous. I've known Honoré almost the entire time he's been here, even before his parents came, and he was *not* involved with that young woman. I'm certain of it." Grace shook her head as if to remove cobwebs from her mind.

It sounded like the countess was trying to disabuse her of any romantic idealization of Honoré Palmer. I was sure that she was wrong about his relationship with Denise Laporte but perhaps she was just repeating what the police suspected, in order to scare Miss Brown off.

Grace took a deep breath and let it out through her mouth. "She said that a young man like that doesn't know his heart and can be too free and open. She said she understood how I might be attracted to him, as she had seen the same thing happen with her own daughter who, she said, believed herself in love with the young man." She bit her lip before speaking again. "She begged me to break it off with Honoré, to allow him to contract a marriage that she said would be welcome to both families. I feel it is right to end our friendship."

I was saddened to think that the wishes of the Palmer and Zugenev families would come between two young people who had seemed to be forming an attachment. The proposed marriage between Honoré and Sonya was beginning to sound even more like a business arrangement. I was grateful that such considerations had never come up while Stephen and I were courting.

"I believe it is over between us," Grace continued. "I, too, have heard he'll probably become engaged to Sonya very soon. I understand. Sonya has been able to clear him from the accusation that he was responsible for Edith's death, which is incredible. But I want him to know...can you please tell him...that he should tell the police that we were together the afternoon when Denise Laporte was killed. There's no reason, now, for him to try to protect my reputation. It is nothing compared to the threat of the police believing he had something to do with her death. Will you tell him that for me? And tell him I am not distressed, I understand. I only hope that he and Sonya are happy and that his father is well."

She stood there in her black mourning, a small figure in a room that was entirely black and white—the floor tiles, the woodwork, the curtains, and even the paintings. It was very stark. I felt sorry for her and if, as I suspected, the Johnstones or someone in their circle was responsible for the thefts, I was sure she knew nothing about it. But Honoré might know something about the thefts. Perhaps that was what he was hiding from us. I could not tell.

Grace said goodbye and headed back to the main room, where she would have to endure the parade of gowns for her friend's trousseau, all the while conscious that her own romance had come to an end. It was an unpleasant prospect. But then, so much about the Johnstones was unpleasant. I needed to think about what Grace had told me.

It was refreshing to step through the wide blue door and out onto the busy sidewalk of rue de la Paix. Having a lot to think about, I decided to walk back to the rue Brignole. It was a warm and sunny day. Ladies strolled under parasols, holding the arms of men wearing light gray suits and the straw hats of summer. The street was wide with broad sidewalks, and horse-drawn carriages and an occasional motorcar paraded down the middle. I turned towards the column in Place Vendôme, which could be seen at the far end of the street. I had gone only a few steps when I recognized M. Worth standing, gesturing emphatically, at the edge of the sidewalk. He was talking to M. Poiret, who smiled as he stared up at workmen on ladders leaning against the storefront before them. I looked up to see what it was all about and everyone else in the vicinity looked up, too. A canvas cloth dropped down and I saw a flourishing series of gold letters that spelled out *Paul Poiret* above the glass walls below. It seemed M. Poiret had started his own house of fashion.

THIRTY-TWO

J ean-Philippe Worth shook his head and stalked away, back to
the great blue door of the House of Worth, only two buildings
down the block. M. Poiret greeted me, as I stood with my mouth
open. "Mme Chapman, congratulate me. Today is the first day of
the Paul Poiret *maison de couture*, my own house of fashion!"

"Congratulations. I had no idea you planned to open your own
shop. Was M. Worth also surprised?"

He laughed. "You might say so. Come." He took my elbow
and led me through the glass door. "*Magnifique*, is it not?" He
swept an arm around the room. It was modest compared to the
House of Worth, of course. A single large room, with light from
the floor-to-ceiling glass windows that faced the street. Tables
of luscious fabrics were placed close enough to the windows to
lure passersby. As you got deeper into the room, iron chandeliers
in the newest curlicue style hung from the ceiling, and S-shaped
plush couches, as well as exotic looking carved tables, were placed
around a large oriental rug. I realized that M. Poiret, too, was
using Art Nouveau elements in his design. There were vases and
lamps with the curvy, fantastic shapes that made you think of a
dream, or of how the world looked when it flashed by as you rode
a carousel. The gowns and walking suits displayed on several wax
figures were of a simple form that somehow fit with the climbing
vines and curlicues of the room's decorations. It made a strong
impression on me.

M. Poiret seemed satisfied by my reaction. "*Bon*. You like it, yes?"

"It's quite wonderful."

He grinned at me. "Perhaps you must have one of my creations."

"I'm sure I couldn't afford it."

"Ah, but you see, one of the things I learned from Worth and Doucet—you dress the women who are admired by other women and then they all come. It is an investment. I know several actresses from my time at Worth. I will offer them something unique. They will wear it, and everyone will be amazed and say, 'I must have that as well!'" He was rubbing his hands together in anticipation.

"I'm afraid no one would see it, if I wore your creation," I told him. "I'm only a social secretary, not an actress. And, right now, poor Mrs. Palmer is not attending social functions because her husband is still recovering."

"So I have heard. I am very sorry for what has happened. But Mrs. Palmer, now there is a lady whose style is copied by everyone." There was a glint in his eye, so I knew he had hopes that I would somehow help him to sell his wares to my employer. Poor Bertha, she was not in any shape to care for new gowns. But I would not confide in him about that.

There was a handsome walking suit on one of the wax figures. I stepped towards it, but M. Poiret led me to another figure wearing a coat of black wool that hung straight down in graceful folds. "You see this? The Princess Bariatinsky, she refused it! And M. Worth, he complains to me. She tells him when fellows run after her sleigh she has their heads cut off and she says, 'We put them in sacks just like that.' Sacks! Can you imagine? It was the end. It was, as you say, the last straw. I can no longer work there. You will see. The great Réjane, the actress, you know? She will wear it. She was made famous by the cloak I made for her in *Zara*. She knows how to carry it off."

Somehow I doubted that wearing his creation was what had made the actress famous. More likely it was *she* who had advanced *his* career by the move, but I hid a smile. Turning to admire a beautiful gown in transparent tulle over taffeta, with a high waist and a very straight skirt, I said to him, "So, it's not just the fried potatoes anymore?"

He grinned. "No, indeed. It will be everything. You will see. I will revolutionize the couture. It is my time."

I suppose he had to have that amount of confidence to start such a bold enterprise two doors down from the House of Worth. "Well, I wish you very good luck. It must have taken a great deal of money to start out on your own like this."

"Luck, it helps with the money," he told me. "But, for the success, it is talent that is needed. For the money, some luck at the racetrack, some interested investors, some lady friends who have money, it is all that is required. But now the talent will make the success."

I saw two saleswomen in the corner of the room. The stock and the staff must have been quite costly. Suddenly, I recognized Mlle Arquette as one of the women. I must have looked surprised, as M. Poiret said to me, "Yes, you see Mademoiselle has come with me." He beckoned her over. "She recognizes the talent, the future!"

I exchanged greetings and the woman gave me a little curtsy. I could see why M. Worth was not happy with the move of his protégé. But, then, apparently M. Worth had not liked the designs of M. Poiret—it was his brother, Gaston, who had hired the younger man. I had assumed that Mlle Arquette was a fixture at the House of Worth. It seemed I was wrong. Either she had a lot of confidence in the designs of the young Poiret or she had some other link to him that made her give up her position to join the new house. It was curious.

I wished them success again and left the new store, deciding to continue walking back to the rue Brignole. I had a lot to think about. I wondered about how Poiret had been able to come up with all of the money that must have been needed. I couldn't help thinking of the jewel thefts and how timely they might have been for a young designer who needed cash to start his own maison de couture. He and Mlle Arquette had both been present at the events where the robberies happened. And as for Denise Laporte, they both would have known the young woman. Despite reports that her lover was a foreigner and the claims that her lover was Mr. Palmer, I wondered if Poiret could be the father of her child? Certainly they would have met at Worth and possibly—if she made demands just when he was about to put all of his resources and energy into starting his own establishment—it might have caused a problem for him. If he had committed, or participated in, the robberies and she knew about it, her silence would be critical to the success of his plans. I could picture him fuming at hearing of the rejection of the coat by the Russian princess. What would he do if he then had to face the demands of a pregnant mistress? Would he succumb to rage? It was not a pretty picture but it was possible.

Still, all of this was nothing but imagining. The father of Denise Laporte's unborn child might have been anyone. The police thought that it was Honoré Palmer, as the countess suggested to Grace. I knew that couldn't be, but why not Poiret? Or even Lord James? M. Jean-Philippe Worth was known to have kept a mistress in the past. After all, his daughter was the child of such a relationship. And what about Mlle Andrée? Could she have discovered a liaison of her father's and been moved to strangle the girl? Or what about her fiancé, Louis Cartier? In some ways I would have preferred to find the culprit in the Johnstone household, but it seemed unlikely to me that Mr. Johnstone would have had such a relationship. I was ashamed to admit that I found Lydia so unlikeable that I could imagine her strangling the girl, but what would her motive have been? I knew it was even more likely that the man in Denise's life was someone I knew nothing about but somehow I was still convinced that her death was related to the jewel thefts. They had stopped while Honoré Palmer was imprisoned. Now that he was released, would they start again? I supposed women with valuable jewels must have heard about the thefts and would now be on their guard. Perhaps they were all taking the advice of Mr. Johnstone and wearing fakes until the police caught the thief.

I was lost in my musing when suddenly I heard my name called. Looking up, I saw that I was in Place Vendôme, in front of the new Ritz hotel. Turning, I saw Consuelo Vanderbilt stepping down from her carriage. She greeted me with a warmth that could only come from a young woman who was bored by the formal duties that fell to her so often. I had to remind myself that she was now the Duchess of Marlborough. She swept me up, insisting I join her in the hotel's garden café. My company would allow her to dismiss both her female companion, who followed her like a lap dog, and the male relation detailed to accompany her. I took pity and agreed to lunch with her.

How could I refuse an invitation to join the throngs of beautifully dressed women seated on light green chairs, at tables covered with white linen and decorated with delicate vases of irises and lilies? We were promptly seated under one of the pastel-striped awnings in the garden, which was tucked away at the center of the building, surrounded by pots of rose bushes, and open to the sky. Across from us there was a line of small green trees with lights strung festively in their branches. The entire area hummed with the conversations of women under their enormous hats, all of them wearing high-necked summer frocks of silk trimmed with falls of delicate lace. There was a scent of roses in the air.

We were quickly supplied with a porcelain teapot and cups. The gleam of silver and shine of crystal made it all seem very new. The linen napkins at each place were even trimmed with lace. Sitting down with a view of the pretty garden, I looked across at Connie's dark brown eyes, set in her oval face. She did indeed look a bit desperate in her boredom. As she told me of the many formal receptions and salons she was required to attend, my mind was moving in the background, forming a plan.

She seemed to want to hear about my life outside the stiff circles she inhabited. In an unfailingly polite manner, she questioned me closely about all of my activities. I could see she was envious of the time I'd spent with Mary Cassatt at Beaufresne. She pouted and complained she would never be allowed to get away like that. I was going to explain the very unhappy circumstances that had led to my flight from Paris, but on the spur of the moment I decided, instead, to recruit her. If there was anyone who could be more enticed by the opportunity to help trap a jewel thief, I doubted I was acquainted with them. And if there was any risk in my plan, I thought the Duchess of Marlborough was well able to cope with it. Besides, she was there, and she was in need of some excitement. That was my only excuse for involving her. But, for myself, I needed to take some action. I was at a dead end when it came to discovering how the two women had died and who was ultimately responsible. But it still seemed that we ought to at least be able to identify the jewel thief. And I was convinced that if we did so the threads would lead us back to the strangling death of one woman and the fall to her death of the other. The current stalemate was so frustrating that I was sure the action of laying a trap would shake something loose, so I was determined to at least try.

THIRTY-THREE

I left the duchess, feeling it was I who had done her a favor, rather than the other way around. She was almost too enthusiastic, but I was satisfied. It didn't stop me from being troubled by the whole situation of the Palmers but I felt I had a plan to address at least one part of the dilemma—the thefts. I had doubts, of course, but I had to do something, and I suppose being freed from my duties as social secretary and mother left me ripe for mischief—like one of my children with nothing to occupy him or her. I did miss the little monsters, but I knew they were having a splendid time running around Miss Cassatt's garden and pestering poor Mathilde. I needed to do what I could to help the Palmers and then either bring the children back or return to them in the country.

One unpleasant task I felt compelled to tackle was confronting Honoré Palmer. I needed to know if what Grace Greenway Brown had told me was the truth. It was not a conversation I wanted to have with him in the company of others when he acted as host at dinner that evening. But when he excused himself to visit his father, who was still not joining the household for dinner, I also rose, pleading a headache from my excursions during the day. Stephen managed to hide his surprise, trusting I would explain later. I got a book and parked myself in the hallway outside the elder Mr. Palmer's room. I hoped Bertha would not see me, but it was worth the risk to be in a position to force Honoré to talk to me.

When the door opened I heard murmured good nights, so I stood. My luck held, as it was Honoré who left, quietly closing the door behind him. "Mrs. Chapman. Are you wanting to speak to my mother? I could tell her you're here."

Before he could reenter the room I stopped him. "No, Mr. Palmer, actually I was hoping to speak to you." He looked confused. Why would his mother's social secretary need to speak to him? "I saw Miss Brown today and she asked me to give you a message."

His eyes widened and his face fell into an expression almost of grief. It took him a moment to recover. Glancing at the door, as if to make sure no one within could overhear, he extended a hand. "Please, won't you come to the library with me? I don't want to discuss it here."

I led the way quietly down the stairs and to the tall door of the library. He opened it, and led me into the book-lined room, furnished with chairs upholstered in soft leather and a large desk in one corner. French windows were partially open to the garden. The room was beside the suite my family occupied. We took armchairs opposite each other, facing the fireplace, which was empty on such a mild summer night. He had composed himself during our walk down and waited for me to speak.

"Miss Brown confided in me that the two of you had been spending time together. She's anxious that you should feel free to tell the police, and your parents, that you were with her the afternoon that Miss Laporte was killed." He grimaced at the mention of his parents. "She says that this will make it clear to them that you could not have been the one responsible for the milliner's death. She said she is willing and able to support you in such a statement. You were with her that afternoon, weren't you?"

"It seems so long ago now, doesn't it?" he asked. He looked pale and strained, but not agitated, as if he were resigned to my questions. "Yes, we had met many times before and, that afternoon, while her friends rode the Ferris wheel, we took the opportunity to walk through the fairgrounds together." He smiled faintly at the memory. "Miss Brown did nothing wrong. I first met her here in Paris before my parents arrived. We became friends. She is a completely innocent and proper young lady. It was my idea to meet in secret. It was foolish, but I assure you, Mrs. Chapman, it was entirely innocent. It was just that my mother and Mrs. Johnstone did not get along."

"You formed an attachment? You became close? It seems to me that Miss Brown is most anxious about your welfare."

He stiffened. "No, no. You misunderstood her. I'm afraid my actions have jeopardized her reputation as well as the well being of my parents. It was my foolishness that led to secretiveness, it was only a whim," he insisted, as if trying to convince himself. "My mother introduced me to the Countess Olga and her daughter. Sonya has been very good to me. That is where my affections lie. We are very close...very close. I was wrong to mislead Miss Brown with my attentions. That was before I met Sonya, and it's entirely my fault if she or anyone else got the wrong impression from our meetings. Entirely my fault." He wasn't looking at me as he declared this.

"And what about Denise Laporte? Were you also seeing her before you met Sonya Zugenev?"

He looked surprised. "Good Lord, no," he said. "I didn't know Denise Laporte. The police want to believe I did, but it's not true."

Perhaps the countess had merely repeated something she heard from the police, or perhaps she had jumped to a conclusion about his relations with the dead milliner. On the other hand, it could be that Countess Olga had exaggerated, in order to shock Miss Brown into giving up her connection to Honoré.

"I see. And what about Miss Stuart? Did she also have the wrong impression?"

He grimaced, as if he had closed his mouth on a sore tooth. "That poor young woman was so wrong about so many things. She said she would expose us to my mother and Mrs. Johnstone—

I mean Miss Brown and myself. She never said anything about Miss Laporte. Miss Stuart was desperate for money. She had debts. Mr. Johnstone was outraged when he heard of them, and he was going to send her home. But there was nothing I could do for her. I hadn't the funds to help her, and I told her so. And she was wrong in any case. There was nothing between Miss Brown and myself. I'd met Sonya by then." Again he stared into the empty fireplace.

"You weren't meeting Miss Stuart that night on the balcony, then?"

"What? No, I just happened to be there." He shivered and I remembered how he looked that night, staring over the railing at the body below.

"I thought Sonya Zugenev said you were with her."

"What? Yes, yes. I was with Sonya. We went out onto the balcony. We looked over the railing and we both saw...what we saw. Sonya screamed then."

I was unconvinced. It seemed to me he was a young man who was caught in a web that would prevent him from escaping a destiny planned for him by others. He seemed resigned to his fate—to return to Chicago with an aristocratic bride and enter the political game as his mother wished—as the way to make reparations for the damage he had caused. I was sure he felt responsible for his father's alarming collapse and his mother's anguish. But I was not at all convinced that he had really relinquished his feelings for Grace Greenway Brown. It made me wonder how big a shock it would be to him if the intrigues I was planning to expose turned out to be as rotten as I suspected. But my suspicion was not enough, I had to be sure.

"Oh, there you are." Lord James was at the door. "I'm sorry, am I interrupting? We were supposed to go out tonight. Did you want to put it off, Honoré?"

"No, no. That's all right. If you'll excuse me, I'll just get my coat and be right with you." Honoré hurried away, leaving me with the Englishman.

"Mrs. Palmer asked me to take him out, to a café. She said he was too much at home and she asked me to try to relieve the gloom, don't you know."

I considered the tall young man. He presented some possibilities. "The jewel thefts stopped while Honoré was arrested, didn't they?" I realized the question was somewhat abrupt, but I was determined to continue my investigations into the thefts.

"I believe so. I haven't heard of any more."

"I'm afraid the police may still suspect him, even if he *has* been released. And if another robbery happens, now that he's free, they're bound to think it was him."

He frowned. "Don't worry. We'll be at a cabaret. There won't be any society women with their jewels there. No danger of that."

"No, but until the thief strikes again, at a time when Honoré Palmer could *not* have done it, he won't be cleared of suspicion. Don't you see?" He looked surprised but I proceeded to quickly outline part of my plan, warning him not to tell Honoré, but recruiting him to help. Leaving Honoré in the dark was part of the plan that was coming together in my mind.

"Certainly. I'll be escorting Miss Johnstone. I'll do anything to help. But aren't you taking a big risk with the Duchess of Marlborough's jewel? As you say, the thief is bound to be tempted by the Sunrise Ruby, everybody's heard of it. It's the most perfect pigeon's blood ruby I've ever seen. She wears it in a gold necklace. It's spectacular. What if it's stolen? Can you be absolutely sure if that happened they wouldn't still blame it on him? Are you sure you want to tempt the fates that way?"

At that moment Honoré returned and Lord James was forced to leave without having his questions answered. In truth, I knew that I was tempting the fates, as he said. And his wariness was not uncalled for. Nonetheless, I was determined to proceed with my plan. I didn't share my suspicions with him, in case they turned out to be wrong, but I wondered exactly how shocked Lord James himself would be by the outcome.

THIRTY-FOUR

My next recruit was also somewhat skeptical. "You've convinced the Duchess of Marlborough to wear the Sunrise Ruby of Burma to the Fourth of July celebration at the United States pavilion, and you expect the thief to attempt to steal it?" Countess Olga's forehead wrinkled in a frown as she thought about this.

I'd visited her at her home in Faubourg Saint-Germain to tell her about my idea, not wanting to speak of it in front of the Palmers. The less they knew of my plan the better. Especially if it didn't succeed. We sat in a luxurious parlor, decorated in the style of Louis XIV, with spindly gilded chairs upholstered in embroidered silks, and very tall ceilings and windows. She had called for tea in a Russian samovar and small cakes sticky with honey.

"Yes. It's the only way to clear Mr. Palmer's name. The fact that the thefts stopped while he was imprisoned has made it seem suspicious to the police. They still believe he's behind them. If we can draw out the thief or thieves at a time when he's not present, at least they'll have to admit he isn't responsible for the robberies. Then, perhaps, they'll look beyond Honoré for the person who really strangled Miss Laporte."

She looked thoughtful. "But it is possible the thief might succeed in stealing the ruby, isn't it? My jewels were retrieved, but only when that poor woman fell from the balcony and Mrs.

Palmer's pearls were returned only when a dead body was found."
She shivered. "The other jewels are gone, is it not so? Andreé
Worth still does not have her sapphire. Does the duchess realize
the risk she is taking?"

"Yes, yes. She's perfectly aware. To tell you the truth, I think
she's thrilled by the thought of it. I suspect that particular
necklace may have been a gift from her husband that she does not
particularly value." I shrugged. "In any case, she knows the risk
and is eager to take it. But what I wanted to beg of you is to help
me keep an eye on the necklace. You yourself have experienced
a theft, and you can be present at places, like the ladies' parlor,
where the thief might strike."

She didn't immediately agree to help. "You believe that is
where it happened? It is possible, of course. It was in the ladies'
parlor that I realized my jewels were gone, but I am not sure
about the other thefts."

"It's hard to say positively, since we don't know who's behind
them. But we do know that on every occasion that a jewel was
stolen, staff from the House of Worth were present and helping
in the ladies' parlor. It's a place where a woman might remove a
jewel while having her hair arranged or might be distracted by
other things. It's at least possible."

"You suspect the House of Worth staff, then?"

"Who knows? But Inspector Guillaume is convinced that these
robberies repeat a string that happened during the 1889 exposition.
Surely Jean-Philippe Worth and his staff could have been present
then, as well. Who better to recruit young people who are in debt
to help with the thefts? They couldn't risk carrying the jewels out
themselves but how simple to remove them from one lady in the
parlor, pass them to another and have her deliver them at a later
date in exchange for money? Eleven years ago there might have
been young people seduced into doing it, and now, well, there is
his daughter, Andrée, and her fiancé, Louis Cartier. Who better
to know who has, and will wear, which jewels than the designer

who designs the gown to be worn with a specific jewel and who better to know which jewels are worth taking and how to sell them than a jeweler?"

"You think Worth and Cartier might work together on this? And involve their own children? It is too scandalous."

"It's only a theory. But perhaps it worked years ago when they were younger, and the temptation to do it again when there is another exposition was too great. But that's only one possible solution. Did you know that Paul Poiret has opened his own house of fashion?" She didn't. "And Mlle Arquette has left Worth to join him." She raised an eyebrow. "Yes, I was surprised, too. It must have taken an awful lot of money to go out on his own like that. He has a storefront just a few doors down from the House of Worth and he has several other saleswomen, in addition to Mlle Arquette. He claims the money came from his winnings at the races and wealthy backers, but what if he's the thief? He also might have done the robberies eleven years ago or he might have just heard of them and, with the help of Mlle Arquette, he might have imitated the Pied Piper of the past. She would have been in a position to find young women who needed money, like Edith, to help with the thefts, and he could have found young men, at the horse races or other gambling places, who needed money enough to participate."

The countess still looked doubtful but she didn't argue with me, so I continued. "And another possibility is Mrs. Johnstone, or she and her husband. Think of it. They were here eleven years ago. At that time their sons were with them. They could have recruited other young people to help with the robberies. I always thought it was a mistake to assume the Pied Piper was a man. Mrs. Johnstone's ambitious and, while they are supposed to be wealthy, perhaps part of that wealth is from the thefts at the last exposition. What if this time they arranged for Mr. Johnstone to be one of the main organizers and brought their daughter to lure other young people into the plan? What if Edith Stuart was part of it, but she got greedy? What if she threatened to expose them? I thought it was too harsh of Mr. Johnstone to send her home, but what if that was to keep her quiet and, when she wouldn't go, well, perhaps someone *did* throw her from that balcony.

"And Denise Laporte was helping in the ladies' parlors, too. What if she died, not because of the man who fathered her unborn child, but because of something she saw? Perhaps she saw the thefts and tried to get money from the thieves to support herself and her child."

"What is it you wish *me* to do?"

"Only to be on guard, to watch. I was thinking we could ask you to spend as much time as possible in the ladies' parlor when the duchess goes there. I can't be by her side all the time or people will be suspicious. But you could follow her in, or even precede her, to fix something or to fix Sonya's gown."

"Sonya should not be a part of this."

"Certainly, certainly. We won't tell her anything about it." The other possible outcome would be that no one attempted to steal the jewel because Honoré *was* really behind the thefts. It was something I wouldn't mention to his future mother-in-law, and I tried to keep it from my own thoughts as well, but, if I was all wrong in my suppositions, it was still possible. If Honoré was involved, who could tell if little Sonya had not been seduced into helping him? I didn't believe it but, until we found the real thief, it would be possible for others to believe. To stave off these thoughts I had a different story to tell. It was pretty fantastic, but I said it anyway. "There's always the slightest possibility that it's Inspector Guillaume who's the Pied Piper."

She looked shocked. "You cannot mean it. The policeman? It is not possible."

"It's unlikely, I know, but he's the one who told us about the Pied Piper in the first place, and who would be better positioned to recruit young people? Once he was called in to investigate the thefts, who would be in a better place to plan more of them and make sure they were successful? I hear that he recently married the daughter of the Commissaire of Police. He was promoted very quickly. Can he be trusted? I know it's hard to believe, but what if he's the one behind the thefts?"

"If the inspector was involved, then laying a trap could be very dangerous."

"Yes, but it would also be much harder to make sure Honoré is completely cleared of all suspicion by any other action." I thought her concern for her daughter's future would ensure her cooperation and I was right.

"Yes, I will help. But you and I alone will do this?"

"Not entirely. I'll ask Lord James to help. But not the Palmers, they will know nothing. My husband and perhaps a few others will also help. Of course the duchess knows and, at worst, she could lose her jewel, but if Honoré is not there, at least we can make sure he can't be charged with the thefts and the police will be forced to look elsewhere. I assure you, the duchess is completely willing to cooperate."

"Then how can I refuse?"

I left the splendid old aristocratic mansion satisfied that I could count on her to join in with my plan. But she was only one piece on the board, and I had others to position.

It had been a simple matter to convince Lord James to participate as well. Having enlisted the duchess, the countess, and the English nobleman, I reluctantly concluded that I should also consult with Inspector Guillaume.

THIRTY-FIVE

Y ou have persuaded the Duchess of Marlborough to wear the very famous jewel to the reception at the pavilion of the United States in order to tempt the thief?" Inspector Guillaume hulked large, but calm, behind his wide desk. It occurred to me that if I had come to Detective Whitbread in Chicago with my plan he would have jumped up and started yelling at me. The Frenchman was taciturn in comparison.

"Yes. She's quite willing to do it," I said. I was still standing, although he'd offered me a chair. I was too full of my plans to sit down. "You've got to see that this will prove Honoré Palmer could *not* have been involved with the thefts. And, if he's not the thief, it's very unlikely he would have harmed either of the dead women, don't you see?"

He crossed his arms over his chest and raised a hairy eyebrow.

"Sonya Zugenev has already said he could not have harmed Edith Stuart. And now Miss Grace Greenway Brown has told me that she was with Mr. Palmer all afternoon the day that Denise Laporte was killed. He couldn't have done it."

"M. Palmer is most fortunate in the testimony of his young lady friends."

I silently cursed the French preoccupation with love. It seemed to me the inspector would never believe anything a woman said about a man for whom there might be any suspicion of an attachment. I despaired of it. "What will it take to convince you that Mr. Palmer is innocent?" I asked.

He sighed. "Do sit down, madame."

Reluctantly, I perched on one of the hard chairs opposite him. From the corner of my eye I could see the miniature guillotine. I glared at the inspector. I had to get him to give up the notion that Honoré was responsible for any of this.

"We have been to the rooms that Denise Laporte shared with her lover," he told me. "My men learned that there had been a tall Englishman and a woman there before them." He raised an eyebrow.

"Well, yes. Lord James and I discovered the address, from an artist that Denise posed for." I was determined to keep Miss Cassatt and M. Degas out of it. "We spoke to the landlady, but she couldn't tell us much that was useful." Nothing she had told us could eliminate the vile suspicions of Honoré that the police were pursuing.

"Really? Perhaps the questioning of French citizens should be left to the French policemen."

"What do you mean? Did you find out something?"

"The identity of Denise Laporte's lover," he said. "But we have reason to believe that man could not be the Pied Piper."

Then it wasn't Honoré Palmer, since they still thought he was the thief. Inspector Guillaume sat with his eyes partly hooded, looking like a cat that was playing with a mouse. What was he hiding? I was losing patience. "But it is not Mr. Palmer, is it? Do you believe me now...that Mr. Palmer is innocent?"

He unfolded his arms and bent forward to page through a pile of papers stacked on his desk. "We must find the thief, the Pied Piper. Once he is caught, M. Palmer will be cleared...if he is not the man."

"What makes you think it has to be a man?" I asked. It had annoyed me from the beginning that the police made this assumption. It showed a prejudice I didn't share. In fact, I was certain a woman was involved.

He held up a folder that was thick with papers. "Here is the file from the thefts at the earlier exposition. There were several suspects but we were unable to prove the guilt of any of them. They were all men. We have been investigating their whereabouts and backgrounds. Two are dead. Another is in jail. Three have disappeared. They most certainly left France. We have sent for information from Germany, England, and America, where they may have gone. We await more information. It was believed the man worked with at least one woman who was not one of the young people of good family who we knew were corrupted. Her identity was never exposed." He still seemed very certain that the mastermind behind the thefts was a man. That undermined some assumptions I had been making.

"How long will it take to track down the men from before? The Exposition could be over and he or she could disappear again, couldn't they? Wouldn't it be better to do what I propose? How could such a major jewel thief resist the Sunrise Ruby of Burma? Especially since he or she has concocted a method that was so successful already? Surely the thief won't pass up the chance to at least try to take it. And, when that happens, I assure you it will *not* be Honoré Palmer."

"You are aware that the robberies ceased when M. Palmer was under arrest? In fact, he has been present at all of the events where jewels were stolen. Even if you were correct about Mr. Palmer, what makes you think the thief will strike this time if the young man is *not* present?"

It was true. The thief seemed intent on implicating Honoré by only committing the crimes when he was present. Perhaps it was done in an effort to make him look guilty, I couldn't tell. I had hoped to keep him away, but I could see the inspector had spotted a flaw in my plan. "We'll just have to get him to come and make sure the thief knows it." Bertha Palmer would not be happy. She was still avoiding engagements, with her husband's illness as her excuse. She made sure her son also refused invitations. But I was confident I could convince him to attend, even if we had to hide it from his mother. After all, Honoré wanted to clear his name.

I was arguing with the inspector about the feasibility of my plan when there was a knock on the door and a uniformed officer delivered a large envelope. Inspector Guillaume dismissed him and emptied the contents onto his desk. It was from Scotland Yard. It was followed by a telegram from America.

To my surprise, he allowed me to stay as he reviewed the information. I helped to interpret the English language documents. Our joint review uncovered a number of interesting and suggestive facts that not only reinforced some of my suspicions about the thefts, but clarified the motive for the death of poor Denise Laporte. Guillaume confirmed some of the details with further telephone calls and telegrams. He sent some of his men out to gather additional evidence. By the end of the day, we both realized what had really happened. They even arrested a guard from the Worth exhibit.

Suddenly, the outline of that horrid crime—the murder of Denise Laporte—crystallized in my mind. With this new knowledge, I was more uneasy about risking the lives of some of my confederates, but Guillaume quite sensibly pointed out that provoking a confession was the only way we could be sure to put a stop to what was happening. He also warned that if Honoré Palmer attended and the jewel was stolen, he could still be seen as the guilty party. In that case, he would be forced to arrest the young man. There was no guarantee that my plan would work.

That discussion sent me hurrying back to the Duchess of Marlborough with an additional request. She was entirely willing to help in the matter. And she accompanied me on one last sad excursion to prepare ourselves for the confrontation.

By then the trap was set. I had only to wait for the culprit to walk into it to see it sprung.

THIRTY-SIX

J uly fourth dawned bright and warm. Festivities were scheduled for the whole day, beginning with a breakfast hosted by the French, followed by the dedication of the statue of Lafayette at the Louvre, a luncheon, and then a parade from the museum to the fairgrounds, ending at the United States pavilion. There one of the wealthy American bankers was hosting a five-course dinner, followed by dancing on the main floor.

Mrs. Johnstone was in her glory, preening herself in three different Worth outfits during the course of the day. I heard she started with a tight fitting, shiny black walking suit that imitated one of Bertha Palmer's, only with too much jet, and then, for the luncheon, she wore a bright pink silk gown with a white lace fichu and a large black velvet rose in the middle of her bosom. By evening she was resplendent in a gown of pale gold silk, embellished with sequins that almost formed a suit of armor over her chest. Reserving the fourth floor ladies' parlor as her changing room was her prerogative until each event began.

She had made all of the arrangements this time, but whatever problems arose—from a lack of silverware, insufficient carriages for the official guests, or cold beef due to the distance between the kitchen and dining tables—it was all blamed on the French staff. Not surprisingly, she took credit for any successes, like the weather, or the very French strict adherence to the schedule.

She'd been forced to invite the Palmers, due to Bertha's official position. But, of course, they declined. Everyone knew that Potter Palmer was still recuperating, so that was expected. On the other hand, when the Palmers asked my husband and me to represent them, we readily agreed and Mrs. Johnstone had to accept our presence.

By the time the day came, everyone knew the Duchess of Marlborough would attend as an American, and that she would be wearing the Sunrise Ruby. It was all the talk of the expatriate American drawing rooms, some expressing admiration for her boldness in the face of the thefts, others condemning her actions as rash. The whispered gossip was concerned with whether an attempted robbery would demonstrate the innocence of Honoré Palmer or, if there was no such attempt, and he was not present, would that condemn him. His mother counseled him to avoid all gossip by remaining at home with her and his father. But, as I had promised the inspector, my husband and I convinced the young man to attend. We all three avoided the earlier ceremonies, arriving just in time for the dinner and dancing.

"Are you quite sure it is safe?" Countess Olga asked me, once we were seated at a table with her.

"He wanted to come. He wants to show everyone that he's blameless and unashamed of his actions. He believes this is the only way to proclaim his innocence. Besides, he was anxious to dance with Sonya," I told her. What I didn't tell her was that Inspector Guillaume had assigned two of his best men—who were dressed in evening clothes—to watch him the entire evening. They would be able to vouch for his whereabouts, should anything untoward occur.

The countess was once again wearing the white and silver gown encrusted with pearls and finished off with the Zugenev family jewels. But she had substituted a spray of diamond flowers in her hair, instead of the tiara, and the bracelet that had played a part in the tragedy the last time we were at the pavilion was missing from her arm. Her daughter wore a new ball gown of ivory silk decorated with sprays of artificial pink roses and white jasmine-like flowers that crossed the bodice, running down the skirt to where the hem was looped up over an underskirt, almost like curtains. Sheer chiffon puffed sleeves covered her shoulders. It seemed bride-like in its simplicity. There would be no call for a thief to target her, since she wore no jewels, other than tiny pearl drop earrings. Seated beside Honoré, she looked up at him with timid admiration. She was quite a lovely young woman.

Inspector Guillaume was also present in evening dress. He walked over to our table and laid a heavy hand on the young man's shoulder, leaning forward to speak to the rest of us. "It is most pleasant to see all of you here. I hope M. Potter Palmer is feeling better. As I am sure you are aware, my men are here in full force tonight." He nodded towards a uniformed officer at the door. "The English duchess declares her confidence by wearing a precious stone. She is most brave, is she not?" We all looked at the head table, where the Duchess of Marlborough sat with the Johnstone family and the ambassador. I spotted Lord James in their party. Of course he would be seated with his future in-laws. He blushed when he nodded to us.

"We are here to represent Mr. and Mrs. Palmer, Inspector. Unfortunately, Mr. Palmer is not sufficiently recovered to attend. But fortunately Mr. Honoré Palmer was able to accompany us." I said it as a sort of challenge and he stared at me for a moment, then nodded.

"The day has been most successful so far, and it will continue without any disturbing incident, I promise you," he said. Bowing, he moved off.

Naturally, that caused all of us to remember the last time we had been in the pavilion and the tragic end to that evening. I could see the memory gave Honoré some distress. Looking across to the head table, I wondered what the Johnstones were thinking. Surely they must recall Edith Stuart, as we all did. I noticed Miss Brown staring in our direction.

"It is so good you have come," Sonya told Honoré. "I can be sure to dance now, is it not so?" I suspected that she had also noticed Miss Brown's eyes on our party. Poor Miss Brown.

"Yes, of course. I'll be happy to dance with you," Honoré said, after a pause. No young man ever looked less like he wanted to dance, but he was nothing if not schooled in politeness. I thought, rather cynically, that he would make an adequate politician, after all.

After the meal, we were directed to the main hall at the center of the building where the chairs and couches had been moved out of the way for the dancing. A five-piece orchestra was tuning up. I glanced up at the second floor and saw that the curtains had been closed to prevent anyone from accessing the balcony where the tragedy had occurred. There were two Marines standing at attention in front of the stairways. Mrs. Johnstone was making a statement. She was dropping the curtain on the tragedy of Edith Stuart and nothing of that sort would be allowed to happen again on her watch.

As before, I wore the gown with cherries at my waist, along with my mother's pearls. I was quite confident that the jewel thief would have no interest in my simple necklace. I danced with Stephen, then we retreated to the side for a brief rest. Careful to be discreet, I watched as Mrs. Johnstone monopolized the Duchess of Marlborough, making a great fuss over her and the man beside her. It was her husband, the duke, making a rare appearance with her. He had just arrived, having been detained by some business dealings, and thus had missed the dinner.

The ruby was large and very, very red. I had heard it was called a "pigeon's blood red" because it was darker than other types of rubies and I had also learned that variety was only found in Burma. The gem itself, and its golden setting, glowed against the duchess's white skin, complementing her patterned velvet gown of black, which was imprinted with white lilies and sprinkled with a few small red satin rosebuds. With her long neck and elaborately arranged dark hair, she was stunningly beautiful. We traded nods cautiously across the room, not wanting to be seen too much together.

"The duchess looks magnificent and she's worn the jewel, just as everyone expected," Stephen said. "Are you quite sure this is safe?"

"No, but I'm sure she's willing to take the risk. She looks bored. Why don't you dance with her?"

"Me?"

"Yes, we want everyone to get a good look so they know it's real, don't we?"

"Your wish is my command." He made a little mock-bow and left me, making his way towards the duchess.

I looked around and saw M. Worth and M. Louis Cartier on the right side of the room, while Paul Poiret looked smug as he twirled an American heiress past them on the floor. There was a look of distaste on M. Worth's face but he merely turned away to talk to Louis. I imagined M. Poiret was trying to convince the heiress to patronize his new fashion house. I saw Stephen bow to the duchess and her husband. She accepted his invitation to dance and they made a fine couple on the floor. I watched as Countess Olga headed for the elevator. She was leaning on her most ornate silver-headed cane. As we had planned, she would visit the ladies' parlor on the fourth floor, where Mlle Arquette was in charge. She stopped briefly to smile at her daughter, who passed by on Honoré's arm. I noticed Miss Brown was not dancing. Instead, she, too, was watching Sonya and the gallant young Mr. Palmer.

When the music ended, Stephen steered his partner to my side. "Emily, thank you for sharing your charming husband with me," she said.

At just that moment, Lord James sidled up to us, seemingly from nowhere. "I say, Duchess, you're a very fine dancer. They must have splendid dances in Newport. Perhaps I'll find out, now that I'm engaged to an American. And there she is." He pointed towards Lydia who was walking onto the dance floor with her father for the next waltz.

"She's most charming. The Johnstones have been so kind to me this evening."

"Oh, they loved having you at their table, you can depend on that, and everyone is thrilled to see your magnificent jewel." Really, I thought he was almost being obnoxious. There was no need to call attention to the prize. But, with his next words, I realized he was attempting to forward the plot. I wished he would leave it alone and let things develop naturally, but there was no stopping him once he'd begun. "If you don't mind my saying, Duchess, I think there's a little loose stone in the setting, on your left shoulder." While she craned to look at the necklace he apologized. "I wasn't going to say anything, but I'm terribly afraid it might fall out." He looked at me for approval but I ignored him.

It was true that one of the smaller gems in the necklace appeared to sit unevenly in the gold filigree, so I made a suggestion. "You might want to just check that it's not too loose, Duchess. We have a ladies' parlor on the fourth floor. Let me show you to the elevator and I'm sure we can get help if you need to adjust it."

"Oh, yes, that would be good. I wouldn't want to lose any part of it." She ducked her head and grinned at me with what she must have thought was a surreptitious look of conspiracy. I took her elbow to show her to the elevator, shaking my head slightly at Lord James as we left him. He was very proud of himself for giving us an only too obvious reason to visit the fourth floor, since he knew I expected any attempt to steal the jewel to be made there. As we walked around the room I felt the eyes of my husband and Inspector Guillaume following me.

On the fourth floor, we found Mlle Arquette assisting Countess Olga in rearranging her hair. A jeweled comb seemed to have fallen out, spoiling her elaborate pile. The vendeuse quickly made a space for the duchess on one of the white wire chairs with satin-covered seats that had been placed in front of gilt-rimmed mirrors for the use of ladies in need of making repairs. Another seamstress sat in a corner helping a woman mend a ripped seam on her gown.

Mlle Arquette was helping the duchess to remove the necklace and spread it on a cloth on a small table before her, when we heard the elevator open again. We all turned to see Sonya arrive with Grace Greenway Brown by her side.

"Mama, there you are. I was bringing Miss Brown…she almost tripped on her hem, there is a tear, you see." Sonya bent to show her mother, and Mlle Arquette hurried over to help, passing in front of me. Sonya spoke to her in French, all the while reaching out for the scissors Mlle Arquette held in her hand. Suddenly there was an exclamation and a cry of pain. When I could see her again, Sonya was clutching her arm. A streak of red was quickly blossoming into a stream against the white of her skin and the pale ivory silk of her gown. Mlle Arquette pulled the scissors out of the young woman's hand and spoke rapidly in French.

Then, everyone was on their feet, trying to help. A towel was brought, and a seat shoved behind Sonya so she could collapse onto it. Her immediate impulse to excuse her clumsiness was followed by alarm as the red stain spread, staining the smooth silk and pink fabric flowers in her lap. She was soon as pale as the white of the room, and the red-stained towel dripped. Countess Olga knelt beside her, looking up at me with alarm.

"My husband's downstairs, he's a doctor. He can help," I reassured her. "Here, take her in the elevator. Call for him as soon as you get downstairs."

It was a tiny elevator, so we put Sonya into it, supported by her mother on one side and Grace on the other, and sent them down. I leant over the balcony and was relieved to see Stephen passing below me. I called out to him and was surprised that he could hear me over the noise of the crowd and the orchestra. He looked quizzically up at me and I pointed down towards the door of the elevator, just as it opened and the women stumbled out. I was heading for the stairs, to run down after them, when I heard a gasp behind me. Turning, I saw the duchess with an astonished look on her face. Mlle Arquette was beside her. "It's the ruby. It's gone."

THIRTY-SEVEN

I raced down the stairway, shoving several people aside as I went. Reaching the bottom, I nearly collided with Stephen as he rushed to the elevator. The waltz was still playing and people further into the room were unaware of the emergency. I was grateful for Stephen's presence. I had expected a distraction so that the ruby could be taken, but I hadn't anticipated an incident such as this. I wasn't able to focus on the problem of the theft with Sonya hurt in this way.

Despite his damaged arm, Stephen was able to lift her and carry her to a table just inside the empty dining room where he laid her out and quickly unwrapped the wound then wrapped it again more tightly, continuing to hold it firmly with his good hand. "It'll be all right," he said, looking across the young woman's prone body to where I stood, shocked by the sight. "It'll take a few minutes, but the bleeding will stop."

Countess Olga took up a place by her daughter's head and gently smoothed her hair. I saw Sonya look up with adoration in her eyes and, at that moment, I realized how very devoted to her mother she truly was. Inspector Guillaume firmly shoved aside several gawpers who were in the way, so he could position himself looming over the petite countess. I looked past him and saw Lord James pushing Honoré forward through the crowd, until the young man stood at the foot of the table, with the tall Englishman behind him. They both looked shocked. Grace clung to one side of the table to keep from falling. She took a large breath, as if to steady herself in the face of this catastrophe. Then, as we all watched, Sonya fainted.

"It's all right," Stephen told us. "She's suffering from the shock. Someone find some blankets so we can keep her warm. It's not a deep wound and the blood is starting to clot. She'll be fine. Let her rest."

Inspector Guillaume spoke some commands to his men and they soon returned with blankets. When Sonya was made comfortable, with Stephen in attendance, people began to recover. The inspector instructed his men to clear the room of spectators so that only those of us involved remained. He indicated that Honoré, Lord James, and Grace should stay. Meanwhile, Mrs. Johnstone and Lydia stood on either side of Lord James and refused to budge. With a nod, Guillaume indicated they could remain with the rest of us.

When the others had been herded out, he turned to look down on Countess Olga. "Pardon, Countess, here is a chair." He helped her to sit beside her daughter, taking her cane from her hand as he did so. She tried hard to cling to it, but he pulled it from her with a quick movement. Disregarding her protests, he twisted the lion's head at the top and spilled out the contents from the bottom of the cane. Dark rubies glowed in the lamplight, red as the blood had been when it flowed from her daughter's arm only moments before. The inspector let the shocked silence hang in the air, waiting for her to speak, but she remained silent, only glancing once at Honoré and Lord James, who stood at her daughter's feet.

"Do you care to explain, Mme Countess?"

She shrugged and her features hardened. Her expression was grim. She stared down at her hands, which were clasped in her lap.

"Madame, your position will not save you. It does not matter, now, that you are an aristocrat. Your husband's position, your house in Faubourg Saint-Germain, none of that will save you.

And do you even implicate your own daughter in this? Surely you are not working alone. Tell me who else is involved and, perhaps, we may be able to save your daughter from disgrace and even imprisonment. Will you do nothing to save her?" We all looked at Sonya, who was covered with maroon blankets, her face white against them. Stephen shook his head in disgust. The tiny woman in the chair withdrew into herself, refusing to look up or to respond. I thought she would remain that way like a rock, but suddenly she broke her silence.

"It was him," she said, pointing to the end of the table. "It was M. Honoré Palmer. He forced us to do it. He knew I needed money. He came to me. He seduced me. He made me help him and once I did so, he threatened to tell the police it was me, to have me arrested. He said his family would protect him, no one would believe me. I don't know if they knew what he was doing. But he knew about the earlier robberies...his parents were here the last time. I don't know if they were involved, if they knew the thief they called the Pied Piper, or if he only hoped to blame it on some figure in the past. He did it." Her voice rose, she was nearing hysteria.

I looked across at Stephen who continued to hold Sonya's arm. He looked alarmed. I could see that Inspector Guillaume was completely surprised by this accusation and he, too, looked very uncomfortable. The countess was suggesting that the influence of the Palmers' would prevent the police from pursuing Honoré. I had not expected her to accuse him like that and it was troubling. Expunging the stain on young Palmer's reputation had been the whole point of trapping the thief. My plan seemed to be unraveling.

Mrs. Johnstone spoke up. "I told you it was that Palmer boy, but with all their influence he'll never pay for it."

Honoré stared down the length of the table, a look of horror on his face. He saw it all closing in on him again. Even Lord James looked startled. "Honoré, what have you done?" he said, as he took a step away from his friend.

At that moment, one of the policemen escorted the Duchess of Marlborough into the room, followed by her husband. She looked at the jewels that had spilled out on the table. "Yes, those are my jewels, that's the Sunrise Ruby." She turned towards Honoré, who still stood frozen at the end of the table, but she was looking at the figure behind him. "But that man is *not* Lord James Lawford. He is an imposter."

THIRTY-EIGHT

The audience was stunned. Inspector Guillaume stepped forward. "This man is Mr. James Baker—from Manchester, England—not Lord James Lawford. He is a confidence man and thief known as 'Jimmy the Lift' to the English authorities." Guillaume stared at the imposter until the younger man looked away. Then he continued. "This plain Mr. Jimmy Baker was a very popular young man when he was here at the Exposition of 1889. He was known as a man about town and he was a suspect in the jewel robberies at the time, but nothing could be proved. Not then. But now we know who you are."

The willowy young man stood alone now, as Honoré and the others moved away, in order to turn and look at him. His bright blue eyes were hooded and he languidly put his hands into his pockets, destroying the line of his trimly tailored evening wear but giving an unmistakable impression of insouciance. "My good man," he said, "I assure you, you are mistaken."

Mrs. Johnstone was outraged. "Whatever are you talking about?" she asked.

Lydia Johnstone frowned. She was comprehending the accusation but it didn't sit well with her and, the next moment, she stepped between the imposter and the police inspector. "I don't believe it for a minute. You've got it all wrong. We call him Jimmy, all right, but he's Lord James." She shook her finger in Inspector Guillaume's face. "You're just desperate because you can't find the thief, so first you arrest Honoré Palmer and now you're going after Lord James. I say it's some Frenchman and you don't want to admit it, so you accuse anyone who's not French. Lord James is my fiancé, and I refuse to believe what you're saying. Wait till I get my father in here, he'll have something to say to you."

During her rant I could see the man I still continued to think of as Lord James easing his way back a few steps. But Guillaume also saw the move, and he nodded to two of his men to come up behind the Englishman. Cautious as a cat, the imposter was also aware of their movement. For the time being, it was a quiet standoff. The tall lanky figure fell into a graceful stance.

"There is no mistake," the Duchess of Marlborough said. "My husband is well acquainted with the Lawford family. This is not Lord James." Her husband merely nodded.

I could understand how Lydia might cling to her delusions under the shock of this revelation, but it was time to destroy that little dream world she was inhabiting. I glanced back and saw that Countess Olga had slumped in her chair, unable to continue with her lies about Honoré.

"Lydia, what they're saying is true," I told her. "Listen to me. Remember Denise Laporte, the little milliner? She wasn't killed because she was going to expose the father of her unborn child, she was killed because she knew the father was the real Lord James and she knew he was dead. He died of consumption. When this fake Lord James went with me to the lodgings where Denise and her lover lived, the landlady recognized him, but not as Lord James, as Jimmy Baker, his friend and constant companion. It's true. I didn't know because they spoke French, but when Inspector Guillaume went back later and interviewed the woman, she identified him as the friend 'Jimmy' who visited the sick man often in his last days...as he lay dying. When I first learned the truth of Jimmy Baker's identity I wondered why he'd been so willing to go along as my translator on that visit. I quickly realized that he'd cleverly figured out that was the best way to control the information I was able to gather."

Lydia shook her head soundlessly but she grasped the edge of the table, her knuckles white. I stood staring at the false Lord James who now avoided my eyes.

Inspector Guillaume continued. "We finally determined that M. Jimmy Baker was here in 1889 and that it was he who was the Pied Piper. He was the one who successfully organized a group of young people to steal some very valuable jewels. We found people who knew him then. They say he was a charmer, he seduced young foreigners, he recruited them and, when they were caught, they believed he was one of them, an aristocrat down on his luck. They were loyal to him even when disgraced themselves.

"But they were wrong, he was not one of them. He grew up poor and orphaned on the streets of Manchester. By the time his confederates were caught, Jimmy Baker was long gone with a substantial stake and plans for future crimes."

The French police had discovered those details when he was a suspect back in 1889, but they couldn't prove anything. This time they had done more digging. They found out that he had gone on to commit fraud and theft in various parts of Europe, always playing an English nobleman under different names, but each time he managed to avoid arrest.

Lydia twisted round for a quick look at the man she had pledged to marry but then she turned back, remaining between him and the rest of us.

"I imagine he couldn't resist it when there was to be another Paris exposition. His previous adventure had been so successful," I said. I'd had time to think about all of this, and I'd confirmed as much as possible with Guillaume.

"So it was," the inspector said. "He moved to the city early, while the fair was being built, and at this time, we believe, he met the actual Lord James Lawford. He recognized an easy target in that real son of nobility. He charmed the man and his young mistress, and he profited greatly from the acquaintance."

I looked across at the suave young man. I had found him so sympathetic and appealing. His sense of humor, his deprecation, the flattering way he could make you feel superior to anyone in the room. I had been fooled, just like everyone else.

"As the sick man got weaker, the landlady told us how he came to depend on his lively friend to help him, even to retrieve his mail with the quarterly allowance that was regularly sent by his wealthy family. He had been estranged from them for a very long time, so when the real Lord James finally passed away, this man even arranged for the burial. Since there was no one else involved, he was able to bury the man, not as Lord James Lawford, but as James Baker of Manchester. You can visit a small stone marker in the Père Lachaise cemetery where he rests," Inspector Guillaume said.

I had gone there that afternoon with the Duchess of Marlborough. The stone was a small, mean remembrance with a false name for the poor dead man.

Both Lydia and her mother were speechless now with horror, as it dawned on them that it was a policeman who was telling the story, so it must be true. The rest were spellbound. The false Lord James merely rolled his eyes to look at the ceiling and kept his hands in his pockets, which helped to keep the policemen at bay as they waited for a signal from the inspector.

"Presented with such an opportunity, how could he resist? The real Lord James was a man who avoided all contact with his relatives except for that regular allowance. What a waste to let it all go unclaimed," I said. "So, of course, it was as nothing to Jimmy Baker to assume the identity of the dead man. And it only made his original plan to resume the lucrative jewel thefts more possible. But, for that plan to succeed, he turned to a confederate from his time at the 1889 exposition."

I shifted slightly towards the table where Sonya still lay senseless. Stephen raised his eyebrows at me across her prone figure. "Countess Olga," he said.

"Yes," Guillaume said. "In 1889 she had recently come to Paris to escape her husband."

"*Non.*" The countess looked up, her large eyes wide, seeking sympathy. "It is not as you believe. He forced me to help him. I was alone. I had no one. I had no choice."

"I spoke to the count when he came to Paris," Inspector Guillaume said. "His story is very different from the one the countess tells. As a young man, he fell in love with a woman of Gypsy blood, and against the wishes of his family, he married her. According to him, it was her infidelities and indiscretions that led to their separation. Apparently he had reason to suspect he was not even the father of their daughter, a suspicion that nearly drove him to madness. His family intervened and sent the woman and her daughter away."

"It is not true, he lies," Countess Olga said, then she collapsed in tears.

Ignoring her, he continued. "By the time she came to Paris in 1889, the countess was alone and without friends. Despite the supposed laxity of the European aristocrats of Faubourg Saint-Germain, they turned to her a cold shoulder. Disapproval of her separation from her husband left her stranded in a society that would not accept her. So when a charming young Englishman named Jimmy Baker offered her comfort and companionship, well, you can imagine." He waved a hand in her direction.

How easy it must have been for him to seduce her and, when he shared his need for money, he would have learned that she and her small child were surviving on a stingy allowance from her husband's family. Knowing that, it was easy enough to recruit her. And what better confederate could he have found to be on his arm as he entered the drawing rooms of Paris?

"The two of them were successful, socializing with young aristocrats, getting their help, gaining their friendship. They shared in the success and they shared in the profit. But as soon as we began to suspect him, the very pleasant Jimmy Baker disappeared without a trace."

The countess sat with tears streaming down her face. "Lies, all lies. He seduced me and then he threatened me. I had no one to turn to. You cannot know how alone I was. I feared him and I feared my husband. That is the truth." She was a good actress.

"It must have been a shock when he deserted her," I said, ignoring her protests. "Her situation after that would have been better because of the money they had gotten from the jewels, but things were just as bleak when it came to her social situation. She survived but, when the money from the jewel thefts was gone, she was reduced to living on the allowance from her husband's family again." Now Lydia was listening intently. Perhaps she hoped the countess could be blamed, or perhaps she was finally coming to see her fiancé as he truly was.

"Imagine how excited she was a few months ago, when the man she knew as Jimmy Baker returned as Lord James Lawford," Guillaume said. "He was back, and suddenly there was hope. How wholeheartedly she must have entered into his schemes this time. She was so desperate to escape her current life that she even recruited her own daughter to help with the thefts." He picked up the now empty hollow cane from beside Sonya, who looked so young and innocent, lying there. How could the countess have involved her own child? It was beyond my understanding.

"This time around, when it came to the foreign visitors, almost everyone had sympathy for the poor countess, especially the Americans, like Mrs. Palmer," I said. Countess Olga looked up at me with a glint of anger in her eyes, but she quickly looked down again, assuming her pose as a poor helpless victim. It angered me that she had taken in Bertha Palmer with her act.

"I knew that woman was a disgrace," Mrs. Johnstone said, glaring at the countess with hatred in her eyes. "I tried to tell people but they felt sorry for her. Hmmph."

"You, Mrs. Johnstone, were unusual in your dislike. Countess Olga and her daughter were soon invited to receptions and balls, especially when she was introduced by Lord James himself."

I looked at the tall young man still lounging behind Lydia Johnstone. He was unmoved.

"It was simple for them to identify a truly valuable jewel, arrange for a distraction, and hide it in her empty cane, a trick she had learned in her youth," the inspector said.

"And it wasn't only the countess who had a clever way to carry off jewels," I said. "Jimmy had secret pockets sewn into the lining of his coat, which explains how he was able to steal Mrs. Palmer's necklace, despite its size. While we were all at the House of Worth that day he met Denise and they arranged for him to place the necklace in the Worth display here at the Exposition, where she would be putting the final touches on the hats. In return, he promised to provide her with money for her baby.

"At first we couldn't figure out why he would want to leave the necklace on the mannequin, but then we discovered that his fence worked as a guard in that building. The thieves would place the stolen jewels on the mannequins, where they would appear to be part of the exhibits. As they never met each other, the fence and the thieves would never risk being interrupted and captured as they passed the stolen goods. It was a technique they had used at the last exposition, and it worked again. The guard could enter the exhibits late at night, when no one else was around, and retrieve the jewels."

"We have arrested him, and we have been able to find several other jewelry items that were stolen," Inspector Guillaume said. "Jimmy was very clever, you understand. And, so, to continue his so very lucrative charade, he had only to avoid contact with the English visitors, at least the titled ones, and once he had ingratiated himself with the Americans that was simple enough to accomplish. But his plans began to unravel once the young Mlle Laporte realized that he had assumed the identity of the dead man. *Pauvre petite fille*, she had no idea what a great danger she was to him. Perhaps, Mme Chapman, you can tell us what you think happened to our little milliner."

"Our theory is that when Mr. Baker met Denise at the exhibition she threatened to expose him unless he gave her even more money. He knew that if she did so it would ruin all of the plans that he and the countess had made. So, as soon as the pearl necklace was safely in place on the mannequin, he strangled her. He never imagined that I would recognize the pearls on the evening of the opening, before the fence had been able to retrieve them."

I stared across the room into the icy blue eyes of Jimmy Baker. He clearly held me responsible for the failure of his scheme. I was astonished to think that he had so successfully fooled me into thinking that we were friends, while the entire time he must have been resenting my interference.

As soon as Inspector Guillaume and I had gathered all of the clues and come to the unavoidable realization that Lord James and Countess Olga were responsible for the jewel thefts, and ultimately the deaths of the two young women, I'd sunk into a well of despair. Two people who I'd befriended, and whose company I'd enjoyed, had turned out to be callous criminals. It made me doubt my ability to judge those around me accurately and to determine who could be true friends. I was embarrassed by how blithely I'd fallen into their web of deceit.

The next part of the story was distasteful to me, but I said, "I imagine he had never planned to assume the identity of Lord James for any length of time. It suited him for the duration of the Exposition. He could retrieve the man's quarterly allowance and use his name and position to commit the well-planned thefts and, no doubt, enjoy himself with the lovely countess at the same time. But it was always meant to be temporary. Until they saw the possibility of marrying Americans."

There was a stir in the room, but I kept my eyes on the fake Lord James. Then I glanced back at the seated woman, now hunched over, elbows on her knees, head in her hands. "The countess must have known that when the Exposition ended she would be left in the same position as before. But then she saw the desire of Mrs. Palmer to marry her son into European aristocracy and her obvious plan to concentrate on Sonya as the main candidate. When Countess Olga realized Mrs. Palmer's intention, and when she saw how the American mothers angled for a chance to hook an English aristocrat like Lord James Lawford, she must have thought she'd found the perfect solution. She would marry her daughter to the Palmer heir and see Jimmy married to an American heiress. Jimmy's only interest in Lydia was for her money…and that Nebraska offered him a refuge away from the French police."

We could hear the gasps of Lydia Johnstone and her mother. "No," the younger woman said, stamping her foot. "No. That's not true. He loves me." But when she wheeled around to confront him, he was ready. Extending his long arm around her waist, he twirled her back, then, pinning her arms to her sides, he pressed a knife to her neck and pulled her towards him.

Mrs. Johnstone screamed. The policemen began to move in from behind, but Inspector Guillaume waved them off. Even Countess Olga was stung into attention, and Stephen half rose, still pressing the wound on Sonya's arm.

THIRTY-NINE

Wait," Inspector Guillaume said, to prevent Honoré or one of the other men from attacking. Jimmy Baker pressed the silver knife against a vein in Lydia's throat, his blue eyes glittering above her elaborate coiffure, like those of a cornered animal. She stopped struggling, despite the anger that contorted her face. I realized, then, that he was capable of slitting her throat with the dinner knife he held. I wondered briefly whether he had palmed it during dinner, somehow anticipating the turn of events. It didn't matter. What mattered was whether he was given an excuse to use it.

"It was all her idea, you know," he said, as he nodded toward Countess Olga. "She was greedy. I told her the jewels were enough. They would be plenty. But she wanted more. She even got her own daughter to do her dirty work, didn't she? What kind of mother does that? Greedy bitch." He clamped his arm around Lydia more firmly, all the while watching us with eyelids lowered to slits.

I regretted now that we had not seized him immediately. The plan that we would get a confession by exposing him publicly was foolish, but it was too late for regrets. Despite the earlier deaths, I hadn't been able to believe that he would turn violent. But now his real identity was exposed—a feral wild animal, preying on others, lacking any moral scruples, protecting himself in any way that he could. A sharp but wasted intelligence burned behind that oh so pleasant exterior. We had made a terrible miscalculation, but there was no time for recriminations. We were teetering on a dangerous edge. I had to be careful, but I needed to keep talking.

"The countess must have guessed you were the one who strangled Denise Laporte. She knew about the arrangement with the guard to fence the jewels. Did she threaten you with that knowledge?" He was silent, watching, watching. "I suppose it didn't matter to you. You knew, no matter what, that she couldn't expose you without exposing herself." I saw the hint of a smile on his face. "Did she also know you were being threatened by Edith Stuart?"

"Stupid cow," he said. "That Stuart girl didn't even know what she was saying." When Lydia opened her mouth to speak he pressed the knife into her skin, drawing a small drop of blood at the tip. She held her breath.

"Don't," I said.

He loosened his grip but glared down at the woman he held so closely. "She believed Lydia's story that I was embarrassed to admit a fear of heights and that was supposed to be why I didn't ride the Ferris wheel with the others. As if that would matter to a ruddy rich aristocrat." The cultured accents he must have spent time honing fell away and his natural accent from the streets of Manchester reasserted itself.

"But if Edith Stuart told everyone about it, that would ruin your alibi for Denise Laporte's death," I hurriedly continued, hoping to keep his attention. "She didn't realize that."

"Oh, yes she did. Stupid, stupid cow," he shouted. "She would have had much better leverage knowing the Brown woman was off with Honoré. He'd have paid a fine price to keep that from his mother, but she was too stupid to know it." There was bitter frustration in his anger, but he quickly got ahold of himself, smiling at all of us instead. It was a grim smile.

"So you arranged to meet Edith on the balcony," I continued. "She wanted money from you, in exchange for not telling the police that you weren't with them that afternoon, in order to pay her debts. But if you allowed her to blackmail you, you would never be free of her. So you decided it was time for her to go.

"I think Edith was actually the one who stole the countess's jewelry that night. Instead of offering her money, you recruited her to help with the robberies and promised her money from the thefts. You convinced her, as you had convinced other young people in the past, and as was done with them, her first theft was a test. Unbeknownst to her, Countess Olga was in on it, allowing her to steal her jewels. Once a recruit passed this initiation rite, then they would be used in real robberies. The police knew this from the earlier robberies. But you never really intended to recruit Edith Stuart, you planned to get rid of her while implicating her in the robberies."

Countess Olga jumped up. "I never knew he would kill her. She was only supposed to steal the jewels, like the other ones before. I knew nothing about killing her. You must believe me."

Inspector Guillaume put a large hand on her shoulder, forcing her back down in her chair. Everyone kept their eyes on Jimmy Baker who glared at the countess. "Fool of a woman. She's the one who told Honoré he was to meet the Brown woman on the balcony and then she sent her daughter instead."

"I didn't know Jimmy was going to meet Miss Stuart there and kill her," Countess Olga said. Tears were running down her face and she clasped her daughter's hand.

"No," I said. "You were busy intercepting Miss Greenway Brown. You had Jimmy tell her that Honoré would meet her in an anteroom but you met her to persuade her to give up her attachment to Mr. Palmer. And you sent *him* to the balcony where he thought he was meeting Miss Greenway Brown. Then you sent your daughter after him. It was only later, after Honoré was arrested, that you realized you could convince your daughter to claim she was with him every moment. You saved him from the police and gained the gratitude of the Palmers." I turned to

Honoré. "Sonya wasn't with you when you got to the balcony, was she? And you thought it was Grace Greenway Brown who had fallen, didn't you?"

"The countess told me Grace would be on the balcony. I tried to go alone to meet her, but Sonya followed closely." He looked at Grace. "It's true, I feared it was Grace, until I went down to the street and saw it was Miss Stuart."

Jimmy Baker was still edging back an inch at a time towards the set of doors at the back of the room. "The fool thought the Brown woman was part of the robberies," he spat out, then grinned. All the while the blade he held to Lydia's throat gleamed in the electric lights. I heard Mrs. Johnstone whimper in the background.

"Because you led him to believe that, didn't you?" I said.

"I told him Edith Stuart was threatening to expose Grace as one of the jewel thieves. He believed it. So, after he saw it was actually the Stuart woman who was dead, he thought Grace was the one who threw Edith over the rail. Fool."

"It's not true, I never believed that. He tried to tell me it was so, but I never believed it." Honoré turned to Grace but she patted his arm. I wondered if, unlike the rest of us, she'd been suspicious of the fake English nobleman all along.

"You knew Honoré would be blamed, didn't you?" I said, inching forward as I took up the story again. "And you knew he would never expose Grace, if he thought she was involved. You thought he deserved it, didn't you? His parents could buy him out of it."

"They never suffer, these rich chaps, do they? Not really." He said. I saw a mad grin on his face, partly buried in Lydia's hair. "They get inconvenienced a bit here and there, that's all."

I wondered if I had gone too far in provoking him, as I watched him slide the knife along Lydia's neck. She stopped writhing in fear and froze. She was breathing fast and I was tempted to imitate her, but I suppressed the urge. I felt the blood pumping through all of my own veins as the sense of danger heightened. There was a gleam in his blue eyes that warned he wouldn't hesitate to kill her if he had nothing left to lose.

"But Countess Olga wouldn't allow you to blame Honoré, would she? If he were condemned, then how could she marry him to Sonya? She couldn't allow that. She would only let you escape to America if she could also be there, isn't it true?" Lydia squirmed with anger at this, but he only tightened his grip, grinning over her shoulder.

I felt sick with distaste at the thought of what they had planned, mortified by how easily we'd all been duped by these charming villains. We'd all been pawns in their devious plot, and now we were paying the price for our naïveté. I looked over at Honoré and saw that he looked as if he might faint, clearly crushed by the words and actions of a man who he'd thought to be a good friend.

"You purposely suspended the robberies while Honoré was in jail in order to make it seem that he was the one responsible for them. The countess must have been unhappy with you for doing that, as she wanted the reputation of her future son-in-law to remain unsullied." Baker grinned like an evil imp as he edged another few inches backwards. I shook my head. "But, when I told you and the countess about the plot to have the duchess wear a famous jewel, it became a challenge, one last theft that you couldn't resist."

"Very clever, Mrs. Chapman. A very clever little trap. My hat would be off to you if I were still wearing one, but I'm a little tied up at the moment."

"Why take the risk? My husband was certain that neither of you would respond to the trap. Why should you? You already each had a promise of marriage, an escape to America. We none of us really thought you would go through with it."

"Which is why you brought young Honoré tonight, I assume?"

"Yes, to make it more tempting. The inspector convinced me. We thought you would find a way to steal the ruby in order to implicate him even further. But how could we imagine the countess would allow her own daughter to be harmed for this?" I turned to look at the pile of rubies and the unhappy mother. Countess Olga was nearly as white as her daughter, although she had lost no blood. I turned back to Jimmy Baker. "Why did you risk it? You could have had everything."

Looking down at the young woman he had almost married, he replied. "Yes, and to think I was so looking forward to seeing Nebraska." He was sneering.

Suddenly, Inspector Guillaume flicked his wrist and the two policemen moved in on Jimmy from behind. But he was expecting them. Whirling around, he slashed at Lydia and, pushing her towards them, he charged through the doorway and disappeared into the crowded reception.

FORTY

A police whistle blew and the inspector and his men followed in quick pursuit. Honoré bent over Sonya, while Stephen demanded my help with Lydia. Blood flowed from her wound, but we soon realized that a fleshy part of her upper arm had been gashed, not her throat. Stephen was able to control the bleeding with a cloth, while I gestured for Mrs. Johnstone and the Duchess of Marlborough to take charge of the countess. Then I raced through the crowded reception, following in the wake of other spectators who were spilling out into the rue des Nations.

Under the curvy iron lampposts I could see uniformed police officers and American Marines converging from all directions. I spotted Inspector Guillaume across the road at the edge of the Seine, where only a few brightly lit tour boats floated in the water. He was directing his men to check in both directions. Jimmy Baker must have gotten away. There were cries from the right, and the inspector and Marines rushed off. I was about to follow when there was a swoosh and a slap behind me but, before I could turn, my mouth was covered by a hand and my arms were pinned to my side. I was pulled back into the shadows. Baker had hidden above, in the arched ceiling of the bridge, and dropped down when the others departed.

"Keep quiet," he whispered in my ear. I felt the knife against my throat and I stopped struggling. All I could think of were the faces of my children. This couldn't be happening. I couldn't leave them like this. He seemed to sense my overwhelming fear. "If you keep quiet and don't expose me, I'll have no reason to hurt you," he breathed in my ear. I felt a sort of laugh from his chest against my back. "You've already done your worst then, haven't you, luv?"

It was true. I had already told everyone all that I knew. There was no secret to be kept by killing me, as there had been for poor Denise Laporte and Edith Stuart. I swallowed and breathed a little more easily. He pulled me across the walkway to the edge overlooking the water. I could hear boats passing behind him but he kept me facing the pavilion. A few of the guests were spilling out to the sidewalk looking up and down for the police. They had no idea what was going on. Why hadn't I stayed inside with the others? Why couldn't I have left the pursuit to Inspector Guillaume and his men?

But, suddenly, I saw Grace and Honoré in the light of the door, hand in hand, coming out looking for me, calling my name. Stephen must have sent them. I felt Jimmy Baker stiffen, then he turned me to the right. Inspector Guillaume was leading a group of men coming back towards the bridge. They held torches that flickered in the breeze.

"You stay still," Jimmy whispered in my ear. "I'm quite good at throwing this knife so, if you want to see your children again, don't turn around and don't move." I nodded.

I felt him release me and I staggered a bit. I heard him hiss, so I froze in place. I held my breath. I became a statue. Even when I heard a splash, and knew he must have dived into the river, I remained rigid. I didn't move until both Grace and the inspector saw me and came running. Convulsing with relief, I told them he had jumped.

With much shouting and gesticulation, the men following the inspector turned towards the river and attempted to find the escaped man. It was the only time I saw Guillaume angry, as he rejected assurances that the man was sure to have drowned if he hadn't been spotted. It worried me as well. I clung to Grace and Honoré and reluctantly turned towards the river with the others. We stood there while they searched. The water was deep and there was a current, but doubt remained. I had no great desire to see the swollen drowned body of the man I had known as Lord James Lawford, but, on the other hand, the thought that he was out there free to exercise his skills at fraud and deceit on other innocents was disturbing. And he had murdered. He could do it again.

When we finally turned back to the pavilion, I felt the relief of Honoré and Grace as I leaned on them for support. I knew I should be satisfied that Bertha's son was cleared of all suspicion. No matter how many other sorry stories were exposed by the revelations of that evening, at least the Palmers' world had returned to the steady sunlight they deserved. And clearing Honoré Palmer was what I had wanted so fiercely. At least that was done and we could return to Bertha and Potter with that good news. The joy of the adventure of the Paris Exposition had been shattered but at least some peace of mind could be returned to them...to all of us.

FORTY-ONE

L ook, there's the pavilion. I can't believe this is ending and we'll be back in Chicago in a few weeks," I said, balancing Lizzie on my hip, as Stephen pointed out the boats on the Seine to little Jack. It was November 12th, the last day of the Exposition, and we'd decided to take one more ride on the moving sidewalk that circled above the fair. So I had put on my new Worth walking suit, feeling a little thrill because I knew how well it looked on me, and we bundled up the children for a final outing in the wonderful City of Light. We'd even brought Delia, who was holding little Tommy in her arms. Her eyes looked with wonder at the fabulous sights of the fair. I was glad we'd brought her. It was an experience she would remember for the rest of her life, as would I.

As we passed over the Seine I couldn't help thinking of Jimmy Baker, who I'd first known as Lord James. It was several weeks after that night at the pavilion before his body was found stuck against a tree root further downstream. It was bloated and ugly according to Inspector Guillaume, but they were still able to positively identify him, especially after they found several necklaces and rings in the hidden pockets of his coat. By then the Countess Olga had somehow been ransomed by her wealthy, titled relatives. She managed to avoid standing trial for the thefts as she'd given testimony against the guard who'd served as the fence. So the stolen jewelry had been recovered before she and her daughter were shipped back to Russia, never to return to France. It may have seemed like she had escaped but I didn't envy her the life she faced back in her husband's home.

Lizzie pointed at the big globe as we traveled by it. And we all looked up at the Eiffel Tower, for a final view of that monument to modern industry. As we traveled towards the Palace of Electricity with its magnificent fountain, I strained to see the Textiles Building. While my family watched the scenes of the fair for the last time, my mind drifted away, mulling over the way the experience had changed so many of the people we met that summer.

M. Worth would be dismantling the 'Going to the Drawing Room' exhibit the following day. Despite the gruesome discovery of the body of Denise Laporte, the exhibit had been a huge success. In my mind's eye, I could still see the display of the beautiful gowns, in glowing colors and textures, each wax figure showing a different woman in her best aspect. It was what the House of Worth and the rest of the Parisian fashion industry did so well. It was a sort of mission for them. I had heard that Andrée would be doing what her grandmother had always done, showing off new creations to society by wearing them in such a way as to make potential clients envious enough to flock to the House of Worth, in order to be dressed in something even better. The marriage to Louis Cartier had happened quietly in August, so she would also be able to display the jewels of her husband's family. Her famous sapphire was one of the jewels recovered and she was able to wear it at their wedding ceremony.

And Paul Poiret was determined to challenge the House of Worth by introducing designs for the new century. He had told us all about his aspirations when Bertha Palmer visited his new establishment. Worth had never been the only source of her wardrobe. She patronized Doucet and Paquin as well, so she was willing to taste the new at the recently opened maison de couture of Paul Poiret. She confided in me, after the visit, that she was not at all sure the simple designs with so few tucks and frills, like the cloak that was refused by the Russian princess, would ever be accepted. They were, of course, and in later years Bertha Palmer indulged in the new styles which allowed a woman to dispense with a tight corset.

Bertha recovered from the travails of that time. Once Honoré was cleared, it was as if a great sigh of relief passed through the entire house on rue Brignole. I never spoke with her again about the sad events of that summer, certain that she was as mortified as I was that we'd been fooled so thoroughly by two people who we'd thought were our friends. Shortly after that regrettable portion of the summer concluded the Palmers were invited by Queen Marie Henriette of Belgium to visit a spa as her guests. At first, Bertha thought Potter would never agree to make the trip, but she was surprised when he said he wanted to go. They rested, took the waters, and had a quiet visit with the aging queen. I remained in Paris, our children returned from the countryside, and we were able to be tourists for several weeks. When the Palmers returned, Bertha was rejuvenated and she plunged back into the social whirl of the Exposition.

I enjoyed a reunion with Jane Addams when she came to judge the prizes for the Social Economy category. Bertha had to fight hard to get her appointed to that awards committee but, once that was accomplished, the members promptly appointed her vice chair. During Bertha's absence I'd been able to spend time in the exhibits on trade unions and labor movements, and laws in different countries. But upon her return I was swept once more into a flurry of letter and report writing, and all the other duties having to do with the many receptions, salons, and dinners she organized or hosted. They all had to live up to her standards, and I am proud to say that one magazine back home reported that, "The splendor and originality of her entertainments have made a stir in Paris." In fact, the following spring she was awarded the Légion d'Honneur by the French government, an award that drew considerable envy from her rivals in Chicago.

Potter Palmer continued to recover, using his illness as an excuse to accept only a few of the many invitations they received. But, of course, Bertha was not hindered at all by that and, once he was back to good health, she indulged in her usual flurry of engagements. There was barely a stop between morning drives in the Bois and fashionable rendezvous on rue Royale or boulevard Haussmann. We dined at Paillard's, the Ritz, and the reopened Cubat's near the Rond Point. And we were often at the weekly receptions for Americans that the United States ambassador to France, Horace Porter, gave at the embassy. I barely had time to see my family, but the children were comfortable and amused in the gardens of Paris, while Stephen delivered his paper and then was happy to consort with the scientists at the Institut Pasteur for the rest of his time.

"Come, it's over," Stephen told us as he stepped down to the slower moving platform and then off. Turning, he made sure we all descended safely. Once we'd bundled Delia and the children into a cab and sent them back to rue Brignole, Stephen and I got another to take us to Durand-Ruel's gallery for the final day of Miss Cassatt's show there.

Once again, the white-haired owner of the gallery greeted us and ushered us in. He'd been chatting with M. Degas. I was a little surprised to see the older artist at the closing of the show but when Mary Cassatt came to greet us she said he had come to see a new work of hers that she'd added at the last moment. She swept us through a small crowd and I nodded greetings to some of the women I had met the last time, then she stopped before a medium-sized picture that was propped on an easel at the end of the room.

It was me, sitting sewing on the porch at Beaufresne. I wore a striped dress covered by an apron and behind me you could see the garden. It felt a little strange to recognize myself like that and I avoided looking at my own face bent over a needle and thread. But at my knee was Lizzie, leaning balanced on her elbows on my lap with her head in her little hands, looking straight at the viewer with a sort of childish skepticism, as if weighing something you had just said. It was wonderful, and Stephen exclaimed, "It's you and Lizzie. It's both of you to the life! I wish we could buy it. I'm sure we can't, though," he apologized to Mary.

She was pleased by our reactions. "It's actually already been claimed by Louisine Havemeyer. But I have something for you." Mrs. Havemeyer had joined us, smiling and agreeing it was a wonderful likeness. Mary pulled out a rolled-up sheet of drawing paper from behind the easel and unrolled it for us. It was a pencil sketch of the scene. She'd probably made it as I sat talking to her that day and she gave it to us as a present. We were overwhelmed, but she said it was the least she could do for our service as models.

As the others exclaimed over the sketch, and Mrs. Havemeyer advised Stephen on how to frame it, I stared at the painting. She had captured Lizzie wonderfully and it made me think what a smart and curious little girl our daughter was. She stared back at the viewer with a completely unafraid interest. It made me resolve to never let her lose that fresh and open approach to the world. I thought of all the young women I had met in the fashion houses and at the Exposition. I thought of Denise Laporte, Edith Stuart, and even Lydia Johnstone and Sonya Zugenev. All of them had once faced the world as intrepidly as little Lizzie in the portrait, but they had been changed by their experiences. I promised myself that I would do everything in my power to make sure that Lizzie never lost that sense of fearlessness as she grew.

We joined the others in toasting Mary Cassatt for the success of her show then we had to hurry back to change for the final reception at the United States pavilion. I again wore the gown with the cherries at the waist. Bertha Palmer had insisted I accept it as a gift. She called it a castoff that she would never wear again, so, in addition to the walking suit, I would return to Chicago with a new ball gown. I reflected that I would certainly have fewer occasions to wear it when I resumed the academic life. But I had no regrets about that. I think we were all ready to go home by that point.

At the pavilion, we greeted Mrs. Johnstone. She'd been considerably less hostile since the exposure of the fake Lord James. Lydia had been packed up and sent home to Omaha, Nebraska soon after that incident. I heard that she had taken the trousseau back with her. Mrs. Johnstone was completely opposed to any further engagements to European aristocrats. She had firm plans to find a husband for Lydia back in Nebraska and the decision to complete the trousseau was evidence that she was confident she would be successful in finding a nice American husband for her daughter.

Next, we greeted Grace Greenway Brown, who had remained in Paris with the Johnstones. She'd been re-introduced to Mr. and Mrs. Palmer after Honoré admitted, and apologized for, their secret liaison. The relationship was moved to one of proper courting with chaperones and formality but I could tell that Bertha really liked the young woman. For so long his parents had feared that Honoré had some awful secret. When they discovered that what he was hiding was an attachment to a perfectly suitable young woman, it was a tremendous relief to them.

Meanwhile, Honoré had submitted to every demand of his mother to attend festivities, or avoid them, to keep his father company, and to attend lectures and meetings as his mother's representative. She was preparing him for the political campaign they would face back in Chicago. The last night of the fair, it was a pleasure to see him and Grace together, happily staring into each other's eyes with the consent of their families.

I'd been in the United States pavilion many times since the tragic death of Edith Stuart, but it was with some trepidation that I stepped out onto that balcony for the last time that evening. Sensing that I was uneasy, Stephen reached out to hold my hand as we moved to a place by the railing. I looked down once, and shivered at the memory of that night, but then all eyes were raised to the sky for the fireworks. The fair was lit up with electric lights and we could glimpse the illuminated fountain down at the end of the Champ de Mars, as well as the lighted frame of the Eiffel Tower and the brightly lit '1900' at the top. As the bursts of the fireworks display ended, the lights of the '1900' dwindled until, finally, they were gone and the rest of the electric illuminations were extinguished one by one. It was the end of our visit. I felt a surge of emotion for this beautiful city, which had provided such a wonderful experience, but I also felt a pang of relief to think that in a few weeks we would be back in Chicago. With all its problems and challenges, it was so much more my home than the beautiful, fickle, dangerous city that was Paris. I knew the memories of this trip would remain bittersweet for the rest of my life and I was right.

AFTERWORD

U nlike Emily, my memories of Paris are all positive. It is a wonderful city, which I have visited more than once and hope to visit again in the future. It was on a trip with a friend a few years ago that I first had the idea that Emily Cabot might attend the 1900 Paris Exposition. I had wanted to use Bertha Palmer as a central character and the fact that the "Queen of Chicago" represented the United States at the 1900 Exposition provided an opportunity for a novel featuring her. The 2013 Art Institute of Chicago exhibit *Impressionism, Fashion and Modernity* also provided ideas and inspirations. Although that covered an earlier decade, it highlighted the importance of fashion to the City of Light. I also wanted to include a woman artist in one of the stories, as Emily has met women social workers and scientists in earlier books. Paris was the perfect setting to meet Mary Cassatt, an American artist whom I have always admired.

As always, the collections of the University of Chicago Library, both physical and electronic, were extremely helpful to me. I was able to consult some guidebooks for the 1900 Paris Exposition that were published at the time, as well as secondary works. Online, I discovered some wonderful resources on YouTube. There are actual films that were taken at the Exposition, showing the moving sidewalks and many other parts of the fairgrounds. I'm sorry I missed the 2014 *Paris 1900* exhibit at the Petit Palais. However, I was able to find a French TV show about that exhibit on YouTube—*Paris 1900: La Belle Époque, l'Exposition Universelle, l'Art Nouveau* (https://youtu.be/8MZGusqwKPo). There are many other sources and images available that describe that exposition.

For Bertha Palmer's life, *Silhouette in Diamonds: The Life of Mrs. Potter Palmer* by Ishbel Ross (https://archive.org/details/silhouetteindiam000337mbp) was my primary source. And the Chicago Historical Society publication *Bertha Honoré Palmer* by Timothy A. Long was a source of images as well as biographical information. I also used a number of newspaper articles from the time as sources of anecdotes. The Renoir painting of the two young circus performers hangs in the Art Institute of Chicago now, and the story of how it traveled with Bertha Palmer on her journeys was told during one of the institute's lectures that I attended.

As it turned out, Bertha was successful in her endeavor to get Honoré into politics. He was energetic and capable when he ran for alderman. At one point, his opponent circulated a report that Honoré had joined the waiter's union. When Honoré heard that, he rushed down to his father's hotel, donned the white coat of one of the waiters and called the press to take pictures saying he was proud to wear the uniform of such an honorable profession. He was successful and served two terms as an alderman before leaving the political life to work in the family business. He and Grace Greenway Brown were married in London in 1903. Their activities as depicted in this novel are entirely of my imagination.

Researching the House of Worth was very enjoyable, as I was able to study many wonderful photographs of the beautiful gowns they created. Most important for that aspect were *The Opulent Era: Fashions of Worth, Doucet and Pingat* by Elizabeth A. Coleman, and *The House of Worth: Portrait of an Archive* by Amy de la Haye and Valerie D. Mendes. Once I started researching the couturiers, I was happy to find that I could read some of their opinions in their own words—Jean-Philippe Worth published several works, including *A Century of Fashion*, and the flamboyant

Poiret published an autobiography titled *King of Fashion*. The walk through the rooms of the House of Worth with the various types of fabrics, which I describe in the first chapter, is roughly based on descriptions from letters of Isabella Stewart Gardner, written some years before the time of this story. I have taken liberties with the dates of Poiret's employment at the House of Worth. In reality, he worked there from 1901 to 1903, when he left to establish his own maison de couture.

There are many sources for information about Mary Cassatt, Edgar Degas, and their gallery owner and agent M. Durand-Ruel. Most important for me was the biography *Mary Cassatt: A Life* by Nancy Mowll Mathews.

The topic of Americans in Paris around 1900 is fascinating. I found the works of Edith Wharton and Henry James particularly useful for their portrayals of Americans going to Europe and trying to buy culture, in order to bring it back to the United States. With the exception of the Palmers and Grace Greenway Brown, the Americans in Paris depicted in this book are all fictional.

When I needed a French police detective, I searched around for a model and learned that Georges Simenon's fictional character Maigret had been inspired by a real policeman, Inspector Marcel Guillaume. Guillaume's investigation of the fictional crimes in this story is another product of my imagination, rather than factual circumstances. For information about the structure of the French police I consulted *The Police of France* by Philip John Stead. Thank you to the Boston Athenaeum for getting that book so promptly on interlibrary loan for me.

This book was so much fun to research, as far as the visual aspect goes, that I created a Pinterest board that readers may find of interest: https://www.pinterest.com/fdmcnama/death-at-the-paris-exposition/. Another board was created by my publisher, Allium Press, and it can be found at: https://www.pinterest.com/alliumpress/death-at-the-paris-exposition/.

Many thanks to my writing group The Complete Unknowns, especially Anne Sharfman and Nancy Braun, for input on this book, and also to Ros Hoey, who once again was a beta reader for me. And, of course, the biggest thanks to my editor, Emily Victorson of Allium Press of Chicago.

ALSO PUBLISHED BY ALLIUM PRESS OF CHICAGO

Visit our website for more information:
www.alliumpress.com

THE EMILY CABOT MYSTERIES
Frances McNamara

Death at the Fair

The 1893 World's Columbian Exposition provides a vibrant backdrop for the first book in the series. Emily Cabot, one of the first women graduate students at the University of Chicago, is eager to prove herself in the emerging field of sociology. While she is busy exploring the Exposition with her family and friends, her colleague, Dr. Stephen Chapman, is accused of murder. Emily sets out to search for the truth behind the crime, but is thwarted by the gamblers, thieves, and corrupt politicians who are ever-present in Chicago. A lynching that occurred in the dead man's past leads Emily to seek the assistance of the black activist Ida B. Wells.

◆

Death at Hull House

After Emily Cabot is expelled from the University of Chicago, she finds work at Hull House, the famous settlement established by Jane Addams. There she quickly becomes involved in the political and social problems of the immigrant community. But when a man who works for a sweatshop owner is murdered in the Hull House parlor, Emily must determine whether one of her colleagues is responsible, or whether the real reason for the murder is revenge for a past tragedy in her own family. As a smallpox epidemic spreads through the impoverished west side of Chicago, the very existence of the settlement is threatened and Emily finds herself in jeopardy from both the deadly disease and a killer.

THE EMILY CABOT MYSTERIES
Frances McNamara

Death at Pullman

A model town at war with itself . . . George Pullman created an ideal community for his railroad car workers, complete with every amenity they could want or need. But when hard economic times hit in 1894, lay-offs follow and the workers can no longer pay their rent or buy food at the company store. Starving and desperate, they turn against their once benevolent employer. Emily Cabot and her friend Dr. Stephen Chapman bring much needed food and medical supplies to the town, hoping they can meet the immediate needs of the workers and keep them from resorting to violence. But when one young worker—suspected of being a spy—is murdered, and a bomb plot comes to light, Emily must race to discover the truth behind a tangled web of family and company alliances.

◆

Death at Woods Hole

Exhausted after the tumult of the Pullman Strike of 1894, Emily Cabot is looking forward to a restful summer visit to Cape Cod. She has plans to collect "beasties" for the Marine Biological Laboratory, alongside other visiting scientists from the University of Chicago. She also hopes to enjoy romantic clambakes with Dr. Stephen Chapman, although they must keep an important secret from their friends. But her summer takes a dramatic turn when she finds a dead man floating in a fish tank. In order to solve his murder she must first deal with dueling scientists, a testy local sheriff, the theft of a fortune, and uncooperative weather.

THE EMILY CABOT MYSTERIES
Frances McNamara

Death at Chinatown

In the summer of 1896, amateur sleuth Emily Cabot meets two young Chinese women who have recently received medical degrees. She is inspired to make an important decision about her own life when she learns about the difficult choices they have made in order to pursue their careers. When one of the women is accused of poisoning a Chinese herbalist, Emily once again finds herself in the midst of a murder investigation. But, before the case can be solved, she must first settle a serious quarrel with her husband, help quell a political uprising, and overcome threats against her family. Timeless issues, such as restrictions on immigration, the conflict between Western and Eastern medicine, and women's struggle to balance family and work, are woven seamlessly throughout this mystery set in Chicago's original Chinatown.

Beautiful Dreamer
Joan Naper

Chicago in 1900 is bursting with opportunity, and Kitty Coakley is determined to make the most of it. The youngest of seven children born to Irish immigrants, she has little interest in becoming simply a housewife. Inspired by her entrepreneurial Aunt Mabel, who runs a millinery boutique at Marshall Field's, Kitty aspires to become an independent, modern woman. After her music teacher dashes her hopes of becoming a professional singer, she refuses to give up her dreams of a career. But when she is courted by not one, but two young men, her resolve is tested. Irish-Catholic Brian is familiar and has the approval of her traditional, working-class family. But wealthy, Protestant Henry, who is a young architect in Daniel Burnham's office, provides an entrée for Kitty into another, more exciting world. Will she sacrifice her ambitions and choose a life with one of these men?

◆

Company Orders
David J. Walker

Even a good man may feel driven to sign on with the devil. Paul Clark is a Catholic priest who's been on the fast track to becoming a bishop. But he suddenly faces a heart-wrenching problem, when choices he made as a young man come roaring back into his life. A mysterious woman, who claims to be with "an agency of the federal government," offers to solve his problem. But there's a price to pay—Father Clark must undertake some very un-priestly actions. An attack in a Chicago alley…a daring escape from a Mexican jail…and a fight to the death in a Guyanese jungle…all these, and more, must be survived in order to protect someone he loves. This priest is about to learn how much easier it is to preach love than to live it.

Set the Night on Fire
Libby Fischer Hellmann

Someone is trying to kill Lila Hilliard. During the Christmas holidays she returns from running errands to find her family home in flames, her father and brother trapped inside. Later, she is attacked by a mysterious man on a motorcycle. . . and the threats don't end there. As Lila desperately tries to piece together who is after her and why, she uncovers information about her father's past in Chicago during the volatile days of the late 1960s . . . information he never shared with her, but now threatens to destroy her. Part thriller, part historical novel, and part love story, *Set the Night on Fire* paints an unforgettable portrait of Chicago during a turbulent time: the riots at the Democratic Convention . . . the struggle for power between the Black Panthers and SDS . . . and a group of young idealists who tried to change the world.

◆

A Bitter Veil
Libby Fischer Hellmann

It all began with a line of Persian poetry . . . Anna and Nouri, both studying in Chicago, fall in love despite their very different backgrounds. Anna, who has never been close to her parents, is more than happy to return with Nouri to his native Iran, to be embraced by his wealthy family. Beginning their married life together in 1978, their world is abruptly turned upside down by the overthrow of the Shah and the rise of the Islamic Republic. Under the Ayatollah Khomeini and the Republican Guard, life becomes increasingly restricted and Anna must learn to exist in a transformed world, where none of the familiar Western rules apply. Random arrests and torture become the norm, women are required to wear hijab, and Anna discovers that she is no longer free to leave the country. As events reach a fevered pitch, Anna realizes that nothing is as she thought, and no one can be trusted. . .not even her husband.

Her Mother's Secret
Barbara Garland Polikoff

Fifteen-year-old Sarah, the daughter of Jewish immigrants, wants nothing more than to become an artist. But as she spreads her wings she must come to terms with the secrets that her family is only beginning to share with her. Replete with historical details that vividly evoke the Chicago of the 1890s, this moving coming-of-age story is set against the backdrop of a vibrant, turbulent city. Sarah moves between two very different worlds—the colorful immigrant neighborhood surrounding Hull House and the sophisticated, elegant World's Columbian Exposition. This novel eloquently captures the struggles of a young girl as she experiences the timeless emotions of friendship, family turmoil, loss…and first love.

A companion guide to *Her Mother's Secret*
is available at www.alliumpress.com. In the guide you will find photographs of places mentioned in the novel, along with discussion questions, a list of read-alikes, and resources for further exploration of Sarah's time and place.

Bright and Yellow, Hard and Cold
Tim Chapman

The search for elusive goals consumes three men...

McKinney, a forensic scientist, struggles with his deep, personal need to find the truth behind the evidence he investigates, even while the system shuts him out. Can he get justice for a wrongfully accused man while juggling life with a new girlfriend and a precocious teenage daughter?

Delroy gives up the hard-scrabble life on his family's Kentucky farm and ventures to the rough-and-tumble world of 1930s Chicago. Unable to find work, he reluctantly throws his hat in with the bank-robbing gangsters Alvin Karpis and Freddie Barker. Can he provide for his fiery young wife without risking his own life?

Gilbert is obsessed with the search for a cache of gold, hidden for nearly eighty years. As his hunt escalates he finds himself willing to use ever more extreme measures to attain his goal...including kidnapping, torture, and murder. Can he find the one person still left who will lead him to the glittering treasure? And will the trail of corpses he leaves behind include McKinney?

Part contemporary thriller, part historical novel, and part love story, *Bright and Yellow, Hard and Cold* masterfully weaves a tale of conflicted scientific ethics, economic hardship, and criminal frenzy, tempered with the redemption of family love.

Shall We Not Revenge
D. M. Pirrone

In the harsh early winter months of 1872, while Chicago is still smoldering from the Great Fire, Irish Catholic detective Frank Hanley is assigned the case of a murdered Orthodox Jewish rabbi. His investigation proves difficult when the neighborhood's Yiddish-speaking residents, wary of outsiders, are reluctant to talk. But when the rabbi's headstrong daughter, Rivka, unexpectedly offers to help Hanley find her father's killer, the detective receives much more than the break he was looking for.

Their pursuit of the truth draws Rivka and Hanley closer together and leads them to a relief organization run by the city's wealthy movers and shakers. Along the way, they uncover a web of political corruption, crooked cops, and well-buried ties to two notorious Irish thugs from Hanley's checkered past. Even after he is kicked off the case, stripped of his badge, and thrown in jail, Hanley refuses to quit. With a personal vendetta to settle for an innocent life lost, he is determined to expose a complicated criminal scheme, not only for his own sake, but for Rivka's as well.

For You Were Strangers
D. M. Pirrone

On a spring morning in 1872, former Civil War officer Ben Champion is discovered dead in his Chicago bedroom—a bayonet protruding from his back. What starts as a routine case for Detective Frank Hanley soon becomes anything but, as his investigation into Champion's life turns up hidden truths best left buried. Meanwhile, Rivka Kelmansky's long-lost brother, Aaron, arrives on her doorstep, along with his mulatto wife and son. Fugitives from an attack by night riders, Aaron and his family know too much about past actions that still threaten powerful men— defective guns provided to Union soldiers, and an 1864 conspiracy to establish Chicago as the capital of a Northwest Confederacy. Champion had his own connection to that conspiracy, along with ties to a former slave now passing as white and an escaped Confederate guerrilla bent on vengeance, any of which might have led to his death. Hanley and Rivka must untangle this web of circumstances, amid simmering hostilities still present seven years after the end of the Civil War, as they race against time to solve the murder, before the secrets of bygone days claim more victims.

Honor Above All
J. Bard-Collins

Pinkerton agent Garrett Lyons arrives in Chicago in 1882, close on the trail of the person who murdered his partner. He encounters a vibrant city that is striving ever upwards, full of plans to construct new buildings that will "scrape the sky." In his quest for the truth Garrett stumbles across a complex plot involving counterfeit government bonds, fierce architectural competition, and painful reminders of his military past. Along the way he seeks the support and companionship of his friends—elegant Charlotte, who runs an upscale poker game for the city's elite, and up-and-coming architect Louis Sullivan. Rich with historical details that bring early 1880s Chicago to life, this novel will appeal equally to mystery fans, history buffs, and architecture enthusiasts.

The Reason for Time
Mary Burns

Whole minutes passed when I didn't think of my man and the swimming lesson set up for the next day, if no one was murdered before then, or the cars stopped, or a bomb go off somewhere…

On a hot, humid Monday afternoon in July 1919, Maeve Curragh watches as a blimp plunges from the sky and smashes into a downtown Chicago bank building. It is the first of ten extraordinary days in Chicago history that will forever change the course of her life.

Racial tensions mount as soldiers return from the battlefields of Europe and the Great Migration brings new faces to the city, culminating in violent race riots. Each day the young Irish immigrant, a catalogue order clerk for the Chicago Magic Company, devours the news of a metropolis where cultural pressures are every bit as febrile as the weather. But her interest in the headlines wanes when she catches the eye of a charming streetcar conductor.

Maeve's singular voice captures the spirit of a young woman living through one of Chicago's most turbulent periods. Seamlessly blending fact with fiction, Mary Burns weaves an evocative tale of how an ordinary life can become inextricably linked with history.

CPSIA information can be obtained at www.ICGtesting.com
Printed in the USA
BVOW02s1220050916

460686BV00003B/17/P